THE BODY IN THE HOT TUB

Bertie abruptly stopped speaking. We'd been walking while we were talking, drawing closer to the raised platform. I took another step and saw what Bertie had seen. A fluffy, yellow bath towel, the kind found stacked in each of the inn's rooms, was draped over one of the back benches.

"What?" asked Aunt Peg.

"It turns out we're not alone." Bertie giggled.

Funny, I thought, that we weren't able to see whoever was sitting in the tub. Not that I had a lot of experience with hot tubs, but I thought people usually sat in them with head and shoulders above the water, perhaps even above the lip of the tub itself.

It was one of those moments when you instinctively know something is wrong, but your brain flatly refuses to process the information.

Aunt Peg, however, had no such problem thinking things through. She glanced at the discarded towel, then at the splash of water on the platform's boards.

"Oh, dear," she said, pushing me out of the way to step up onto the deck.

Even as Aunt Peg gasped, Bertie and I were already hopping up to stand beside her.

A man was floating face down in the hot tub. His dark hair was shiny and slick under the lights from above. His arms were outstretched, well-manicured fingers reaching for something he'd never touch.

Bertie went pale. "That can't be good."

My sister-in-law, the master of understatement.

Books by Laurien Berenson

A Pedigree to Die for

Underdog

Dog Eat Dog

Hair of the Dog

Watchdog

Hush Puppy

Unleashed

Once Bitten

Hot Dog

Best in Show

Jingle Bell Bark

Raining Cats and Dogs

Chow Down

Hounded to Death

Doggie Day Care Murder

Published by Kensington Publishing Corporation

Hounded to Death

Laurien Berenson

KENSINGTON BOOKS
KENSINGTON PUBLISHING CORP.
http://www.kensingtonbooks.com

KENSINGTON BOOKS are published by

Kensington Publishing Corp.
850 Third Avenue
New York, NY 10022

All Kensington titles, imprints, and distributed lines are available at special quantity discounts for bulk purchases for sales promotion, premiums, fund-raising, educational, or institutional use.

Special book excerpts or customized printings can also be created to fit specific needs. For details, write or phone the office of the Kensington Special Sales Manager, Kensington Publishing Corp., 850 Third Avenue, New York, NY 10022. Attn: Special Sales Department. Phone: 1-800-221-2647.

If you purchased this book without a cover, you should be aware that this book is stolen property. It was reported as "unsold and destroyed" to the Publisher and neither the Author nor the Publisher has recieved any payment for this "stripped book."

Kensington and the K logo Reg. U.S. Pat. & TM Off.

ISBN-13: 978-0-7582-1605-2
ISBN-10: 0-7582-1605-X

First Hardcover Printing: September 2007
First Mass Market Paperback Printing: August 2008
10 9 8 7 6 5 4 3 2 1

Printed in the United States of America

1

On the road again . . .

The refrain from some half-forgotten song was playing on an endless, rolling loop in my brain. It made a fitting backdrop to the day's activities, but it was slowly driving me crazy.

Anyone who was a dog show enthusiast was accustomed to spending a lot of time traveling to far-flung locations. That was the nature of the game. But this trip was different.

For one thing, there weren't any dogs in the car. None of my beloved Standard Poodles—clipped and bathed, beautified almost beyond the point of common sense—had accompanied me on this jaunt. Instead my two companions were Margaret Turnbull, my Aunt Peg, and Bertie Kennedy, my best friend and sister-in-law.

Three women on the loose—or as loose as one could be in a minivan heading down the highway toward Pennsylvania.

Aunt Peg was the one who had proposed the trip.

And although I often try to fight the impulse, as usually happens I'd ended up falling in with her plans.

As for Bertie, I think she felt that five days away from the responsibilities of home and family would be just the thing to recharge her batteries. Her daughter, Maggie, was ten months old. She'd consumed most of Bertie's time and attention since her birth just before Christmas, but now she'd been left in the care of Bertie's husband, my brother Frank.

Bertie was currently riding shotgun in the front seat.

"This is going to be great," she'd said delightedly when we'd hit the road an hour earlier. "A girls' road trip. Just like Thelma and Louise. Except that we won't die in the end."

Which . . . you know . . . set the bar and gave us something to aspire to.

"You're being awfully quiet back there," Aunt Peg said. Her gaze found mine in the rearview mirror.

Aunt Peg was driving, of course. She plots her own course and it's left to those around her to either keep up or get left behind. The fact that we were doing better than seventy miles an hour on the Garden State Parkway was apparently not sufficient incentive for her to keep her eyes, or her mind, on the road.

"I'm singing to myself," I said.

"You are not." Bertie swiveled in her seat. "I've heard you sing. If you were singing, my ears would be hurting."

I loved Bertie dearly. That didn't stop me from reaching up and poking her.

"Maybe if you two would let me have a turn in the front seat, I'd be more likely to join in the conversation."

"We put you back there for your own good."

Peg flipped on her signal and changed lanes simultaneously. Not to worry. New Jersey drivers are used to that kind of behavior.

"To protect me from your driving?"

"My driving skills are excellent, thank you very much. I haven't had an accident since Nixon was in office."

Aunt Peg was in her early sixties, but age hadn't curtailed a single aspect of her behavior. I was three decades younger and would have considered myself lucky to possess half her drive and enthusiasm.

"Bertie and I were only thinking of your comfort. We assumed you'd be happier having the backseat all to yourself. After all, you're the one who needs the extra room."

Aunt Peg was referring to the fact that I was four months pregnant. Increasing as they used to say in earlier times, before women had minivans to cart around their expanding bodies.

Yes, I had begun to outgrow my clothing. But needing an entire bench just to sit by myself? Thankfully I wasn't expanding that fast.

"Speaking of which," said Bertie, "how are you feeling?"

Let's recap here for a minute. When my lovely red-headed sister-in-law had been pregnant the previous year, she'd sailed through that nine months with the same aplomb she brought to most endeavors. No matronly maternity clothes for her; she'd simply borrowed some of Frank's shirts and jeans, refashioned them around the slight bump in her figure, and made do. She'd eaten whatever she wanted, glowed like an angel, and handled her clients' dogs to numerous wins nearly right up until the day she delivered.

Remembering that was enough to make me feel like giving her another poke.

Bertie must have read my mind because she moved out of easy range. "Everything okay?"

"Just fine," I replied.

Which was true if you didn't count the fact that I felt grumpy, and lumpy, and had to pee every five minutes.

"I'm delighted to have your company," said Aunt Peg. "But under the circumstances, frankly I was a little surprised that Sam let you go."

Sam was my husband. We'd eloped in the spring after an extended engagement. But despite the brief duration of our marriage, not only had I not had a hard time getting away, but Sam had all but packed my bag and pushed me out the door. He'd claimed to be acting for my own good.

It was amazing how many times that phrase seemed to have popped up lately. This current pregnancy was my second. The first had taken place ten years earlier and produced my son, Davey, who had remained at home with Sam. I supposed I'd forgotten in the intervening time how involved other people tended to become when a woman was carrying a baby. Not to mention how many decisions they felt qualified to make on her behalf.

Sometimes it seemed as though the general consensus was that pregnancy was not only changing my body but also addling my brain.

Nevertheless I knew that Sam had been trying to do the right thing. He had wanted me to slow down my schedule, and somehow that solicitude on his part had morphed into my accompanying Aunt Peg on a small vacation of sorts.

During the school year, I work as a special needs tutor at a private academy in Greenwich, Connecticut.

Luckily, however, Aunt Peg's proposed getaway had come up in the middle of October and coincided with fall break. Which was how I'd come to find myself in the backseat of a minivan, on my way to a dog show judges' symposium at the Rockwall Mountain Inn in the Poconos.

"Sam knew I'd be in good hands." I was careful to keep any trace of irony from my voice.

"Good luck with that," said Bertie. "Not that I don't love Maggie to bits, but taking care of a baby is a full-time job. This trip is going to be my great escape and I intend to make the most of it."

"Really?" Aunt Peg slanted a look down her nose. "What exactly do you have planned?"

Usually those looks are aimed at me. Most times they make me squirm with discomfort. Not Bertie; she just grinned.

"You know," she said, "the usual. Sleeping until seven-thirty, wearing clothes that don't have spit-up on the shoulder, enjoying a little privacy in the bathroom. All those wild things."

"Good." Aunt Peg nodded with satisfaction. "That won't interfere. While I'm busy with lectures and such, you'll be the one taking care of Melanie."

"*Taking care of Melanie?*" I echoed incredulously from the backseat. If they could talk about me in the third person, so could I. "Melanie is a grown woman, thank you very much. She doesn't need to be taken care of."

"You know how she has a propensity to get herself into trouble." Aunt Peg blithely ignored my protest.

While I was busy sputtering, Bertie came to my defense.

"Funny thing about that," she said to Peg. "When it comes to trouble, I seem to recall you've found your share."

"Nonsense. That's been nothing more than a bit of bad luck and poor timing."

"And general nosiness," I said.

Aunt Peg mustered a credible show of outrage. "Perhaps you might be thinking of yourself, because you certainly can't be referring to me. I'll admit that on occasion I might feel obliged to step in and lend a hand when a problem arises unexpectedly. But mostly I keep my opinions to myself and let other people find their own way. Why, if I were a country, I'd probably be Switzerland."

"Switzerland," I said faintly.

The mind boggled. Aunt Peg thought of herself as a neutral country. And here I'd always imagined her more like an elite special forces unit. Something along the lines of Mossad.

"Don't worry," said Bertie, "I'll do my best to keep an eye on her."

She looked back and winked.

"Neither one of you needs to worry," I said firmly. "My schedule is going to be totally filled with panels and seminars. With so many events crammed into the agenda, I doubt there will be time for any of us to get into trouble."

"Amen to that," said Peg.

"This is my first symposium," said Bertie. "Tell me what to expect."

"I'm only one ahead of you," I admitted. "This is just my second."

My tenure in the dog show world was relatively new. Not like Aunt Peg, who'd been involved for decades, first as a Standard Poodle breeder, and then more recently as a judge. Initially approved for the three varieties of Poodles—Standard, Miniature, and Toy—she'd quickly moved on to add more breeds to her resume.

The surest way to judging success is to gain approval in multiple groups, and Aunt Peg was well on her way. The Non-Sporting group was already hers, and by the end of the year she would have approval for all the Toy breeds as well.

Bertie, on the other hand, was a professional handler. Her knowledge of judges and judging came from the other end of the leash. She had neither a breeding program, nor strong ties to any one particular breed.

Her forte was presentation. Breeders who lacked either the skill or the desire to handle their own dogs in the ring hired her to do it for them. She had handled hundreds of dogs to their championships and dozens to coveted group and Best in Show victories.

Part of Bertie's job was to study judges she exhibited under and figure out exactly what each one wanted to see in a dog. It was a skill she excelled at. Even so, the thought of becoming a judge herself still seemed like a foreign concept to her.

To tell the truth, it did to me too. Not that I would have dreamed of admitting as much to Aunt Peg. She would have seen such a notion as heresy.

"There was a symposium held in conjunction with Westminster last year," I said. "That was my first. It covered a bunch of breeds and ran all day Saturday and Sunday."

"I was busy showing at specialties then," Bertie said with a sigh. "Nobody plans these things with handlers in mind."

Casual spectators think of the Westminster dog show as the crown jewel of the dog world. It's the show that has the cachet, the television coverage, and Madison Square Garden. But for many of the exhibitors who come to New York, wins at the specialty shows that precede the main event are equally important.

"That's why you're in luck now," said Aunt Peg. "This should be a tremendous learning opportunity both for aspiring judges and for those of us who are already approved. Aside from the various breed lectures, there will be panels on the mechanics of the judging process, on bookkeeping, hassle-free traveling, and even on fulfilling the requirements to apply for a license. A wealth of knowledge will be offered this week and I'd be hard pressed to see why anyone wouldn't want to take full advantage of it."

"I don't know," said Bertie. "I doubt if all the attendees will have the same high-minded goals that you do."

"What do you mean?"

"I wouldn't be surprised if half of them are looking at this week as a tax-deductible excuse to party. Why else would the sponsors have chosen to hold the event at a mountaintop resort?"

Bertie had a point. Dog show exhibitors were no different than anyone else. Remove them from the boundaries and constraints of their daily lives, isolate them all together in a convivial atmosphere, and there was no telling what kinds of trouble they might get up to.

Which led me directly back to our earlier conversation.

"Switzerland," I muttered under my breath.

Now all I had to do was hold on tight to that thought.

"What, dear?" Aunt Peg asked.

"Nothing." I rubbed a hand over my stomach. The small swell I felt there gave me comfort. "I think my stomach was rumbling."

"Little Brutus must be talking to you," Bertie said.

"*Little Brutus?*" Aunt Peg craned her head around. "I should hope not."

"Bertie's just upset because I won't let her help Sam and me pick out names for the baby. She's taken to offering suggestions."

"Excellent suggestions," Bertie sniffed. "If I do say so myself."

"Right," I said. "This from a woman who almost named her daughter Godot."

"She was late. I got tired of waiting. I might have been a little cranky when I came up with that name."

"*Might* have been?" Trust me, I'd been there. There was no "might" about it.

"And anyway, now I've got all week to work on you. Without Sam to back you up, you'll never be able to withstand my influence."

"You wish."

"Five whole days," Bertie said with a happy sigh. "You know what's the best thing about leaving all the men home?"

"We don't have to shave our legs?"

"Not what I was thinking, but good answer."

"About that no-men thing," Aunt Peg said casually.

That stopped the conversation cold.

"That doesn't exactly apply to me," she said.

She was right in that she hadn't left a man at home. In fact, since her husband's death three years earlier, Aunt Peg had had only one relationship I'd been aware of; and that, unfortunately, hadn't lasted long.

But somehow I had a sneaking suspicion that wasn't what she was referring to.

Bertie and I exchanged glances. She shrugged slightly, apparently as baffled as I was.

"Go on," I said.

"There's actually another reason I signed up to come to the symposium. I happen to have a new boyfriend. His name is Richard Donner and he'll also be attending. I'm quite certain we're all going to get along famously."

2

"Wow!" cried Bertie. "Good for you."

I just stared.

It wasn't the thought of Aunt Peg with a man that made my eyes widen. It was the fact that she'd apparently managed to slip this one into place in her life without my noticing his existence earlier.

Aunt Peg was sneaky, that was a given; it was one of her better attributes. But truly, I had thought I was more observant than to let something of this magnitude slide by.

Maybe the consensus was right and pregnancy *had* addled my brain.

"So," said Bertie, "you're going to Pennsylvania to meet up with a hot date. Tell us everything."

"His name is Richard Donner."

"We already have that much," I said impatiently. "Where did you meet him?"

"Over the Internet."

The comment was delivered with total nonchalance.

As if she thought that feigned indifference on her part might ward off the anticipated outcry. It didn't.

"You must be joking!"

"Perfect." Bertie giggled. "Did you go to one of those sites like match dot com? Have you met your perfect match? This is so romantic—"

"It is not romantic," I said sternly. "In fact it might be only one step away from lunacy. What do you know about this man aside from the fact that he owns a computer?"

Peg was unruffled. "I know he likes dogs."

"Everybody likes dogs."

"Bob's next door neighbor doesn't."

Bob was my ex-husband, and Amber was a cat person. All of which was beside the point.

"Have you met him in person? Do you even know what he looks like?"

"I've seen his picture. To borrow a word from Bertie, he's hot."

"If what he showed you was the right picture," Bertie mentioned.

Peg's gaze swung her way. "What do you mean?"

"Plenty of people misrepresent themselves on the Internet. Child molesters go to chat rooms and pretend to be twelve-year-old girls—"

"You think I've gotten myself mixed up with a child molester?" Aunt Peg sounded incredulous. Also annoyed.

"I'm just using that as an example. You have to be really careful when you use those Internet dating sites—"

"How would you know?" I asked.

Bertie ignored me. "Of course everyone wants to present themselves in the best light. So you add a couple inches to your height, shave off twenty pounds, say you have a master's degree when you barely graduated from high school."

"People *do* that?" Aunt Peg, a woman who had never felt inadequate in her life, still sounded incredulous.

"That and more," I confirmed. "For all you know, you might have seen a picture of what this Richard person looked like ten years ago."

"Or maybe one of his next door neighbor," Bertie said.

"You're being ridiculous," Aunt Peg scoffed.

"No, we're not."

"You're mad, both of you."

"We're being cautious."

"And realistic."

"Cynical," Peg said firmly. "With very little faith in the goodness of human nature apparently."

"When it comes to the Internet, buyer beware."

"I think you're both missing the point. I'm not trying to *buy* anything."

Aunt Peg took a moment to lift her foot from the gas pedal and study some approaching road signs. She didn't want to miss the turn onto 80 West. And maybe she was hoping a pause in the conversation would result in a change of subject.

Not a chance.

"So you haven't actually met this guy in person yet?" I said once we were on the new highway.

I was beginning to relax a little. If all they had done was exchange a few e-mails, maybe there was still time to ward off impending disaster.

"Believe me, it isn't from lack of desire on either of our parts. But unfortunately we're geographically incompatible. Richard lives in Ohio."

Thank goodness for small favors.

"So you're meeting halfway in Pennsylvania?" said Bertie. "Great idea. How did you ever convince him to sign up for a dog judges' symposium?"

"It required no convincing on my part at all. Richard had received a brochure and was already planning to attend."

"Wait a minute," I said. "But that means—"

"That Richard is a judge too?" Aunt Peg's tone was smug. Once again she'd managed to pull one over on her younger relations. "Quite so."

"For real?" asked Bertie. "You actually met a dog show judge on an Internet dating site?"

"No, dear. I met him on a message board on a web site dedicated to the betterment of purebred dogs."

My stomach rolled. Maybe it was the baby. Maybe it was the fact that I hadn't eaten yet that morning. Or maybe it was simply proximity to my ever-exasperating Aunt Peg.

"Why didn't you say so in the first place?" I asked.

"What, and deny the two of you the opportunity to make perfect fools of yourselves? Trust me, driving in a mostly straight line for three hours isn't that entertaining. Listening to you two flap and flounder in outrage is the most fun I've had all day."

"Even so," I said.

"She has a point," Bertie added.

"How can she have a point?" Aunt Peg demanded. "She hasn't said anything yet. In most places where people speak English *even so* isn't a point."

"Just because Richard Donner is a dog show judge doesn't mean he's a good person."

"Of course not," Peg agreed. "You and I have both met our share of idiots who think that a small amount of knowledge coupled with the ability to look good in a plastic rain hat and a pair of rubber boots qualifies them to define breed type. But how am I ever going to find out what kind of person he is if we don't get together?

"For all I know, Richard might be the man I'm meant to spend the rest of my life with. And wouldn't it be a shame if I passed up a chance like that simply because our first contact happened to have taken place over the Internet?"

"Well . . ." I said grudgingly.

"Well, what?"

"You may be right."

"Of course I'm right."

Like that was anything new.

We drove in silence for several minutes.

I stared out the window at the passing landscape, thought about home, and wondered what everyone was doing in my absence. Davey was likewise out of school this week. He and Sam had a number of outings planned, but right now I was willing to bet that they were simply out in the backyard, enjoying the crisp fall weather.

I imagined Davey was probably playing in his tree house. Sam would be raking leaves. Sooner or later, one of them would pick up a tennis ball and start a game of fetch with the Poodles.

Gone less than two hours, I felt a pang of homesickness. Probably latent nesting instincts coming to the fore.

Having expected to sail through this pregnancy the same way I'd done nine years earlier, I'd been in for a rude awakening. This time I felt as though I was on an emotional roller coaster. No wonder Sam had been so happy to send me away for a week.

"Funny thing," Aunt Peg mused in the front seat. "I had thought it would be Richard's age the two of you would object to."

I gulped. *His age?*

What about his age?

Life with Aunt Peg; it was a constant round of waiting for the other shoe to drop.

"How old is he?" I asked.

"Forty-nine."

Bertie laughed out loud. "No wonder you thought he was hot," she said.

The Rockwall Mountain Inn turned out to be a rustic retreat, located at the end of a long, winding driveway that carried us up the side of a small mountain.

"Smell the fresh air," Aunt Peg said happily as the road began to climb. "Look at the views!"

A nice thought, but since the driveway was surrounded on either side by a dense wall of very tall fir trees, the view consisted mostly of pine needles and bark.

Then we reached the top and the trees fell away. The dark road opened out into a wide parking lot with sweeping mountain vistas and miles of blue sky.

"Wow." Bertie exhaled. "Whoever chose this place really knew what they were doing."

"That would be Margo Deline, the symposium director," Peg said crisply. "The woman is one of life's great organizers. She always does a bang-up job."

The hotel consisted of a cluster of four low buildings, each one fashioned to look like a large log cabin. Wrap-around porches lined with rows of Adirondack chairs invited guests to sit and enjoy the dramatic views. The inn was billed as a resort and spa, and signs outside the main building pointed us toward the swimming pool, tennis courts, hot tub, and health club.

"Damn," said Bertie as she pulled her suitcase out of the back of the van. "I didn't bring my tennis racquet."

"You don't play tennis."

"I would if I had time."

"No, you wouldn't, you'd just sleep."

"Well," she admitted, "there is that."

"Stop squabbling, you two." Aunt Peg paused in front of a set of wide double doors that led into reception.

The handle was fashioned from what looked like a large tusk. Boar? Elephant? Water buffalo? Aunt Peg tapped the appendage with her fingernail.

"Plastic," she said with satisfaction and threw it open.

The lobby was a two-story great room with an enormous stone fireplace on one end and a wide, bending staircase on the other. Between the two, a gallery opened out into the upper hallway, giving strolling guests a vantage from which to watch the action below. The reception desk was located beneath the overhang, the wall behind it decorated with various pieces of artwork, most of them attributed to local artisans.

Within minutes, Aunt Peg, Bertie, and I had been registered and delivered to our rooms. Bertie and I were sharing; Aunt Peg had her own, adjoining room next door. Upon entering, we found information packets waiting for us on the desk, describing the week's activities.

I set down my suitcase, opened the packet, and pulled out the top sheet.

"Tonight the only thing on the schedule is an informal opening reception." I read the invitations aloud. *"Come and join us in the Elk Room. Rally round the blazing fire to greet old friends and make new ones. Cash bar."*

Bertie hooted. She lifted her hands, let her body fall backward onto one of the double beds, and landed with a gentle plop.

"You know what that translates to. *Let's get everybody roaring drunk on the first night and set the tone for the rest of this shindig.* If nothing else, it'll be interesting to watch. I always wondered what kind of wild and crazy people dog show judges turn into when no one else is around."

"Very funny. Next you'll be imagining them howling at the moon."

"Who's howling?" Aunt Peg asked. She stuck her head through the door between the two rooms. "I don't hear a thing. And if somebody has a dog here, I am not going to be amused."

"Nobody's howling yet," said Bertie. "Give them time. Maybe after dark."

"Oh, I see. You were talking about people. More's the pity."

Aunt Peg, I noted, didn't deny the possibility. I supposed that, being both older and wiser, not to mention a judge herself, she had more experience in dealing with her peers than Bertie and I did.

I grabbed my suitcase and hefted it onto a nearby rack. If I didn't unpack first, Bertie would nab all the drawer space and I'd spend the rest of the trip with my clothing piled in inconvenient spots around the room.

Aunt Peg sighed and sank down in an upholstered chair. It didn't look very comfortable but she didn't seem to notice.

"This is never going to work," she announced. "I don't see how it can."

"What won't work?"

"Me, you, all of us. A hundred avowed dog lovers

here for a week and none of us allowed to bring along a single dog for companionship."

Bertie blinked and sat up. "I think you're meant to enjoy the companionship of your fellow judges."

"Pish," said Peg. "Can a person gaze up at you adoringly? Rest his head in your lap? Laugh at all your jokes, even the bad ones?"

Well . . . yes, I thought. Maybe it *had* been too long since she'd had a relationship.

"I'll never be able to sleep a wink." Peg sounded grumpy. "Do you know how many years it's been since I slept in an empty bed without a single Poodle to snuggle up to? Honestly, aside from the fact that I miss their company, I feel naked without my dogs. I don't even know what to do with my hands."

"You could bunk in here with us," said Bertie.

"Don't be silly. That's not even remotely the same."

"There's always Richard," I said without thinking. As soon as the words were out, I could have kicked myself.

Aunt Peg arched a brow. "That's putting the cart before the horse, don't you think?"

"Or maybe giving the milk away for free?" said Bertie.

"Nobody's going to be giving anything away." Peg was firm. "For free or otherwise. At least not until we test the waters a bit and see how compatible we are in person. That *is* supposed to be the purpose of dating another person, isn't it? Things can't have changed that much since the last time I was out and about."

"Don't look to us for dating information," Bertie said. "Melanie and I are just a couple of old married ladies. If there's any excitement to be had this week, you're the one who's going to have to supply it."

"How very depressing for you, as I intend to have a

rather peaceful week myself. I'm simply going to give my Poodle lecture, attend a few judiciously chosen seminars, and maybe enjoy a quiet dinner or two with Richard if time permits."

"Right," I snorted.

Like most things, Aunt Peg seemed able to manipulate time to suit her will. And unless I missed my guess, Richard was going to find himself being rushed off his feet.

I snapped my suitcase shut. The small noise was enough to draw Bertie's attention.

She surveyed the results of my efforts, then looked at her own, still-full suitcase sitting on the floor by the door. Immediately she rolled off the bed, grabbed her bag, and dragged it over to the room's single dresser where I had already staked out two of the three drawers.

"Don't you have to, like, pee or something?" she asked.

Actually I did. But we had traveled together before and I knew perfectly well that Bertie had no honor when it came to her wardrobe and the concept of first dibs. There was no way I was letting her unpack unsupervised.

"Don't think I don't know what you're thinking." I shoved the middle drawer shut with my knee. "You snooze, you lose."

Aunt Peg looked at us. "Are you two going to be like this all week?"

"Probably," I said.

Bertie nodded.

"I was afraid of that," said Peg.

3

The reception was supposed to start at six-thirty, but even before the appointed time people began to gather in a cozy bar area off the lobby. When that room was full, partygoers spilled out into the great room where a roaring fire crackled in the fireplace.

The idea of being fashionably late is a concept entirely unknown to Aunt Peg. Immediate gratification is more her style. And since Bertie and I had accompanied her downstairs, that meant we were among the first to arrive. By the time a crowd had begun to gather, we already had our drinks and had staked out a prime location near the door.

Aunt Peg watched that portal like a hawk, alternately greeting or commenting on the new arrivals. While I was busy reading the name badges that most people had affixed to their lapels, Aunt Peg seemed to know just about everyone on sight.

"Tubby Mathis," she said, when a portly man with bushy eyebrows and thinning hair entered the room. "He judges hounds, after a fashion. I can't imagine what he's doing here. His mind is a closed book. I don't think he's learned a single new thing in the last decade."

"Maybe he's hoping to get laid," Bertie said.

I choked on my Shirley Temple.

"Then he must be an optimist," Peg said, dismissing him.

A well-matched, middle-aged couple came through the door next. If it's a truism that longtime dog owners often look like their dogs, it's equally true that longtime spouses also tend to acquire a similar veneer. Both members of this pair were fit and tan, as if they'd just returned from a vacation on some exotic beach.

They were holding hands as they entered the room, but almost immediately both were hailed by friends and pulled in different directions. They exchanged a brief look—shorthand between people who knew each other very well—and went their separate ways.

"Charles and Caroline Evans," said Aunt Peg. "They belong to several kennel clubs, principally Windemere in northern Maryland. Both of them judge all over the country and Charles is a well-regarded speaker as well. He's scheduled to give the keynote address tomorrow on 'The Future of Dog Shows.'"

"I've shown under Caroline," said Bertie. "She does sporting dogs and hounds. She can be tough, but she's fair."

"The same is true of Charles," Aunt Peg replied. "He's got the Working, Herding, and Terrier groups. One of the reasons they're so much in demand is that between them they can cover so many breeds."

"How long have they been married?" I asked.

Peg gave me an odd look. Anything that doesn't pertain to dogs is immaterial, or at least of lesser importance, in her view.

"Forever. What difference does that make?"

None really, I thought. And the question was out of character for me. Or at the least usual me, the one I had known before I became pregnant. But now, along with rocketing emotions, I seemed to have lost my usual air of cynicism. Instead I was filled with a dreamy sort of optimism that looked for the good in everyone.

"I just thought it was sweet that they were holding hands."

Aunt Peg snorted. "There's nothing sweet about those two. Smart, driven, eminently respectable? Yes. Sweet, no. Not even on a good day."

"Hey, look," Bertie said as a pale, lithe beauty swept through the doorway. The woman had the practiced strut of a supermodel and a look of disdain on her face. "There's Alana Bennett. I'm going to go say hi."

Bertie was no slouch herself when it came to looking good. She was probably the only woman in the room who didn't feel even the slightest bit threatened by Alana's arrival. When the two of them joined up and walked to the bar together—silky blonde and fiery red-head, heads dipped toward each other as they talked and laughed—there wasn't a man at the gathering who didn't take notice.

"It's a good thing Bertie has a decent head on her shoulders," Aunt Peg remarked, tracking the pair's progress for a moment before turning back to the door.

"Why?"

"Because her friend Alana is a bit of a flit. In my day she would have been known as a good-time girl. I'd be shocked if she came to the symposium because she's interested in getting her judge's license. More than likely she's just here to socialize."

"What's wrong with that?"

I may have sounded a little defensive, and with good reason. I was eons away from applying to become a judge, if indeed I ever did. But I had plenty to learn in the meantime and this symposium, coming up at just the right time, had seemed like a nifty vacation opportunity. Did that make my intentions any more pure than Alana's?

"You're a different case entirely," said Aunt Peg.

It was spooky how often she was able to read my mind, probably a skill she'd honed through decades of nonverbal communication with her Poodles.

"You'll go to lectures and take a few notes, meet some new people over meals, maybe have a massage and take a hike in the woods, then go home feeling that you've had a successful stay. Alana, on the other hand, will drink too much and party too hard. She'll flirt with half the men here, and won't think her week is successful until at least one fight has broken out on her account."

My gaze drifted toward the bar where Alana was now draped languidly over a stool, a pose that showed off her long, bare legs to perfection. "What's her connection to the dog show world?"

"Tenuous at best. Several years ago she was involved with an older man who had a wonderful line of Old English Sheepdogs. She started going to shows with him and must have enjoyed herself because even after their relationship was history she continued to put in an appearance, usually at upper tier shows like Tuxedo Park or Ox Ridge.

"She fashions herself as some sort of freelance do-gooder, the moral arbiter of the dog world. Every six months or so she's passionately devoted to a new cause, which could be anything from genetic research to saving pound puppies."

"She sounds fascinating," I said, mostly because I can never resist goading Aunt Peg.

"What she is, is dizzying. Try to keep up with her at your own peril. I haven't got the energy."

Energy, my aunt had in abundance. Patience, she did not. I suspected it was the latter that kept her on this side of the room while Bertie and Alana were now holding court on the other.

"Oh dear," Aunt Peg said suddenly.

"What?"

"He's here."

"Who?"

She didn't answer, and after a moment I realized I should have known. Richard Donner must have arrived.

I looked in the same direction she was staring and saw a perfectly ordinary-looking man. His dark hair was seasoned with gray at the temples, his nose was a shade too big for his face. But his shoulders were broad and his torso still lean. Wearing corduroy slacks and a blue cashmere sweater, he had the easy stride of a former athlete.

He paused in the doorway for a moment and surveyed the activity in the room. I thought perhaps he was looking for Aunt Peg, but then he turned and waited for an older woman behind him to catch up. She was nearly a foot shorter than he was and her white hair was sprayed up like a halo around her face.

Richard leaned down and said something, his lips close to her ear, and she nodded and smiled. When the older woman headed toward the bar, Richard placed a determined smile on his face and came toward us.

"Quick!" Aunt Peg said under her breath. "What should I do?"

"Smile."

"I'm smiling," she said through gritted teeth. "What else?"

"Act natural."

"Natural? *Natural*? There's nothing the least bit natural about this whole situation. What the hell does that mean?"

My aunt is not a woman given to swearing. Nor one who usually succumbs to nerves. I was seeing a whole new side of her, and it was not necessarily her most appealing one.

"How do I look?" she demanded.

Any second Richard would be upon us. Just as well because then she would have to stop spitting out rapid-fire questions.

I leaned over and whispered, "Perfect. You look perfect."

Her shoulders relaxed ever so slightly and I hear her exhale a soft breath. Then she held out both hands to clasp the one Richard was offering.

"I'm Peg," she said simply.

"I know," he said. "I could tell that from across the room. You're the most striking woman here."

Jeez, I thought. *Good answer.*

"And this is my niece, Melanie."

Richard and I scoped each other out.

"Pleased to meet you," he said after a moment. "If you're anything like your aunt, I'm sure you're a formidable woman."

So my aunt's new beau was a man of many compliments. But praise that had sounded just right when directed at Peg seemed over the top when applied to me.

"I find myself growing more and more like her all the time," I said mildly.

Beside me, Aunt Peg was beaming. Not just smiling,

but actually beaming. Either she was really, really happy, or else she was so tense that her fine motor skills had short-circuited.

I was hoping for the former, but I was beginning to suspect the latter.

"Perhaps I should leave you two alone so you can get to know one another?" I asked.

"Yes, please," Richard said smoothly.

"No!" cried Peg.

That settled it. Nerves, it was. I was torn between feeling compelled to come to her aid and wanting to enjoy the moment at her expense.

Petty of me, I know. But it wasn't like she didn't make a habit of abandoning me to the wolves.

"I'll tell you what," said Richard. "I'm going to go to the bar and get a drink. Maybe while I'm there, I can refresh yours?"

Aunt Peg nodded.

She was drinking scotch neat. Considering that her usual beverage of choice was tea, it wouldn't take too many more of those before the occasion acquired a pleasing, rosy hue.

"While I'm gone, you two can decide what you'd like to do."

Richard took Peg's tumbler and disappeared into the crowd.

"Don't leave me here alone with him," she said as soon as he was gone.

"Why not? I thought you were looking forward to meeting him."

"I was. But now that the time has come, I find it's harder than I thought. Do you have any idea how long it's been since I tried to make small talk with an attractive man? What if I say something stupid?"

I chuckled under my breath. "My being here won't prevent that."

"All right, then, what about awkward silences? Who's going to smooth those over?"

"Why should there be any silences? Don't you already know Richard? How long have you been corresponding?"

Aunt Peg considered. "Three months at least. But writing is entirely different. You can go back and edit what you say. There's time for a second draft. In e-mail, I always sound brilliant."

Hard to believe she could suffer a crisis of confidence, isn't it?

"If you want me to stay," I said, "I will."

"Thank you." Peg looked past me and scanned the room. Fresh drinks in each of his hands, Richard was threading his way back toward us through the crowd. "Next to you, I'm sure I'll come off wonderfully."

That was me, ever useful.

Richard had not only wrangled a pair of drinks; he'd also met up with a couple of friends along the way. Perhaps he'd hoped that enlarging the circle of conversation might put Peg more at ease. Or maybe he simply hadn't wanted to feel outnumbered.

Introductions were quickly performed. Derek Ryan was a Beagle man from northern Kentucky. He had a strong handshake, kind eyes, and a habit of standing much too close. Marshall Beckham looked like a stork. He was tall, slender, and serious; and when he heard Peg's name, he immediately shifted his attention her way.

"Peg Turnbull?" he repeated. "You're Margaret Turnbull, of Cedar Crest Kennels fame?"

Peg nodded graciously.

"I saw you win the group at Westminster! Champion Cedar Crest Chantain, wasn't it?"

She nodded again. Marshall was speaking much too fast for any of us to get a word in.

"I can't believe it. This is fantastic! What a turnout there is here. First Charles Evans, the man is one of my heroes . . . and now I'm meeting Margaret Turnbull. Somebody pinch me. That win at Westminster was quite a coup for an owner-handler! And what a lovely dog."

"Thank you. Beau was always one of my favorites."

In the face of Marshall's barrage of words, Aunt Peg was finally beginning to relax. Dog talk always did the trick. She was an old hand at that.

"I have Bichons," Marshall said. "And I handle them myself. Certainly not with your flair, but I pride myself on doing okay. I know you've recently been approved for the breed and I hope you'll consider coming out to Ohio to judge. I'd be delighted to have your opinion of my dogs."

Peg smiled. "All I need is an invitation."

Now that they'd navigated their way to common ground, the conversation was up and running. And the fact that Peg had been revealed as a minor celebrity in the dog community didn't hurt either. Richard regarded her with fresh appreciation and she basked in his attention.

No need to worry about her saying anything stupid. She could have told him that the moon was blue and he would have agreed.

After the first few minutes I began to feel superfluous. Slowly I edged back from the closely grouped circle. None of them even noticed my retreat. Toting my warm ginger ale, I headed in the direction of the bar.

Bertie hailed me as soon as I reached the counter.

"Hey!" she cried, her voice raised to be heard above the din. "Come and meet my friend Alana."

As Bertie introduced us, Alana looked me coolly up and down. I recognized the tactic. She was checking out the competition and doing her best to make me feel about three inches tall in the process.

Don't get me wrong. In most situations I can more than hold my own. But there was something about the way Alana ran her flat gaze over my body that made me feel fat and unappealing. As if I'd been mentally compared to her svelte beauty and found wanting.

"Stop it," Bertie ordered. She smacked her friend on the arm. "Melanie is my sister-in-law and my best friend. She's not someone for you to chew up and spit out."

Bertie turned to me. "Don't mind Alana. She doesn't have many women friends."

"I can see why not," I said.

Bertie slid off her stool and offered it to me.

Gratefully I hiked up and sat. It was nice to get off my feet.

Alana cocked a brow.

"Pregnant," I said. "Deal with it."

"Well, shit," said Alana. "Why didn't you say so in the first place?" She leaned over and gave me a hug. "Congratulations! When's the baby due?"

"March."

"Boy or girl?"

"We don't know yet."

Alana waved to the bartender. "This deserves another drink!"

News of my pregnancy had an immediate softening effect on her. Either she was genuinely happy for me or else this development had changed my status in her eyes. I'd been removed from the ranks of competitors and placed in a new category where friendship might be possible.

"Not for me," I said. "I find I have a limited tolerance for ginger ale. In fact I seem to have a limited tolerance for just about everything these days."

"I don't blame you a bit," said Bertie. She'd been pregnant just a year earlier. The experience was still fresh in her mind.

"Neither do I," Alana echoed in the spirit of our new kinship. She picked up her new drink and downed half of it in a single gulp. "If you ask me, tolerance is a highly overrated virtue."

Bertie leaned over and said, "How's Peg doing? She seems to be surrounded by men. Is one of them the famous Richard?"

"Broad shoulders, blue sweater."

"Not the tall one with the besotted look on his face?"

"No, that's Marshall Beckham. An aspiring owner-handler. Apparently he thinks he's in the presence of some sort of minor deity."

"Peg's been known to have that effect on people." Bertie shifted around and had another look. "Richard looks all right, doesn't he? I'd say there's definite potential there."

Alana leaned toward us to join the conversation. "Who are we talking about?"

"Richard Donner," I said. "Do you know him?"

"Sure," Alana replied. "The guy who travels with his mother."

The din in the room made conversation difficult and for a moment I wondered whether I'd heard her wrong. Then I remembered the sweet looking, little old lady

Richard had entered the room with earlier. Could that have been . . . ?

"There she is." Alana raised a not-too-steady hand and pointed. "The woman with the ratty little Chihuahua sticking its head out of her purse? That's Florence Donner. She and Richard go everywhere together."

4

I almost laughed. Then I caught myself.
Whatever mean-spirited thoughts I had harbored earlier—payback for all the times Aunt Peg had maneuvered me into in an embarrassing situation and then left me there to fend for myself—she certainly didn't deserve something like this.

"You're not joking, are you?"

"Why would I joke about something like that? It isn't the least bit funny. If you ask me, it's kind of pathetic. A grown man traveling around to shows with his seventy-year-old mother. You'd think he'd want to get a life."

My stomach sank. Apparently Richard *had* wanted to get a life. And he begun that quest by wooing Aunt Peg over the Internet.

"Florence Donner and Richard Donner are mother and son?" Bertie said, surprised. "I never made the connection."

My gaze swung her way. "You know her?"

"I've shown under her. She judges some of the Toy breeds."

"Is she any good?"

The question, though not germane, was almost automatic. Dog show exhibitors' fortunes rise and fall with the quality of the judges they show to. We're always on the quest for good judges and we'll travel almost any distance to find them.

Bertie shrugged. "She's not bad."

Alana looked at us. "What's up with you two? Why are you so interested in Richard Donner?"

"He and my aunt have been corresponding by e-mail for the last few months. Apparently they've become quite good friends."

"Is that her over there talking to him now?"

I nodded.

"Your aunt is Peg Turnbull?"

"That's right."

"Well then," said Alana, sliding down off her stool. "There's only one thing to do."

"What's that?"

I figured she was going to advise us to warn Aunt Peg about this unexpected development. But Alana surprised me. She grabbed my arm and headed determinedly into the crowd.

"Let's go introduce you to Florence."

"Bertie!" Swept along like a tug in the wake of a much larger barge, I cast a beseeching glance back over my shoulder.

"Coming." She slapped her glass down on the bar and followed. "I wouldn't miss this for anything."

Florence Donner was speaking with several people, but the impetus of our approach, which had already caused the crowd to part before us, now made her companions draw back as well. Alana smoothly inserted her-

self into the space they'd vacated, so accustomed to that
sort of deference she didn't even notice it.

"Florence," she said.

"Alana." The older woman tipped her head slightly
to one side. "Imagine seeing you here."

Had the temperature in the room cooled suddenly,
or was it just us?

Then I noticed that the little fawn-colored Chihuahua,
whose domed head had been sticking up through the
opening at the top of Florence's commodious purse,
had abruptly tucked himself back inside. Apparently I
wasn't the only one present who was skilled in reading
the nuances of human behavior.

Ignoring Florence's less than welcoming demeanor,
Alana reached back and hauled Bertie and me forward.
"I'd like you to meet Melanie Travis and Bertie Kennedy.
They're friends of mine."

"Really? How very fortunate for them."

I held out my hand and after a brief hesitation, Florence Donner followed suit. Her slender fingers felt dry
and fragile in my grasp. I didn't dare actually shake her
hand for fear I might break something.

"You." Florence's sharp gray eyes focusing on Bertie.
"I've seen you before."

"You have a good memory," Bertie said. "I showed to
you last year at Harrisburg."

"Of course I have a good memory. I remember every
dog I've ever judged. And most of the people too. Did
you win under me?"

"Yes, with the Pomeranian. No, with the Pug."

Florence clapped her hands in delight. "So the jury's
still out on how you feel about me, isn't it?"

Bertie grinned. She was enjoying herself too.

"The Pug could have done better on the day. The Pom?" She shrugged. "Not so much."

"So you say. But did you have your hands on the other dogs in the ring?"

"No, but—"

"But nothing! That's the beauty of being the judge. You're the only one who has *all* the information. And the only one whose opinion counts."

Florence nodded briskly. The debate had been settled to her satisfaction and she would brook no further argument. Aunt Peg was going to have her hands full with this one.

The two women were either going to end up the best of friends, or else they were going to kill one another. And I suspected I was going to have a ringside seat for much of the action.

"Nice to meet you both," said Florence. "Now it's time for me to collect my son from whatever mischief he's gotten himself up to. He and I will be dining together this evening."

In an unconscious gesture, her hand lifted to pat the side of the copious purse. The bag undulated in reply.

I couldn't imagine having a dog small enough to fit in a pouch under my arm. Nor would my Poodles enjoy tucking themselves away in a dark cubbyhole.

"That's Richard over there, isn't it?" Alana said innocently. She waved a hand in Aunt Peg's direction.

"So it is. That woman he's talking to looks familiar. Do I know her?"

"That's Peg Turnbull from Connecticut," said one of Florence's earlier companions. He stepped back in to rejoin the group. "You know, Cedar Crest Standard Poodles?"

"Is she indeed?" Florence's lips drew together in a

thin line. "I believe that's the woman Richard has been corresponding with. On the way here, he announced that he was looking forward to making her acquaintance. He admitted that they'd met on the Internet, of all things. Can you believe that?"

Her friends responded with general muttering and shaking of heads.

"It's a nasty business if you ask me. In my day, people knew how to conduct themselves. If you wanted to meet new people, you found someone to make a proper introduction. But now computers bring all sorts of unwanted business right into people's homes. It's not the way things ought to be done."

Opinion delivered, Florence left us. Shoulders back, head held high, she sailed across the crowded room.

There was no time to get to Peg first and warn her. Indeed there was no time to do anything but follow along in the hope that I might somehow be able to mitigate the approaching disaster.

As we crossed the room, I waved frantically in Peg's direction. I knew she saw me out of the corner of her eye. I watched her glance quickly at Richard, then make the decision to ignore my rude behavior.

Sometimes Peg has only herself to blame.

"Richard? Darling?" Florence's voice was smooth as honey. "I find myself growing hungry. Perhaps you'd be good enough to escort me to dinner?"

"Mother! There you are. There's someone I'd like you to meet."

As Richard turned to greet the older woman, I saw Peg process what he'd said. Her eyes widened; her face blanched. Then she had the nerve to glare at me like this calamity was all *my* fault.

But when Richard turned back to her, Aunt Peg

quickly wiped her features clean. She gazed at Florence and forced a smile. Never had I seen my aunt put her acting skills to better use.

"Your mother's here at the symposium with you?" Aunt Peg sounded as though a large lump of clay had lodged in her throat. "What an unexpected surprise."

"I knew you'd be pleased." When neither woman made the first move, Richard reached out, took their hands, and joined them in the middle. "I have no doubt that the two of you are going to get along beautifully."

"Beautifully," Florence echoed. She moved a proprietary step closer to her son, like a mother lion staking out her territory and daring the foolhardy interloper to challenge her supremacy. "But that's for later. Now I'd like to be taken in to dinner."

"So you shall," Richard said smoothly. "I'm afraid I've made other plans but Marshall and Derek would be delighted to have you join their party."

"*Other* plans?"

"Yes, Mother. Peg and I are going to enjoy a quiet dinner alone."

"But—"

Richard circled an arm around his mother's shoulders and deftly swung her away. He beckoned to Derek and Marshall and they fell into line.

"Would you excuse us for a minute?"

"Of course," Peg murmured.

Our eyes were riveted on the foursome as Richard and his friends surrounded his mother and maneuvered her away. Unfortunately for the sake of our curiosity he chose to take their argument out of the room.

Peg frowned into the vacuum created by their absence.

"Am I mistaken," she asked, "or did that woman have a dog inside her purse?"

Under the circumstances, I'd have thought that was the least of her worries. But trust Aunt Peg to gloss over the big problem and focus on the dog.

"It's a Chihuahua," I said.

As if that mattered.

There could have been a rabid Bullmastiff tucked beneath Florence's arm and that still wouldn't have been the most bothersome thing about the woman's presence at the symposium.

"What's a Chihuahua?" A woman I hadn't yet met came over and stood beside Peg.

My aunt is tall but this woman nearly matched her in stature. She had sharp features, which were arranged, at the moment, in a ferocious scowl. With her chestnut hair scraped back off her face in a tight ponytail, and her dark eyes scanning the room even as she paused beside us, she looked like a Doberman on the prowl.

"Margo! I've been wondering where you were." Aunt Peg greeted her friend with a quick hug. "Quite a turn-out you've come up with. Well done. This is my niece, Melanie."

So this was Margo Deline, the woman whose organizational skills Aunt Peg admired, the one who'd lured a diverse group of people to the Pennsylvania mountains to focus on learning more about dogs.

"It's a pleasure to meet you," I said.

"We'll just see about that."

She grasped my hand and pumped it firmly.

"Now, Margo," Aunt Peg reproved. "We just got here. Don't try to scare Melanie off already."

"Don't worry," I said. "I'm accustomed to my aunt's

company. It takes more than a determined woman to scare me."

"I see she has your number," Margo said to Peg. Then she turned to me and stared hard. "Now, what's this I hear about a Chihuahua?"

I felt like a second grader being called before the principal. And being asked to tattle on someone else.

I'm a teacher; I'm used to being on the other side of the equation. So I didn't even hesitate before spilling my guts.

"One of the judges has a dog in her purse," I said.

Margo sighed. "Let me guess. Florence Donner?"

"How'd you know?"

"She takes that silly little animal with her everywhere. Once she even carried him into the ring when she was judging. Left him sitting on the judge's table while she went about her job. Her steward just about had a fit.

"Don't get me wrong, I love dogs as much as the next person, perhaps more. But Button has been so thoroughly spoiled by that woman that he hardly even qualifies as canine."

"Margo has sporting dogs," Peg interjected.

It sounded like a non sequitur but she knew I'd follow her train of thought. Margo liked dogs that were big and sturdy and useful. Dogs that would leap into icy waters to retrieve game by day and drape their heavy bodies over their owners' feet to warm them at night.

"I have nothing against little dogs," Margo said firmly. "Just little dogs who are where they're not supposed to be. Every single piece of literature we sent out about the symposium stated in bold letters 'No Pets Allowed.' But of course Florence would be the one to assume that she's above the rules."

"I just met Florence earlier," I said. "She seemed like an interesting woman."

"That's one way to put it." Margo reached over and patted my arm. "And aren't you a dear to be so tactful? I guess I'd have to say that Florence is like that dog of hers, more than a little spoiled. In her whole life, very few people have bothered to tell her no, and she certainly doesn't see why anyone should start now."

That didn't bode well for Peg's and Richard's budding relationship, did it?

I glanced at my aunt. Her brow was furrowed; she was deep in thought. She looked like the *Before* picture in a Botox commercial.

"What will you do about it?" I asked. With luck, Florence might be asked to take her contraband pet and leave the symposium.

That optimistic thought didn't last long.

"There's not much I can do, is there? Both Florence and Button are already in residence. As long as she keeps him mostly out of sight, I imagine I'll just have to pretend I don't notice anything out of the ordinary."

Margo turned back to Peg. "Listen, that isn't why I wanted to talk to you. Florence Donner is small potatoes compared to the other potential problems we've got brewing. Two things. First, what have you heard about Charles Evans and the speech he's planning to give tomorrow?"

"Nothing." Aunt Peg perked up. There's nothing she enjoys more than the prospect of mayhem. "What's going on?"

"I'm not sure. Nobody has said anything to me directly, but there are several unsavory rumors floating around. I've heard that his keynote address is going to be highly controversial. It's scheduled to take place in the largest lecture hall and the room is going to be packed. I hope he isn't planning anything outrageous."

"Charles, outrageous?" Peg looked dubious. "That would be most unlike him."

Even though I didn't know the man, I had to agree. He certainly looked like a straight arrow. I remembered Aunt Peg had said that Charles would be talking about the future of dog shows. The topic sounded innocuous enough.

"That's what I thought," Margo said. "And it's not like anyone actually expects him to prognosticate from the podium. Charles chose the topic and I thought it seemed like something harmless and entertaining that he could have some fun with. But now I don't know . . . I've heard just enough innuendo to make me start to worry."

"There's an easy solution to that, you know." Peg nodded across the room to where Charles and Caroline were standing in a group of fellow judges. "Why don't you march over there, pull him aside, and ask him to tell you what he's going to say? You'd be well within your rights as director of the symposium to demand a heads-up."

"You don't think I haven't already tried? Charles can be slippery as a fish when he wants to be. He's very aware of his position in the dog show world and not above using it to his advantage. I'd barely even gotten the question out before he totally dismissed me. He said he wouldn't dream of spoiling the effect his speech was going to have by talking about it ahead of time."

That didn't sound good.

Aunt Peg frowned. "What about Caroline? What does she have to say?"

"I've known Caroline for a hundred years," said

Margo. "She and I started out doing obedience together back in the Dark Ages. I wouldn't say we're best friends, but if she thought I needed a warning, I'd like to think I could count on her to pass one along."

"And?"

"And nothing. Caroline says that Charles keeps certain things private, even from her. She has no idea what he's planning."

We all stood there and considered that.

"We've been no help with your first problem," Peg said after a minute. "You mentioned two. What's the other?"

Margo looked resigned. "More unsubstantiated rumor, I'm afraid. Apparently one of our esteemed judges has gotten himself caught with his hand in the cookie jar."

"Taking bribes in exchange for wins?" Aunt Peg elucidated just in case I hadn't caught on.

She needn't have worried. A story like that wasn't a new one. For as long as I'd been showing dogs, I'd heard similar rumors. An infraction of that sort was enough to end, or at least severely curtail, a career. But as long as the talk remained just that, nothing ever came of it.

"Just so. I've heard that a disgruntled exhibitor is about to turn him in."

"Who's the judge?" I asked, beating Aunt Peg to the punch.

"Unfortunately, I haven't a clue. If I did, perhaps I could put a lid on the scandal before it blows up in our faces. I've worked long and hard pulling this symposium together, and I have a great deal invested in its successful outcome. I have no intention of letting Charles Evans, or anyone else, ruin it for me."

"Forewarned is forearmed," said Aunt Peg.

And wasn't that a pleasantly cheerful thought on which to start the week?

5

The reception was beginning to wind down. That was fine by me because after two Shirley Temples, a slew of introductions to people whose faces I could barely remember, and more inane chatter than I usually heard in a week, I was worn out.

Richard came back and collected Aunt Peg. Florence was nowhere to be seen; presumably Derek and Marshall had escorted her to dinner.

Bertie and Alana had disappeared together while I'd been busy talking to Margo and Aunt Peg. I could have hunted them down but the prospect of food held little appeal, and the prospect of Alana's company held even less.

There was a granola bar in my purse upstairs that could double for dinner. Better still was the thought of stretching out on the bed and putting my feet up. Sad but true; it was eight-thirty on a Monday night and I was just about done for.

As I walked up the wide staircase to the second floor of the inn, leaving the noise and the revelry behind, I ran my hand over my stomach. I felt the slight swell and imaged the tiny person nesting within. Life as I knew it had changed dramatically over the last few months. My breasts were tender, my ankles swollen, my energy level flagging.

You better be worth it, I thought with a smile.

I hadn't expected a response and yet I wasn't startled when one came.

I am, said a voice in my head, clear as a bell. *You know I am.*

No arguing with that.

Once in the room, I immediately kicked off my shoes and unbuttoned my waistband. A sigh of relief followed. That felt much better.

Then I pulled out my cell phone and pushed the buttons to connect me with home. As I listened to it ringing, I piled up a nest of pillows on the bed and lay down gratefully.

I imagined Davey running to pick up the phone, Sam pausing in what he was doing to hear who was calling. All the little routines of home, going on in my absence. The Poodles would follow Davey out to the kitchen; several would bark to add to the excitement.

I could have called Sam's cell phone, but that would have spoiled Davey's fun. When you're nine, things like picking up the phone are still exciting.

I felt a swift stab of homesickness as I heard a click and Davey yelled, "Hey!"

"Hey yourself, it's Mom."

I could hear the Poodles in the background and I quickly picked out Faith's distinctive voice. She was the first dog I'd ever owned and she'd become my canine soul mate. Since Faith can pretty much read my mind, I assumed she knew it was me on the phone.

"I figured it was you," Davey said, sounding very pleased with himself. "How are the Poconos? Are they big? Do they have snow on them?"

Told that I'd be spending the week in the mountains, my son had pictured me scaling the Alps or living at a Mount Everest base camp. Unfortunately my real life wasn't that exciting.

"They're medium-sized and I haven't seen any snow yet. Actually the weather here is pretty much like it is at home."

"Oh. No skiing?"

"Not this week. And probably not at all for me until after the baby is born."

"The baby needs a name," said Davey.

This was a familiar complaint. Davey is very organized and he likes the world around him to be the same.

"Sam-Dad and I are working on it," he said.

"Good. What have you come up with?"

"We're thinking maybe Rufus."

I swallowed a laugh. "Really."

"You know, in honor of Sam's Scottish heritage."

"Sam doesn't have a Scottish heritage."

"That's not what he told me." This time it was Davey who let a giggle escape.

"Okay," I said. "Rufus sounds good. What if it's a girl?"

"It won't be."

"It might be."

"It won't."

The utter confidence of youth. While I loved the idea of a baby daughter myself, I was really hoping he wouldn't be disappointed.

"How's everything going at home?" I asked.

"Mom, you've only been gone a day. Not even."

"Yes, but I know you guys. And things can go wrong in less time than that."

"No problems here," said Davey. "Everything's cool. Wait! Here's Sam."

"Hi, Mel." Sam's voice replaced my son's on the line. "How's everything going?"

"Great. If you don't count the fact that Aunt Peg came to this symposium to rendezvous with her new forty-nine-year-old boyfriend whom she met over the Internet, that some sort of judging scandal is brewing, and that the organizer of the event is afraid the keynote speaker is up to something nefarious."

"In other words, business as usual," said Sam.

"Pretty much."

"How are you feeling?"

"Good." I leaned back on the pillows and closed my eyes. "Tired."

"Don't do too much. You're there to enjoy yourself, take in a few lectures, learn a little something, have a week off. A low-stress vacation."

"There is such a thing?"

"Damn straight. You're on it. Let me talk to Bertie. I want to find out if she's keeping an eye on you."

"Not here," I said with a yawn. "She's out partying the night away with her new friend, Alana."

"Not Alana Bennett?"

"The very same."

Like Aunt Peg, Sam had been involved in the dog show world for eons. Her knowledge and connections were legendary, but his were pretty impressive too.

"Tell Bertie to keep her hand on her wallet and her back to the wall," said Sam.

"Will do. Aunt Peg has already said much the same thing. Now, what's this about Rufus?"

Sam's deep laugh rumbled through the phone. "Just trying it on for size."

"And your supposed Scottish heritage?"

"Supposed, hell. I look fine in a kilt."

"No arguments from me, not that I've ever had the pleasure. Maybe when I get back?"

"Anytime, babe."

"Now listen," I said on a more serious note. "Talk to Davey about the fact that he might be getting a little sister. He's waited so long for a sibling, I'd really hate for him to be disappointed."

"I know," said Sam. "Me too. I'll work on it."

"One more thing. Reach down and give Faith a pat. Tell her it's from me."

"Already done," said Sam. "She's been sitting on my lap listening to your voice while we've been talking."

My heart softened. "I love you."

"I know."

"Do better."

"You're the love of my life and you always will be."

"That works."

"For me too," said Sam.

Bertie got back to the room just before midnight. She beat Aunt Peg by at least an hour. So it was no surprise that my aunt was looking rather bleary eyed at breakfast the next morning.

Not that I was eating breakfast actually. But I was sitting at a table with the two of them, sipping a glass of orange juice and trying to be sociable.

Aunt Peg's a multi-tasker. She had a fork in one hand and the day's agenda in the other.

"Margo has really outdone herself," she said. "This schedule has something that should be of interest to just about everyone."

"Better still," said Bertie, "if we get tired of sitting through lectures and panel discussions, all the inn's facilities are available to us. I've got my eye on the spa myself. I'm pretty sure I could use a mud bath or a massage."

I watched enviously as she cut off a large square of waffle and stuffed it into her mouth. Bertie never had to worry about her weight. Not only that but whatever carousing she and Alana had been up to the night before, she didn't seem to be suffering any repercussions.

"Richard wants to try out the hot tub," said Peg. "He asked if I'd brought a bathing suit with me. Can you just imagine?"

"Sure," I said, lying with conviction. I'd never seen my aunt in a bathing suit and I doubted I ever would. "Speaking of Richard, how was your dinner?"

"It was fine."

I sat and waited. Aunt Peg ignored me and returned to eating her omelet. Obviously she thought her first answer had been sufficient.

Which of course it hadn't.

"Fine?" Bertie said after a minute. "Just fine?"

Peg looked up. "What do you mean *just* fine? Fine is a good thing."

"Fine is an okay thing," I said. "It's damning with faint praise. It certainly doesn't sound very exciting."

"Oh, pish. Who wants excitement at my age?"

Bertie and I exchanged a glance. As if we were going to buy *that.* Especially considering the source.

"We want details," I said.

"Well, I'd like to win the lottery," Aunt Peg replied, "and I don't see that happening either."

She looked at her watch, pushed back her chair, and stood. "My dear friend Wanda Swanson will be starting her Saluki lecture shortly and I intend to be sitting front row center when she does. I trust you two can manage to keep yourselves occupied without my guidance?"

Bertie and I agreed that we could.

"In that case, I shall see you later. We'll meet at quarter to three outside the main lecture hall. Does that suit?"

Charles Evans would be giving the keynote address at three. Before speaking with Margo the previous evening, I wasn't sure I'd bother to attend. Having been forewarned, however, that Charles's presentation might be the most exciting thing to happen all week, I now had no intention of missing it.

Bertie obviously felt the same way. We both nodded. Aunt Peg gathered up her things and left.

Bertie glanced down at the schedule. "Let's see, the first track offers a choice between Salukis and Irish Setters. Or I can cut out on them both and get a little pampering." She considered for a moment. "Not much choice there, I'm going for the pampering."

"It's Irish Setters for me," I said. I'd always been intrigued by the beautiful, russet dogs.

"Go for it," said Bertie. "I'll catch up with you later."

If I had been paying more attention—which translated in my mind to *if I wasn't pregnant*—I would have realized that Caroline Evans was the judge leading the discussion of Irish Setters. I settled down near the front of the room and watched Charles's wife take command of the podium with authority. She was petite in stature but her forceful demeanor made her seem bigger. When Caroline was ready to start speaking, the room, filled nearly to capacity, immediately quieted.

What followed was a talk that was every bit as lively and playful as the red setters themselves. Caroline clearly adored her subject. She managed to convey her devotion to the breed while at the same time imparting a huge amount of useful information.

It was easy to understand why Bertie and Aunt Peg had praised the woman's judging skills. If Caroline handled herself in the show ring as well as she did in the lecture hall, even the most knowledgeable exhibitors would have been delighted to have her opinion.

Having skipped breakfast, I took a quick break for an early lunch when the lecture ended. Soup and crackers eaten in a café overlooking the wooded mountainside was about all my stomach could tolerate. That afternoon, I listened to half a session on Otterhounds, then stuck my head briefly into the Kuvasz room.

By then, I'd been inside nearly all day. The building was beginning to feel stuffy to me; I grabbed a jacket and headed outside for a walk.

As soon as I stepped through the door, the crisp, cool autumn air revived my spirits. The tangy scent of pine filled the air. A hiking path angled away from the far side of the parking lot and off into the woods. Striding out, I headed for it eagerly.

After a day of sitting still, it felt good just to be moving again. The only thing keeping the experience from being just right, I realized, was the lack of canine companionship.

I'd grown up without pets, and spent my early adult years similarly dogless. Then Aunt Peg had given me my first Standard Poodle, Faith, and everything had changed. Faith's daughter, Eve, had become part of our family several years later; and now it was hard to imagine how I'd ever lived without either one of them.

When Sam and I got married, he'd added his three Standard Poodles to the mix. Now we had a houseful, and I couldn't remember the last time I'd gone for a walk without at least one Poodle cavorting at my side. Glad as I was to be outdoors on such a beautiful afternoon, I knew I'd enjoy the activity more if I had a dog to share it with.

Lost in contemplation, I actually, for a moment, thought I'd conjured up the dog that suddenly came trotting out of the woods and onto the path in front of me. He was a good-sized German Shepherd, tan with black markings. His body was muscular, but thin. He wasn't wearing a collar.

"Hey, boy," I said.

The dog stopped in his tracks. He seemed as surprised to see me as I was to see him.

"What are you doing out here?" I asked.

Not surprisingly, he didn't answer.

I stopped walking, too. We stood and stared at one another.

After a moment, I held out a hand. The dog lifted a lip, showing a row of strong white teeth.

"Shhh," I said, "it's okay."

But I pulled my hand back, just in case.

The dog had a wary, skittish look about him. He was an attractive Shepherd, clearly a purebred. His eyes were sharp and shifty, though. He didn't look like someone's pet.

"Are you hungry?"

The dog cocked his head. Clearly he was listening to me. Just as clearly, he wasn't about to come any nearer.

Slowly I reached in my pocket and pulled out a granola bar. Probably not the best thing for him, but it was all I had. If the dog was a stray and had missed a couple of meals, he wouldn't be too choosy.

He watched me unwrap the treat. His body was still, his dark eyes riveted.

Once again I held out my hand. Once again he declined to step toward me. Someone, somewhere, had destroyed his trust in people.

"Here you go," I said, giving the granola bar a gentle toss.

I thought he might catch it, but he was too cautious for that. Instead he let it land in the pine needles at his feet. His head dipped down for a quick sniff; then his teeth opened and he snatched it up. Immediately then, he spun around and disappeared back into the trees.

"You're welcome," I called after him.

I might as well have been talking to myself.

The woods were thick with underbrush, but the Shepherd slipped through the thick cover effortlessly. No sound alerted me to the direction he had taken. When I stepped off the path and peered into the trees, I saw no sign of him. The dog had vanished as suddenly as he'd appeared.

If I hadn't still been holding the empty wrapper in my hands, I might have wondered if I'd imagined him.

6

"There you are," said Aunt Peg. "Bertie and I were wondering where you'd gone off to."

The two of them were waiting for me outside the door to the main lecture hall. It was nearly time for Charles's speech, and judging by the crowd that had gathered, most of the symposium participants planned to attend. The room's double doors were wide open; even so, with the crush of people in the entryway, there was a wait to get through.

"I hear you're supposed to be keeping an eye on me," I said to Bertie.

She flushed guiltily. "Frank made me promise. I think Sam put him up to it."

"And you gave in? You of all people should know better. I'm pregnant, not incapacitated. When you were pregnant, did anyone follow you around?"

"Actually, yeah . . . Frank did. It just about drove me crazy. Eventually I had to tell him that if he didn't stop, I'd reconsider the whole idea and not have the baby."

"I'll bet that worked," Peg said dryly.

She ushered Bertie and me into the flow of traffic. "If we don't find seats soon, we'll have to settle for a back corner somewhere. Considering what Margo said last night, I'd just as soon have a good view of the proceedings."

"Have you heard any more about Charles's speech?" I asked, as we found three empty chairs on the aisle in the middle of the room.

"Not a blessed thing. If Charles is up to something, he must be planning to spring it on us as a surprise. Or maybe Margo was mistaken and it was all just a false alarm."

At the front of the room, Margo stepped up to the podium and asked for silence. Stragglers found their seats. Conversations died away. Everyone waited expectantly.

"I'd like to welcome you to the first annual Rockwall Mountain Symposium," she began. "I trust you're all having a wonderful time so far?"

People nodded in agreement. There was a smattering of applause.

"Excellent. It's my pleasure to present our keynote speaker, Charles Evans. For most of you, I would imagine that this is a man who needs no introduction. Charles has been a force in the world of purebred dogs since he won the Junior Showmanship class at Westminster in . . ." She paused as if trying to come up with the year. "Well, let's just say it was quite some time ago."

Charles, standing off to one side, nodded in acknowledgment of the teasing jab. The audience laughed appreciatively.

"In due course Charles became one of the top professional handlers the sport has ever known. Some of the dogs he presented are known in the annals of their breeds as legends. His skill, his flair, his innate ability to bring out the best in every dog he showed changed the look of presentation for the generations of professional handlers that followed."

She was laying it on pretty thick. I wondered if Margo was hoping that if she piled on the accolades, Charles might be convinced to abort whatever subversive plan he had in mind.

If so, the symposium director was certainly giving it her best shot. The introduction droned on and on. Finishing with his handling career, Margo began to praise Charles's superior skills when he moved into the next phase of his profession and became a knowledgeable and discerning judge.

I slumped in my seat and reconsidered my earlier opinion. Maybe Margo's plan was to bore the audience to sleep before she relinquished the podium in the hope that that would mute the effect of whatever it was Charles had to say.

I took a look around the room. Though a majority of the attendees were already aware of Charles's accomplishments, most were listening politely.

I'd have expected to see Caroline Evans sitting right down in front. Instead she was seated not too far from us. Rather than listening to her husband's introduction, she was fooling with something in her lap. It looked like she was text-messaging someone on her phone. No doubt she'd heard all this before.

When Margo finally stopped speaking and Charles stepped forward, the applause was thunderous. Whether the response was for Charles himself, or whether the audience was simply relieved to finally have the program move forward, it was hard to tell.

"Good afternoon," Charles said.

His voice was deep and soothing. It rolled out across the room like the voice of wisdom. And the voice of authority.

We all sat up and began to pay attention.

He looked around the room. "What a pleasure it is to see so many familiar faces here today. Old friends and, I hope, some new ones too. I'm here to talk to you about the future of a sport that we all know and love. Of course, I'm referring to the sport of dogs."

Despite his opening, Charles spent the next fifteen minutes speaking not about the future, but rather about the past. He gave a brief history of dog showing in the United States and talked about how much the dog world had changed in the thirty-plus years of his own involvement.

Earlier sportsmen, he told us, had defined the different breeds of dogs by their function and usefulness. In the intervening years, however, generations of dog fanciers had revised and reshaped those breeds with the result that the dogs we knew today often looked very different from their forebears.

None of this came as a shock to anyone in the audience. Some of the listeners were nodding as he spoke; others were desultorily taking notes.

Then Charles paused and took a deep breath. "We now come to the heart of the message I want to deliver. Conscience compels me to say something that may not be entirely popular. Something that many of you may not want to hear. Please bear in mind that throughout my entire career, one thing has remained true. I have always, *always* put the welfare of the dog first. It is something I shall also attempt to do today, no matter what the consequences of my actions might be."

People who had begun to relax, sat up straight again. Those who were taking notes, turned to a fresh page.

"Uh oh," Aunt Peg said under her breath. "Here it comes."

I could see Margo, sitting off to one side of the dais. Her fingers were knit together tightly in her lap. Her expression was strained.

Charles, by contrast, looked calm and composed. He grasped the sides of the podium between his hands and gazed out over his audience.

"Unfortunately in its current state, the sport of dogs has become a somewhat unnatural activity. Driven by the desire to produce dogs that will excel in the show ring, putting the need to win above all else, breeders are manipulating canine genetics in the quest to produce a perfect specimen. A quest that has not only proven elusive but has also worked to the detriment of many breeds. One only has to look at the narrow, pointed head of the Collie, the profuse, almost unworkable coat of the Poodle, or the reproductive difficulties of many of the Toy breeds to see how true this is."

"I would beg to differ," Aunt Peg said under her breath.

No surprise, she sounded annoyed. As soon as Charles had uttered the words, I'd known that the reference to Poodles would make her bristle.

"We have taken animals that, in their pure and natural state, are a thing of grace and beauty, of intelligence and fierce loyalty, and we have turned them into little more than puppets for human entertainment."

"What's your point?" somebody called out from the back of the room.

Angry muttering followed. It was, I suspected, directed more at Charles than at the heckler.

"I'll tell you my point," Charles said. Despite the obvious opposition in the room, he remained unruffled.

"Dog shows were originally intended to be a sporting competition to determine whose dogs were best suited for the purpose for which they'd been produced. That is obviously no longer true. In the show ring, we have retrievers who can't retrieve, Newfoundlands who've never been allowed to swim, and terriers who wouldn't recognize vermin if it ran between their legs. One by one, the usefulness of our breeds is slipping away. They're being ruined by what has essentially turned into a canine beauty contest. And that is a damn shame."

The audience—all of them dog lovers, and all of them dog show aficionados—was growing mutinous now. People were speaking loudly among themselves. Other voices joined those of the initial heckler.

Caroline rose, excused herself, slipped from the row of chairs, and left the room.

Charles, still speaking, didn't appear to notice.

"As we look toward the future, we need to recognize that not only are the animal rights groups not going to go away, but they are going to increase their base of support. It would be a show of wisdom on our part to accept the fact that they have some valid points. Rather than dismissing their agenda, we need to find a way to reconcile and to work together with them."

"No way!" someone called out.

A woman I didn't know stood up. "You want us to reconcile with people who think it's all right to stage protests by showing up at dog shows, opening crates, and turning defenseless dogs loose to run in traffic? That's the kind of agenda you think we ought to support?"

Charles looked to see who had spoken up.

"I'll admit that in an effort to get our attention, some of their tactics have been extreme. But that doesn't negate the fact that some of what they're saying has merit. We are the ones who are to blame for letting dog shows reach their current state. We have work to do, people, and it's high time that we accepted that fact."

Charles may have firmly believed what he was saying, but if he had expected to find even a shred of approval or agreement in this room, he had sadly misjudged his audience. He tried once again to drive home his point.

"In a perfect, future world the huge dog shows that we know today, the events that are little more than testimonies to artificiality, would cease to exist. Instead, our breeds would be allowed to return to what they were meant to be in the beginning—friends, companions, helpmates to man. Dogs would be bred for function rather than the need to conform to a pre-set standard. And they—and we—would be much the better for it."

Charles finally stopped speaking. No applause greeted the end of his speech. He didn't seem to expect any.

In this crowd, what he'd said was tantamount to heresy. If he hadn't realized that in the beginning, he certainly had to know it now.

After a moment, he stepped away from the podium and strode off the stage. Margo, already on her feet, turned and hurried after him.

"That was interesting," I said.

"Interesting, my foot," Aunt Peg snorted. "Whatever else Charles hoped to accomplish, he's just committed career suicide."

"He probably doesn't care," Bertie said practically. "Considering that he just issued a call for the abolishment of dog shows."

"Nobody will take him seriously on that score," said

Peg. "They couldn't possibly." She looked around the room. "Where's Caroline? I imagine she's about ready to kill him."

"She slipped out five minutes ago."

"I don't blame her. She probably didn't want to listen to that drivel any more than the rest of us did."

"It wasn't entirely drivel," I said. "He made a few good points."

Aunt Peg disagreed. "A well-reasoned call for reform would have been one thing. But asking us to align ourselves with the animal rights groups? Charles had to have known he was going much too far taking a stand like that."

"Why do you think he did it?" I asked.

Now that the show was over, the room was emptying quickly. We gathered up our things and prepared to leave.

"I have no idea," Aunt Peg replied. "It's hard to imagine that Charles actually believes all those things he said. He's been a highly respected judge, firmly embedded for years in the system he just thoroughly excoriated. So why the sudden turnaround?"

"Maybe he needs new meds," said Bertie.

We both turned and looked at her.

"Just a thought."

Under the circumstances, it wasn't a bad one.

Sad to say that while Bertie and Aunt Peg went off to do fun and exciting things, I went upstairs and took a nap before dinner. When I rejoined them two hours later, Aunt Peg was holding court at a large corner table in the bar.

I recognized most of the people she was seated with.

Richard was there, along with his two buddies, Marshall and Derek. Bertie was sitting next to a woman I didn't know and on the woman's other side was Tubby Mathis, whom Aunt Peg had dismissed so firmly at the last gathering.

I slid into an empty chair beside Bertie, and Richard immediately raised his hand and called for another round of drinks.

"Name your poison," he said to me.

"Just water, I'm afraid."

"Water?" Tubby lifted his head and looked at me balefully. His arms were cradled possessively around a tall whiskey and there were several empty glasses nearby. "You've come to the wrong place if all you want is water."

"I'd like some pleasant company too," I said. "Presumably I might be able to find that here?"

The woman I hadn't met yet barked out a laugh. She reached a hand across in front of Bertie.

"Rosalyn Arnold," she said. "You must be Melanie."

"Don't tell me my reputation precedes me."

"I'm afraid so. Bertie's been wondering where you were for the last half hour."

I sighed. "There seems to be a lot of that going around."

"Wait a minute," said Tubby. "Are you the gal they've been talking about? The one who's pregnant?"

The one who's pregnant? Was that what I had been reduced to now? Had every other aspect of my being been relegated to lesser importance compared to the fact that I was carrying a child?

Resigned, I nodded. "That's me."

"Well, all right, then," Tubby said. "Course you don't want something hard to drink. Barkeep, bring this gal some water. Looks to me like she's probably thirsty."

Oh God. Now every eye in the bar had turned my way. Everyone was checking out the *pregnant* woman who wanted only water to drink.

"What did I miss?" I asked brightly. Anything to change the subject. "What were you guys talking about?"

"Three guesses," said Derek. "And the first two don't count."

"Charles's speech?"

"Got it in one," said Peg.

1

"The man's a jackass," Tubby pronounced. "Always was, probably always will be. I don't see why anyone ought to stir themselves to give credence to anything he says."

"I have to admit I was disappointed," said Marshall. "Charles Evans is such a well known and well respected judge, I expected his speech to be something different, something better than that. But then I thought, here's a man who knows so much more than we do. Even if his ideas seem somewhat radical, perhaps we owe him the courtesy of at least considering his point of view."

"Baloney," said Rosalyn. "I considered it and found it wanting. Now I'm done."

I leaned over to Bertie and asked, "What's her breed?"

Knowing that affiliation was a reliable short cut in the dog show world for finding out more about someone.

"Bedlingtons," Bertie whispered back.

Adorable, soft looking, pale colored terriers. Lamblike on the outside, scrappy on the inside. Perhaps like

Rosalyn herself. At any rate, she didn't seem likely to back down from her opinion.

"I'll say one thing." Aunt Peg entered the fray. "Just the fact that we're sitting here discussing this means that Charles accomplished what he set out to do. I'm betting that he intended to open a dialogue—"

"He wanted to create controversy," Derek interjected.

"And he succeeded," Peg continued smoothly.

"He said that he wanted to abolish dog shows," said Tubby. "Of all the asinine ideas. I can assure you, he won't succeed there."

"Thank goodness for that," Richard commented. He gazed around the table with a smile; it looked like he was hoping to lighten the mood. "Otherwise we'd all be out of luck."

"True," said Rosalyn. "And that's exactly what makes him so dangerous. Because when a man of Charles's stature espouses an idea—no matter how outlandish it might be—people will sit up and pay attention."

"Hear, hear!" said Derek.

I tried to remember what I'd learned about him the day before. It seemed to me that he had Beagles, though I didn't know which size. Nor whether he was an exhibitor or a judge.

"Charles must be getting soft in the head," said Tubby. "It's a wonder Caroline doesn't try harder to keep him in line."

"I take it you've never been married," Aunt Peg said dryly.

"I was married," Tubby replied. "It didn't last."

"I can't imagine why not," Bertie said under her breath.

"Caroline has her hands full with her own career," said Marshall. "Let's not forget that she's every bit as important in the dog show world as her husband is. The two of them are constantly on the road, traveling from one assignment to the next. I'm sure she doesn't have time to monitor everything he gets up to."

"Nobody's asking her to baby-sit him," said Richard. "But it wouldn't have hurt if she'd given Margo a hint ahead of time about what Charles was planning to do. I thought those two women were supposed to be friends."

"Women friends," said Derek. "Now, there's an oxymoron for you."

Tubby looked up from his drink and grinned.

"Excuse me?" I said.

"You know what I'm talking about," said Derek. "Women don't have any idea how to be friends. All they know how to do is compete with one another."

"My dear boy," Aunt Peg said. The words sounded like anything but an endearment. "Whatever gave you such a foolish idea?"

"Life." Derek shrugged. "Experience. Observation. Don't you all agree?"

He looked around the table at the other men present.

Richard lifted his hands and shoulders in a comically broad shrug. "You're on your own with this one, buddy."

"Okay, time out," Rosalyn said. "I sure as heck didn't drive all the way to Pennsylvania to rehash the war of the sexes. Entertaining as your company has been, I think I'm done here. It's time for me to go find the people I'm supposed to be meeting for dinner."

Thankfully, Rosalyn's announcement brought the budding argument to a halt. Everyone checked their watches and thought about their own plans. Drinks were finished, the bar tab settled.

Tubby wandered away and joined another table. Derek and Marshall left together. Richard had a quick word with Aunt Peg, then disappeared too. Having dined the previous evening with my aunt, he would make his mother happy tonight by having dinner with her.

That left Bertie, Peg, and me to figure out what we were going to do next.

"You need a real meal," Aunt Peg said to me. "I bet you haven't eaten a thing all day."

"I had soup. And crackers," I added as an afterthought.

"Barely enough to keep one person functioning," she said sternly. "Much less two."

Point taken.

The dining room was nearly full but the maitre d' managed to find a table for three, situated by a window on an enclosed porch.

"Perfect," Aunt Peg pronounced. She immediately waved over a waitress and placed an order for three tall glasses of milk.

"Three?" I said weakly.

My aunt subscribes to the firm belief that any and all pregnancy related issues can be cured with dairy products. I knew, however, that I'd have trouble keeping even one glass of milk down.

"There's no reason why you should be the only healthy one among us. Bertie and I will join you."

Bertie sent me a dark look, apparently less than pleased at being roped into my calcium support group. But when the milk arrived, she chugged hers down with good humor and even managed, when Aunt Peg wasn't looking, to help make a dent in mine.

Peg, meanwhile, ordered me a steak. It arrived looking thick, well cooked, and dripping with juices. Normally I make a great carnivore but now all I could see was a large dark blob of fat and sinew.

I let the meat sit on my plate while I picked at my

veggies and consoled myself with the knowledge that my body would ask for the foods it needed. Besides, I was up to date on my vitamins.

Over dinner Aunt Peg adopted the role of cruise director and demanded to know how each of us had spent the day. Bertie went first, informing us that she had indeed had a massage. Aside from attending two seminars, she'd also managed to spend some time in the hot tub that afternoon.

"How very eighties," I said with a laugh.

"No, really, it was great. Hot water below, cold air above, the smell of pine trees in the air, a tall hedge all around for privacy. I recommend it highly."

"I'll pass," I said. Water that hot was forbidden for the duration.

Aunt Peg, however, looked interested.

"How does it work?" she wanted to know. "Are you by yourself or in there with others? I assume you must be wearing a bathing suit?"

"I was by myself," said Bertie. "But people share them all the time. It's a very convivial thing to do." She stopped and grinned. "And yes on the bathing suit. In this crowd, I wouldn't expect to see anyone skinny dipping."

"Too bad," Aunt Peg murmured.

I choked on my milk.

She shifted her gaze my way. "How about you? I trust you spent the first day of the symposium profitably?"

Attempting to divert attention away from my mostly full plate, I started to tell her about the lectures I'd attended. Then stopped, as I realized there *was* something I'd done that my aunt would find interesting. In the furor over Charles's speech, I'd forgotten all about my encounter in the woods.

"I saw a dog," I said.

"Button?" asked Bertie. "That Chihuahua seems to be everywhere."

"No, not Button. A German Shepherd, a half wild one."

"Here? At the resort?"

"In the woods. We met up on the walking path. He looked like a stray."

"What made you think that?" asked Aunt Peg.

I had her full attention now.

"For one thing, he looked pretty skinny. For another, he wasn't wearing a collar and he wouldn't let me near him. I even tried offering him some food, but he was too afraid of me to come and get it."

"What kind of food?"

"A granola bar."

Aunt Peg frowned at my response.

As often happened where my aunt was concerned, once again I'd been found wanting. But *come on*, I thought. Did she actually think I should have been out in the woods toting around a pocketful of premium kibble?

Then I paused and reconsidered. This was my aunt I was talking to. Knowing her, she probably did.

"Maybe he doesn't like granola bars," Bertie offered.

"Or maybe he wasn't as hungry as you thought," said Peg.

"No, he was hungry all right. When I threw it to him he grabbed it right up and then ran away."

"Toward the resort or in the other direction?"

"Away, back into the woods."

"I wonder if there are any houses on that side of the mountain. Just because we can't see them from here doesn't mean there might not be people living just down the slope."

"Even so," I said, shaking my head, "he definitely didn't look like someone's pet. He was very wary, and once he realized I was there, he never took his eyes off me. Not even for an instant. I think he was afraid I might try to leap out and try to grab him or something."

"Maybe he's been abused," said Bertie. "That would explain his attitude."

"I wonder if he's been abandoned," Aunt Peg mused. "Unfortunately people seem to find ways to do plenty of stupid things when it comes to the animals they supposedly care for. Perhaps with winter coming, his owners didn't want an extra mouth to feed."

"Nobody would be that callous," I said.

"Yes, they would," Bertie immediately contradicted me. "People dump dogs for all sorts of idiotic reasons. Then they rationalize to themselves that they're doing the right thing. They imagine that someone else will find their cast-off and give him a good home."

"And instead, of course, the reverse is true." Aunt Peg took up the cause of educating me when Bertie paused for breath. "If they're lucky, abandoned dogs will find themselves picked up and taken to the pound, where if they're cute they might manage to be adopted. The unlucky ones are hit by cars, or killed by coyotes, or else they simply starve to death."

The little food I'd eaten turned over in my stomach. I thought of the dog I'd seen earlier with his rough, unbrushed coat and wounded eyes. He needed more in the way of human intervention than just one measly granola bar.

I already had five big dogs at home, I told myself firmly. The shepherd's welfare wasn't my responsibility.

"Shall we?" said Aunt Peg. She was already signaling for the check.

Bertie pushed back her chair. "I'll go up to the room and get our coats."

"Shall we what?" I asked.

It appeared to be true. Pregnancy *had* dulled my brain.

"Go find ourselves a stray dog, of course," Peg said briskly. "What else?"

Just like that the decision was taken out of my hands.

As soon as I'd opened my mouth, I should have realized exactly what would happen next. Present Aunt Peg with a cause and a dog, and you'd have to wrestle her to the ground to regain control of either.

Especially now, when her own family of Poodles remained at home in Connecticut and she was feeling dog-deprived, Aunt Peg couldn't wait to lead the way outside in search of the indigent German Shepherd. She took over like a woman on a mission.

It had grown dark while we were eating dinner, but the area around the inn and its various outbuildings was well lit. Aunt Peg marched down the front steps, stopped and looked around, then headed toward the buffer of tall pine trees that surrounded the parking lot.

"He went in this direction?" she asked, but didn't wait for confirmation.

As it happened, she was heading the wrong way.

"If you were a homeless dog, out alone at night," Aunt Peg said, thinking aloud, "where would you be?"

"If I was a stray but I used to be somebody's pet," said

Bertie, "I might be looking for company. Or maybe a warm place to sleep."

"I don't think so," I spoke up. "I bet he's still hungry. If I were that dog, I'd be out behind the kitchen looking for something to eat in the garbage cans."

"Good thought." Aunt Peg abruptly changed course. Then she stopped for a moment and studied the main building thoughtfully, working out a blueprint in her mind. "Judging by the position of the dining room, I imagine it's safe to assume that the kitchen would be around the back."

"Follow me," said Bertie. "There's a path that leads between the buildings. It runs alongside this hedge. . . ."

Even in the semi-dark she seemed to know where she was going. Aunt Peg and I fell into line behind her.

"You've done this before," I said. "What's back here?"

Bertie laughed. "The famous hot tub of course. It's off in a little alcove between the inn and the health club. We'll see it in a minute, as soon as we come to an opening in the hedge."

Aunt Peg's long-legged stride slowed. Behind her on the path, I was forced to check myself.

"You don't suppose anyone would be out there now, do you?" she asked.

Aunt Peg's curiosity about the facilities had to be due to Richard's suggestion that they sample the hot tub's pleasures together. Surely she couldn't be serious about doing such a thing?

"Easy enough to find out," said Bertie. When a gap appeared in the hedge, she veered right and headed toward a lighted area.

"Wait!" cried Peg. "We don't want to disturb anyone."

"It's a public place. Open to all the guests. If people

don't want to be seen doing something, they shouldn't be doing it out here."

Hoping Aunt Peg would take those words to heart, I followed along behind. On the other side of the hedge, we found ourselves in a small, square courtyard. The area was bounded by trees on two sides, and the back of a building, presumably the health club, on the third.

Overhead lights illuminated the large wooden tub in the center of the square. It sat on a raised platform and was surrounded by benches. As it was above my eye level, I couldn't see the water inside; but steam rose from the tub, attesting to how much warmer than the night air its contents were.

"It's empty," said Aunt Peg. She sounded disappointed.

"It happens." Bertie chuckled. "This week I think most of the inn's guests are more interested in attending the symposium than they are in availing themselves of the amenities."

"That's because this place is called a *health* club," I pointed out. "And that makes people think of stuff like treadmills, stair steppers, and aerobics. Most of them would rather do almost anything else."

"Speak for yourself. Supposedly healthy is the new American way of life. Besides, the building also contains a spa—"

Abruptly she stopped speaking. We'd been walking while we were talking, drawing closer to the raised platform. I took another step and saw what Bertie had seen. A fluffy, yellow bath towel, the kind found stacked in each of the inn's rooms, was draped over one of the back benches.

"What?" asked Aunt Peg.

"It turns out we're not alone." Bertie giggled.

Funny, I thought, that we weren't able to see whoever was sitting in the tub. Not that I had a lot of experience with hot tubs, but I thought people usually sat in
them with head and shoulders above the water, perhaps
even above the lip of the tub itself.

It was one of those moments when you instinctively
know something is wrong, but your brain flatly refuses
to process the information.

Aunt Peg, however, had no such problem thinking
things through. She glanced at the discarded towel, then
at the splash of water on the platform's boards.

"Oh dear," she said, pushing me out of the way to
step up onto the deck.

Even as Aunt Peg gasped, Bertie and I were already
hopping up to stand beside her.

A man was floating face down in the hot tub. His
dark hair was shiny and slick under the lights from above.
His arms were outstretched, well-manicured fingers reaching for something he'd never touch.

Bertie went pale. "That can't be good," she said.

My sister-in-law, the master of understatement.

8

"Bertie, help me get him out of there!" Aunt Peg was already reaching to drag one of the heavy benches closer to the side of the tub.

"You!" Her finger sliced at me like a thin dagger. "Find a phone. Call 911."

The phone didn't require much finding; I had one in my pocket.

While I spoke to the authorities, Bertie and Peg scrambled to the rescue. Aunt Peg reached up over the side of the tub and turned the body onto its back. Charles Evans's face swam into view, his blue eyes open and staring blindly.

"I think I'm going to lose my dinner," I said.

"Not around here," Peg ordered. "If you have to throw up, go do it in the bushes."

Instead I swallowed heavily and tried to figure out how to help. Aunt Peg was holding Charles's torso up and out of the water. However, in order to get him out of the hot tub, she was going to need more leverage from below.

Bertie had obviously already come to the same conclusion. Busy kicking off her shoes and shedding her jacket, she hadn't yet seen what Peg and I had.

I reached down and steadied the bench as she climbed up onto it and hopped over the side of the tub. Bertie landed in the deep water with a small splash. Then she took a good look.

"Damn," she said softly. "It's Charles."

"We know that," Aunt Peg snapped. Her arms had to have been growing tired from the pressure of supporting his weight at that awkward angle. "Now help me get him out of here. Maybe there's still time to save him."

Judging by his pallor I didn't think so, but I wasn't about to argue. CPR sometimes worked wonders. I only hoped that one of the other two knew how to perform the procedure.

Bertie leaned down under the water to grasp Charles's legs.

"Ewww!" she said, straightening abruptly.

"Now what?"

"He isn't wearing any clothes."

Eww, indeed.

"Hang on," I said, climbing up on the bench. "I'll come in and help."

Aunt Peg spared a hand to swat me back down. "No, you won't. Go stand over there."

Out of trouble. Out of the way. As if pregnancy had rendered me not only dull but also useless.

"Like hell," I said.

Bertie reached down again. She circled her hands around Charles's knees, hoisted his torso up out of the water, and passed his legs to me. Charles's skin felt slick and slippery, and every bit as warm as the water it had just been in.

It took all three of us to lift him up and out. Charles was heavy. Deadweight, pardon the expression. We lowered him gently down onto the platform.

Bertie grabbed the towel and dried off as well as she could. The night air was chilly. In another minute she'd be shivering.

I helped Aunt Peg lever Charles up onto his side. We meant to dump the water out of his mouth, but only a small amount trickled out from between his lips. That wasn't a good sign.

When we laid him back down, Aunt Peg cupped her hands around his nose and mouth and began to blow oxygen into his lungs. I never should have doubted her ability to rise to the occasion.

"Anything?" said Bertie, leaning over to have a look. Rivulets of water streamed from her hair. They dropped down on us from above.

Not taking my eyes from the drama in front of me, I shook my head.

Bertie wrung out the now sodden towel and laid it gently over Charles's lower body, an attempt to give him the dignity he was past caring about. Ignoring both of us, Aunt Peg continued to work.

It seemed like eons passed, but finally I heard the sound of sirens racing up the side of the mountain. Over on our side of the main building, floodlights began to wink on. A door slammed. Running footsteps came toward us.

Reinforcements were about to arrive. We'd done all we could; now the professionals could take over.

"Aunt Peg?" I laid a hand on her shoulder.

"No," she said, shaking me off. "I'm not giving up."

"You don't have to give up, help is here."

"Help?"

Aunt Peg stopped and took a deep breath. When she lifted her head and rocked back on her heels, a paramedic slipped in and took her place. She looked like someone emerging from a trance.

EMTs and staff from the inn swarmed around us. I grasped Aunt Peg's arm on one side. Bertie took the other. We got her up onto her feet and led her a little bit away.

Behind us, experts continued the work she had started.

"You did everything you could," I said.

"It wasn't enough," she replied.

The first sirens I'd heard had been those of the ambulance. A police car followed in short order. A fire truck came next, then another police vehicle. Apparently death was an unusual occurrence at the Rockwall Mountain Inn.

Within minutes, the small enclosure surrounding the hot tub was filled with people. Bertie, Aunt Peg, and I had retreated farther and farther away as each new contingent arrived. Now we were standing a good distance from the action, back near the hedge that bordered the courtyard.

Bertie was the only one who was soaked through, but all three of us were wet and we were all shivering. Bertie had put her jacket and shoes back on, but it didn't help. Her teeth began to chatter.

"Let's get you inside," said Aunt Peg. "There's nothing more for us to do out here now."

As soon as we started to move away, a uniformed police officer stepped into our path.

"If you three ladies would please wait here," he said,

"I'm sure the detective is going to want to have a few words with you."

Aunt Peg drew herself up to her full height. "We've had a rather harrowing experience and on top of that, we are cold and wet. When the detective is ready, he may speak with us inside the inn."

"Ma'am." The officer positioned his body so we couldn't get by. "I really would like you to wait here."

"Will you take responsibility if we become ill on your account?"

The officer bit his lip and didn't reply. He didn't move either.

I could feel Aunt Peg growing increasingly annoyed. I also sensed the moment inspiration struck. She grabbed my arm and thrust me to the front.

"This woman is pregnant," she said in a loud voice. "Are you willing to risk harm to her unborn child merely to detain us out here for someone's convenience?"

Peg had uttered the magic words. A fleeting look of panic crossed the poor man's face. Perhaps he was imagining me delivering the baby on the spot.

"No, ma'am," he said, melting back out of the way. "No, ma'am."

Who knew? Aside from its other benefits, it looked as though pregnancy was also a get-out-of-jail-free card.

"Your detective may look for us in the bar," Aunt Peg said frostily. The three of us hurried past him. "Don't make us wait all night."

Once inside the inn, Bertie ran upstairs to change her clothes. My attire was damp in spots but that wasn't why I was shivering. I was cold from the inside out.

Of one accord, Aunt Peg and I headed for the fire crackling in the large stone fireplace on the other side of the great room. Unfortunately, we didn't get that far. Almost immediately, Peg and I were surrounded by other guests.

Everyone had heard the sirens. They all knew that something was happening outside. They'd been asked, however, to remain in the inn until the emergency had been dealt with. Now everyone wanted to know what was going on.

"There's been an accident in the hot tub," Aunt Peg said. She didn't offer any details.

Quickly I scanned the crowd, looking for Caroline Evans. I didn't see her. I did see Margo, however, and she was heading purposefully our way.

Coming up beside us, Margo didn't even break stride. Instead she simply looped an arm through Peg's and quickly drew the older woman off to one side. Much as I really wanted to go stand next to the fire, I found myself following them instead.

"What's happened?" Margo demanded, her voice low and tense. "I heard somebody's dead. Is that true?"

"Possibly," Aunt Peg waffled.

Margo leaned in closer. "Don't bullshit me, Peg. We've been friends too long for that. Just tell me what the hell is going on out there."

"I'm afraid it's bad news."

"Of course it's bad news. It has to be bad news. Out with it."

Aunt Peg grasped her friend's hand and squeezed it. "We found Charles Evans floating face down in the hot tub. We got him out and tried to revive him, but I don't think we got to him in time."

"Charles?" Margo staggered back as if she'd been struck. "Are you sure it was him?"

"Positive," Peg confirmed and I nodded.

Of all the things we weren't sure of, the identity of the man we'd found wasn't one of them.

"But that doesn't make sense. What would Charles have been doing outside in the hot tub at this time of night?"

I'd seen such behavior before: friends and loved ones of a victim trying to deny what they were hearing, coming up with all sorts of arguments to refute a truth they didn't want to accept.

Only hours earlier, Margo had been furious with Charles. She might even—in a moment of supreme annoyance—have wished him dead. But now she looked stunned and disbelieving, unwilling to grasp the enormity of what had happened.

"Oh, dear Lord," she said, lifting a hand to her mouth. "Someone has to tell Caroline."

"Do you know where she is?" I asked.

Margo shook her head. "I haven't seen her since this afternoon, in the lecture hall when Charles gave his speech . . ."

At the mention of the afternoon's events, Margo's voice trailed away. We all remembered what one of Charles's last acts had been. And pondered the implications.

"Maybe Caroline is in her room?" I said.

Margo nodded, though she didn't actually seem to be listening. "I have to find her. It will be better if she hears the news from me than from a stranger."

She turned and hurried away. Watching her go, Aunt Peg looked thoughtful.

"What?" I asked.

"I hope I didn't just make a mistake. Considering that Margo is the director of the event that brought us all here, I felt it was her right to know what had happened. I was speaking to her in a professional capacity, however, not a personal one."

I didn't understand. "She's right about Caroline, though. She needs to be told what happened."

"Of course she does. I'm just not sure that Margo is the right person to deliver the news."

I would have delved further, but Bertie chose at that moment to reappear. She was bundled into a warm, gray sweatsuit and had her still-damp hair slicked back off her face.

"What are you guys doing standing here?" she asked. "I expected to find you in the bar downing a shot of whiskey, or at the very least, some hot tea."

"A fine idea," Aunt Peg concurred. "Lead the way."

None of us wanted to answer any more questions. We skirted around the edges of the room and ducked into the bar. With all the activity taking place elsewhere, the room was nearly empty. We had no trouble finding a table.

Aunt Peg ordered a large pot of tea, staring hard at the bartender until he offered to go over to the restaurant and procure one for us. We sat in silence and awaited his return. When he delivered the tea a few minutes later, we poured it by rote, each of us adding generous quantities of milk and sugar to our cups.

The horror of what had happened outside was still fresh in all our minds. Maybe talking about it would have made us feel better, but none of us wanted to be the first to broach the subject. So instead we sat and sipped our tea and waited to see what would happen next.

Detective Wayne found us there fifteen minutes later. He walked over to the table, stood above us, and gazed downward sternly. He looked large, and unhappy, and somewhat intimidating, as I was sure he meant to.

He introduced himself, then said, "Are you the three women who hauled our victim out of the hot tub?"

One by one, we nodded.

"You were told to wait outside, that someone would be by to question you."

"We were cold and we were wet," said Aunt Peg. "And there wasn't any point to our standing around in the dark. If you have questions, pull up a chair, take a seat, and ask them now."

The ground rules had been laid. Of course we would cooperate, but we would do so on our own terms. And Detective Wayne's bullying tactics weren't about to make us cower.

He stood for a minute, still staring down at us. Then he capitulated. He reached around behind him, grabbed a chair from another table, and sat.

"Tea?" Peg asked politely as if he'd just joined a party she was hosting.

Wayne looked faintly amused. "That's what the three of you are drinking? Hot tea?"

"Actually we don't seem to have gotten much of anything down," Bertie said. "That's why there's still plenty left for you."

He gazed around the table. "I understand one of you is pregnant?"

"That would be me."

"Are you feeling all right? Do you need me to get anything for you? We still have medical personnel outside if you'd like to check in with someone."

"No," I said quietly. "I'm fine." But I appreciated the thought.

"Right. Let me know if that changes."

"I will."

Wayne nodded. "Now then, which one of you would like to tell me what happened?"

"Aren't you going to question us separately?" Aunt Peg asked. "That's how they do it on TV."

Once again, a small smile played about his lips. "Any particular reason you think I should do that here? Right now, all we're trying to do is gather information and find out what went wrong."

"Is Charles dead?" I asked.

"I'm afraid so." The detective's tone was somber. "He didn't respond to efforts to revive him."

So the trained professionals hadn't been able to accomplish any more than we had. I sighed softly. Even though I'd suspected as much, it was hard to hear the words.

"The three of you knew the victim, then?"

"His name was Charles Evans," Aunt Peg said. "He was a highly respected dog show judge."

"I take it he was a guest here at the inn?"

"There's a judges' symposium going on here this week," said Bertie. "Charles was one of the participants."

"And the same would be true of you three as well?"

"That's right," I said. "People have come from all over the country to take part."

Detective Wayne nodded slowly, considering that information. Perhaps it was just occurring to him that there was a time limit to how long he'd have to investigate Charles's death. Within a few days' time, most of the likely suspects would be gone.

"About Charles . . ." I said. "Was his death an accident?"

"I'm afraid I don't have the answer to that yet. We'll know more once the medical examiner has done his job. In the meantime, I'm trying to learn what I can by talking to witnesses."

"Unfortunately," said Aunt Peg, "we didn't witness anything. By the time we arrived on the scene, Charles was already dead."

"Yes, ma'am. How did the three of you happen to be walking back there this time of night?"

"We were looking for a dog," said Bertie.

"A dog," Detective Wayne repeated.

His tone implied that this might be one of the least likely excuses he'd ever heard.

"A stray German Shepherd," I explained. "I had seen him earlier and we were hoping to be able to help him."

"And you were expecting to find this dog in the hot tub?"

See? This is why I don't like talking to the police. They tend to take the most innocent assertions, turn them around, and make them sound like something incriminating. Or something stupid.

"Yes," I said. "We thought he might be going for a moonlight swim."

Aunt Peg kicked me under the table. Hard. "Don't mind Melanie. She's—"

"Yes, I know," said Detective Wayne. "Pregnant."

He reached for the pot of tea and poured himself a cup. Then he took his time adding two sugars and stirring the brew. When he was finished, he didn't bother to drink. The ritual seemed less a matter of thirst on his part than a conscious decision to take a time-out.

"Let's start over," he said. "And let's try and remember that we're all on the same team here. Tell me what you saw."

9

So we did.

Between the three of us—a trio of women all talking at once, finishing each other's sentences, and adding both random and pertinent facts when they occurred to us—we probably managed to tell Detective Wayne a great deal more than he was looking to find out.

We told him about the symposium, what it was, and why we were there. Then we gave him a brief overview of the speech Charles had delivered that afternoon, a description that was interspersed with editorial commentary from Aunt Peg explaining why such views would have proven to be so unpopular with this particular audience.

We told him what little we knew about the stray German Shepherd, and that segued into a lecture from Aunt Peg on the importance of caring dog owners stepping forward and acting responsibly when the need arose. Bertie even took time out to tell him about her spa experience that morning, and how much she'd enjoyed her time in the hot tub.

If the detective spent even one, brief, uncensored moment imagining what the redhead would have looked like in a bathing suit, he was careful to not let it show. I had to give him points for that. Having Bertie as a friend can be a hazard at times; lesser men have fallen to their knees on her account.

By the time we'd finished outlining all of that, we'd drunk the first large pot of tea and requested another. I had also been to the bathroom. Twice.

When I returned for the second time, it looked as though we were finally getting ready to wrap things up. All we had left to do was walk Detective Wayne through the events that had transpired earlier that evening.

Which, to be fair, was the only thing he'd asked about in the first place.

To his credit, Wayne didn't show the slightest bit of impatience with the colorful and circuitous route that had taken him on a conversational merry-go-round before finally bringing him back to his original question. Maybe he was enjoying our company. Or perhaps he just had a thing for hot tea.

"So the three of you were walking on the path that leads around the side of the building . . . by the way, did you ever see the dog?"

"No," I said. "We were planning to check out the garbage cans by the kitchen, but we never made it that far. Aunt Peg wanted to see the hot tub and we detoured that way."

"And that's when you discovered Mr. Evans?"

"That's right." Peg took up the story. "He was floating face down in the water. We immediately jumped up onto the platform and pulled him out."

"The three of you together?"

"I called 911 first," I said. "Aunt Peg didn't want me to help."

No point in repeating the reason for that. We all knew what it was.

"But he was too heavy," said Bertie. "It took all three of us to get him out."

Wayne looked her way. "You climbed into the tub with him."

"Someone had to."

"There are several benches around the perimeter of the platform. One of them was pulled over next to the hot tub."

"We did that," said Aunt Peg. "I needed more height to get enough leverage. Then Bertie used the bench to get over the side."

Wayne processed that. "It didn't occur to you to use the steps around the back?"

Well . . . no. Now that he mentioned it, it did make sense that there would have been an easier way to access the hot tub. But none of us had stopped to think about that.

"Next time we'll try to do better," Aunt Peg said tartly.

"I'm not criticizing your rescue efforts, I'm just trying to imagine the scene. I saw that the bench had been moved from its normal spot and I was wondering why, that's all."

Detective Wayne turned to me. "So the three of you were approaching the hot tub. Tell me what you saw."

"Nothing at first. As you know, it's on a raised platform. So we couldn't see inside it. We just thought it was empty."

"Then what happened?"

"Then we got closer and saw there was a towel thrown over one of the benches. That's when we realized that we probably weren't the only ones out there."

"On your way around the side of the inn, had you seen or heard anyone else in the vicinity?"

All three of us stopped and thought about that. Then we all answered in the negative.

"Then you saw Mr. Evans in the hot tub . . ."

"We didn't know who it was then," said Aunt Peg. "We didn't find that out until I reached in and turned him over."

Detective Wayne walked us slowly through each of the remaining steps we'd taken. Unfortunately the rest was fairly straightforward; none of us had any brilliant insights to add.

"You'll probably want to talk to Margo Deline," Aunt Peg said at the end. "She's the director of the event. And of course Caroline, Charles's wife."

"Already being attended to," the detective said. He pushed back his chair and stood. "Ladies, thank you for your time."

Detective Wayne left the bar. We prepared to do the same.

"Maybe Charles had a heart attack," I said hopefully as Bertie nabbed the check and charged it to our room.

"Maybe he slipped and hit his head," she suggested, scribbling a signature on the bill.

Aunt Peg was ever the realist.

"Maybe someone wanted to shut him up," she said.

The next morning at breakfast, the only thing any-one wanted to talk about was what had happened to

Charles. And since Bertie, Aunt Peg, and I had had a ringside seat for the proceedings, we were the most popular people in the dining room.

The first person who stopped by to see us was Richard. He slipped into the empty chair at our table for four and took Aunt Peg's hand in his.

"I'm so sorry I wasn't there to help in your time of need," he said. "Mother and I were dining in our room. So it wasn't until this morning that we even heard about what had happened. Why didn't you call me? You know I would have come to your aid."

The notion of Aunt Peg calling a man to help her cope with a problem seemed like an utterly foreign concept to me. So I was curious to see how she would respond to Richard's solicitude. And just in case things weren't already interesting enough, Florence was wending her way toward us through the roomful of tightly packed tables.

The woman's large purse was tucked in its customary position beneath her arm, with Button's head poked forward out of the top like the figurehead on the prow of a ship. The little Chihuahua looked around as his mistress navigated in our direction. He seemed to be enjoying the ride.

"Thank you for your offer of assistance," Peg replied. "But I wouldn't have dreamt of disturbing you."

"Don't be silly," Richard chided her. "Mother would have completely understood the need to cut our evening short."

Maybe it was just me, but it had been my impression that Mother was not necessarily the understanding sort. Nevertheless, I was sure we would hear her take on the situation shortly, as Florence was fast approaching.

"Incoming," Bertie muttered under her breath.

I was seized with the sudden impulse to duck.

"Good morning, everyone," Florence chirped.

Her purse bobbled beneath her arm. Button lifted a lip and sneered.

"I understand there was some excitement here last night. And that you . . ." Florence's gaze scanned the table and came to rest on Aunt Peg. ". . . seem to have found yourself right in the middle of it."

"There was an accident outside in the hot tub," said Bertie. "We just happened to be in the right place at the wrong time."

"How very unfortunate for you."

I lifted a brow. "More so for Charles, I should think."

"Richard." Florence tapped her son's shoulder smartly. "Go find us another chair, would you?"

"You can have mine," Peg said smoothly. "We're almost finished anyway."

Almost finished? Not even close. We'd just placed our order. Our food had yet to arrive.

"That won't suit," said Florence. "Since you're the one I want to talk to. Richard?"

"Yes, Mother." He withdrew his hand from Peg's and rose. "Excuse me, I'll be right back."

Florence slipped into the chair he'd vacated and Bertie and I shared a look.

This was a fine mess. Somehow we'd lost Richard—whom Aunt Peg presumably wanted to spend time with—and ended up instead with his mother. Whom none of us were anxious to get to know better.

A waiter delivered our three glasses of orange juice.

Florence immediately absconded with Bertie's. She took a sip, leaned across the table, and said to Peg, "Start at the beginning and tell me everything."

While Bertie ordered more juice, Aunt Peg gave Florence a highly edited version of the previous evening's events. The retelling was over in less than a minute.

"Poor man," Florence said at the end.

She made a stab at looking mournful, but I wasn't fooled for a moment. If that woman was overcome by grief, I was Deputy Dawg.

"Charles deserved to come to a better end than that," she said. "What on earth do you suppose he was doing out there?"

"I'm sure I haven't a clue," answered Peg.

"He didn't say . . . anything?"

"He was already unconscious," I said, "when we arrived on the scene."

"No dying words?"

"No words at all," I said firmly. That was the second time I'd answered that question. "Were you a close friend of his?"

"I'd known Charles for years," said Florence. "Even before Caroline. Since he was a youngster almost. I watched him make his own opportunities and build himself an enviable career. Our sport will be a poorer place without him."

It sounded as though she'd been practicing his eulogy, I thought. And yet, she hadn't actually answered my question.

"Mother?" Richard reappeared. "The dining room is unusually busy this morning. There are no extra chairs, but I've managed to secure a table for two over by the window."

"As you wish," said Florence, rising. She looked at Peg. "We'll have to finish our discussion another time."

Richard hesitated beside Aunt Peg's chair as his mother walked away. "I'm sorry—"

"Go." She flapped a hand, shooing him away.

"I will see you later, won't I?"

"That's up to you."

"Good," he said with a smile. "Then it's a plan."

I waited until Richard was out of earshot and then said, "*Go?*"

"What would you have had me say? Stay here with us and let your mother go sit by herself? That wouldn't have been very nice."

"No," said Bertie. "But it would have been expedient."

"Never come between a man and his mother," said Aunt Peg.

"Too bad," I said, "that his mother doesn't feel as kindly about you."

Margo appeared next.

Our food had just arrived. I'd been feeling well enough, and hungry enough, to order a bowl of oatmeal. There wasn't even time to sample it before Margo was sliding into the seat Florence had recently vacated. She looked frazzled and cranky and there were dark circles under her eyes that even her artfully applied makeup couldn't quite conceal.

"What does a woman have to do to get a cup of coffee around here?" she demanded.

Aunt Peg lifted a hand and summoned a waiter. If he was surprised to find yet another newcomer at our table, he didn't let on.

In mere seconds he was back with a coffee pot. Maybe the look on Margo's face scared him. I know it worried me.

She left her coffee black and drank most of the first cup in a single gulp. It was a wonder she didn't burn her throat.

The waiter, still hovering and holding the pot, refilled her cup as soon as she set it back on the table. Good man.

"Better?" Aunt Peg inquired as Margo expelled a deep breath and sat back in her seat.

"Not yet. Is Charles still dead?"

"I'm afraid so."

"Then I'm going to need a hell of a lot more than coffee to get through the rest of this day. What could he have been thinking?"

"Charles?" I asked.

Silly question, I know. But since he'd been the victim presumably his death had not been his idea.

"Of course Charles," Margo snapped. "Who else are we talking about?"

Aunt Peg's bacon and eggs had arrived with my oatmeal. They were sitting in front of her, untouched and growing cold on the plate. Bertie, meanwhile, had tucked into her French toast like it was the first meal she'd had in a year. She doesn't let anything distract her when there's food in the offing.

"How is Caroline doing?" Aunt Peg asked.

"Better than you'd expect," Margo said. "She's a pretty tough cookie."

"Even so . . ."

Margo shook her head. "If you're waiting for hysterics, Caroline won't be the one to supply them. She has entirely too much dignity to play out her grief in public."

"I assume she'll go home, won't she?" I asked.

"That's not what she said last night." Margo reached over and swiped a piece of bacon off Peg's plate. "Of course I saw her before she'd spoken to the police. She might have changed her plans since then."

The thought of her breakfast disappearing into someone else's mouth was enough to motivate Aunt Peg. She angled her plate away from Margo and began to eat.

"She must have been in shock when she found out," said Bertie.

"I hope," Aunt Peg said, looking at her friend meaningfully, "that you broke the news to her gently."

"I didn't break it to her at all. Caroline already knew."

That bit of information distracted us long enough for Margo to snag a square of toast from Peg's plate.

"How?" I asked.

"I don't know. I didn't ask. It wasn't any of my business, was it?"

I would have made it mine, I thought.

"Speaking of business," said Aunt Peg. "I know how hard you've worked to pull this symposium together. What a shame that last night's events have spoiled it all for you."

"What do you mean?" Margo looked surprised. "Charles's death is certainly unfortunate, not to mention untimely. But I'm afraid I don't see how his demise will have any bearing on my symposium."

Margo was either very naïve or else so totally focused on her own goals that she was failing to see the big picture. I wondered if that was why Aunt Peg had been concerned about sending her to break the news to Caroline the night before.

"For one thing," said Bertie, "look around the dining room. I'll bet there isn't a single person here who's talking about dogs, or the lecture they went to yesterday, or the ones they plan to attend today."

"So there's a temporary departure from the agenda," Margo said, waving off our concerns. "Of course what happened is big news, but people will get over it and the symposium will bounce right back. You'll see. By to-morrow, everything will be back to normal."

"That would be a shame," I said.

"There's nothing shameful about it. It's human na-ture, plain and simple. People pay attention to the things that are important to them—"

"And a murder in their midst isn't important?"

Margo gave me a long look. "Have the police ruled Charles's death a murder? I hadn't heard that."

"Well, no, but . . ."

It was hard to think otherwise, wasn't it? Did she honestly think that Charles had gone outside, taken off all his clothes, and proceeded to drown himself?

"But nothing," Margo said firmly. "This symposium offers an unparalleled learning experience. One that will allow a majority of the participants to enhance and expand their careers. They'd be foolish not to take ad-vantage of such an opportunity while they can."

Eating while I'd been talking, Aunt Peg had man-aged to finish her food. Meanwhile, my oatmeal was still untouched.

"So," said Peg, "does that mean everything will pro-ceed as normal?"

"Absolutely. We're right on schedule and none of this morning's programs have been canceled or modi-fied in any way. Everyone will receive full value for the registration fees they've paid, I certainly don't want to hear any complaints on that score."

"The show must go on," Bertie said.

She was being sarcastic, but Margo didn't seem to notice. She snapped her chin downward in a sharp nod of agreement.

"Precisely," she said.

10

With that pronouncement, Margo got up and left. I doubt if any of us were sorry to see her go. At least now we could stop guarding our food.

I picked up my spoon. Now that my oatmeal had cooled, it didn't look nearly as appetizing as it had earlier. When my stomach flipped over in protest, I gave up and pushed the bowl aside.

"Nice friends you have," I said to Peg.

"Death does strange things to people."

"That woman was strange before Charles died," Bertie commented. Then she looked past me, stood up, and waved.

I turned to see who she was hailing. Alana Bennett was walking through the arched entryway into the dining room. Seeing Bertie, she shifted course and headed our way.

"Are you sure you wanted to do that?" Aunt Peg asked. Her tone made her own thoughts on the subject quite clear.

"Of course," Bertie said as the other woman approached. "Alana always has the best gossip. If people are going to keep trying to pump us for information, don't you think it would be nice if we actually had some?"

"Darling!" Alana cried.

She and Bertie touched cheeks, first one side and then the other.

I felt more sophisticated just sitting there watching them.

Alana reached for the empty chair. Before she'd even settled in the seat, the waiter was back with a fresh place setting and the ever-popular pot of coffee. By now, he was probably envisioning a tip that would put his kids through college.

Alana looked up at him and batted her eyelashes. Flirting so second nature, she didn't even stop to think about it.

"I'd prefer a latte," she said.

"Sorry—"

"Espresso?"

The waiter shook his head regretfully.

"All right." She heaved a loud sigh. "Then coffee will do."

He filled her cup and withdrew.

"I guess you've heard what happened," said Bertie.

"Heard?" Alana looked up from adding sweetener in her coffee. "I was practically there!"

No, I thought. *We* were practically there. And we hadn't seen any sign of Alana.

"When?" asked Aunt Peg.

"You know. When Charles met his demise . . ."

Alana's voice had lowered to a confidential tone. Call me a cynic but I wouldn't have been surprised to discover that she'd already taken half the inn's guests into her confidence. Not only that, but while the gossip was indeed juicy, its validity was highly suspect.

"Funny thing," said Aunt Peg. "We didn't see you."

"Of course not. You weren't there."

"We were," said Bertie. "We were the ones who pulled Charles out of the water and called for help."

"No!"

Some gossip queen. She didn't know the basic chain of events—a progression that, by now, was pretty much common knowledge.

No doubt about it, pregnancy has made me snippy. Either that, or these days I simply have less patience with posers and wannabes.

Alana leaned in closer. "Did you see what happened?"

"No," I said. "Only the aftermath."

"Somebody murdered him."

Her voice was still hushed. It was the same low pitch and timbre that kids used to tell ghost stories after dark at camp. And even though I wouldn't have placed much credence in anything Alana said, I still felt a chill slide down my spine.

"Why do you say that?" asked Aunt Peg.

Alana looked at her as if she was daft. "Because otherwise Charles wouldn't be dead."

"It might have been an accident," Bertie said.

"It wasn't."

Whether I agreed with her or not, I envied Alana's certainty. The woman possessed the boundless self-assurance of someone who rarely found herself being corrected.

Whereas I possess the limited self-confidence of someone who's often wrong.

"When were you outside?" I asked, trying to pin her down. For all we knew, she might have passed by the alcove the previous afternoon.

"Just before . . . you know. Bertie had told me how much she enjoyed using the hot tub." She glanced at Bertie, who nodded. "So I thought I might give it a try myself."

"At night?" asked Aunt Peg.

"Why not? I was busy earlier. Besides, I wasn't looking to share the experience with a bunch of other people. I thought it would be more likely to be empty then."

"Did you see Charles?" I asked.

"Of course. I went walking through the opening in the hedge, saw that the hot tub was already in use, and quickly withdrew. I didn't want to disturb his privacy."

"Then what?" asked Peg.

Alana shrugged. "I went back to my room, changed out of my bathing suit, and settled down to watch some TV."

"Did you see anyone else around?" asked Bertie.

"You mean like some big burly guy, wearing a ski mask and skulking around in the shadows? What do you think?"

I thought the whole story sounded like a crock. But then who was I to judge?

"Have you spoken with the police?" I asked. "Did you tell them you were out there last night?"

"No, why should I? Nobody's bothered to ask me anything, and I'm certainly not going to volunteer. All that does is stir up trouble. No matter what they try to tell you in kindergarten, the police are not really your friends. Besides, it's not like I have anything useful to tell them."

"You seem pretty sure that Charles was murdered," I said. "Maybe you'd like to discuss that with them."

"No," said Alana. "That's what I'd like to discuss with you."

Uh oh, I thought.

"Charles was a good man, perhaps even a great one. Whoever killed him needs to be found and brought to justice."

She set her cup down in the saucer so hard that the china rattled. For a moment, I thought it might break. Coffee sloshed over the rim and onto her manicured fingers. Alana didn't seem to notice.

"That's why I'm here," she said. "I need your help."

"With what?" asked Aunt Peg.

She's usually quicker on the uptake. Perhaps, considering her low opinion of Alana, she simply hadn't been listening. Because I certainly knew what was coming.

"I want you to investigate," said Alana. "I want you to find Charles's killer. He deserves that much, don't you think?"

"Yes," I said. "But no."

"What a stupid answer." Alana sniffed. "Say it again in English."

"You still won't like it."

"Try me."

"She said no," said Bertie.

Alana was unimpressed. "You can't say no."

"Why not?"

"Because Bertie told me."

I leveled a glare at my sister-in-law. Bertie looked as though she wanted to slide beneath the table.

"It's what you *do*," said Alana.

"Not when I'm pregnant."

"Oh that."

I'd played my trump card and it hadn't made the slightest impression on her. Was Alana Bennett the only person who hadn't gotten the memo saying that pregnant women could do whatever they wanted? It looked that way.

"Women have been getting pregnant for centuries," she said.

Even longer, I thought, but I didn't correct her.

"Slave women delivered babies in the cotton fields, then got up and picked more cotton."

"Thankfully," I said, "times have changed."

"Not that much," Alana replied. "Women still have to keep proving themselves if they want to be taken seriously."

"I take myself very seriously, thank you."

"Of course you do. And you should. Because you're good at what you do."

"Which right now is incubating a baby."

"Oh please." Her eyes slid up and down my body. "You hardly even look pregnant. Haven't you ever heard of multitasking?"

Bertie laughed out loud.

"You're not helping," I said. I might have tossed a piece of toast at her except that Aunt Peg had eaten it all.

"Back up a step," Peg said. "Why do you care so much about what happened?"

"Do I need a reason?"

"Yes," the three of us replied in unison.

"Charles was a friend. And he was a nice man. The kind of man who would go out of his way to help someone in need. So it seems to me that that's the least we can do for him."

Alana paused. She looked around the table. "Besides,

if Charles was killed, that means there's a murderer right here among us. Doesn't that worry any of you?"

My hand dropped to my stomach protectively. It seemed to do that a lot these days.

"Certainly it's worrisome," said Aunt Peg. "But would it be too much to hope that the police might do this job for us?"

"They might." Alana pushed back her chair and stood. "I guess we'll just have to wait and see, won't we?"

I looked at my watch as she walked away. It was barely nine o'clock.

"Is it just me," I said, "or is this the craziest morning we've ever had?"

"It's just you," said Peg, signaling for the check. "Eat your oatmeal, dear."

Detective Wayne waylaid us on our way out of the dining room.

"Do you ladies have a few minutes?" he said. "I'd like to ask a couple more questions."

I thought longingly of the Ibizan Hound seminar I'd been on my way to, then fell into line when Bertie and Peg followed the detective into the library. He stopped and shut the door behind us.

"Please take a seat," he said.

We all complied.

"I'd like to run you through the events of last evening one more time. See if there's anything you'd like to add to your story, or any changes you'd like to make to what you previously told me."

"Does this mean you've determined that Charles's death wasn't an accident?" I asked.

Detective Wayne looked as though that was a question he'd rather not have to answer.

So we sat and looked stubborn. At least I liked to think we did.

"Yes, it does," he said finally. "I would prefer it if that information doesn't leave this room."

"It already has," Bertie told him.

"Pardon me?"

"Everybody's been speculating about what happened. Consensus seems to be that Charles was murdered. The fact that you haven't admitted as much doesn't change that one bit."

"I see."

The detective hadn't sat down when we did. Now he dragged over a chair and hunkered down opposite us. Coming down to our level. Trying to encourage us to feel comfortable and talkative. It was beginning to look like we might be there a while.

"The fact that so many people believe that Mr. Evans was murdered leads me to think that he must not have been a very popular man," he said.

"On the contrary," Aunt Peg replied. "Charles had many admirers among the symposium participants. He's had a long and useful career in the dog show world. Which is what made his behavior yesterday all the more puzzling."

The detective leaned forward, bracing his arms on his thighs. "In what way?"

Aunt Peg was talking about the keynote speech of course. We'd explained the night before, but maybe not well enough, because it didn't look as though Detective Wayne had understood. It was sometimes hard to make outsiders see what a small, close-knit community the dog show world really was. And how likely it was that we would collectively hold many views in common.

And one of those views was that the animal rights activists, the people who wanted to stop all dog show and breeding activity, who wanted to ban the keeping of dogs as pets, were unequivocally the enemy of everything we held dear. So for Charles to stand up in front of a gathering of his peers and lend his not-inconsiderable support to their theories was almost unthinkable.

And yet that was exactly what he had done.

Aunt Peg tried once more to explain. And once again, Detective Wayne listened. He made no attempt to interrupt or hurry her along. He simply sat back and took in everything she had to say.

At the end he said, "So you're telling me that Charles Evans might have made himself some enemies yesterday?"

"It's possible, yes."

"We're talking about people who are here, staying at the inn, for the symposium."

"Yes," Peg said again. "However, I must admit I would find it hard to believe that anyone would have resorted to murder to address their grievances. Charles was a reasonable man, at least he always had always seemed so in the past. It's more likely that someone might have attempted to argue him out of his newfound beliefs rather than committing bodily harm."

"Likely or not," said Detective Wayne, "the man was murdered. So somebody must have had strong feelings about him."

He had a point.

"I'd like the three of you to run through that sequence of events once more, if you don't mind."

Superfluous of him to tack on that last part. About us minding, that is. What would happen if I stood up and said, "Thank you, but no, I'd rather go learn about Ibizan Hounds?" I'd probably receive a blank stare and a quick order to resettle my fanny in the seat.

While I'd been busy with my internal dialogue, Aunt Peg and Bertie had begun a recitation of events. By the time I tuned back in, Bertie was already in the hot tub.

"I want you to think about this before answering," said Detective Wayne. "You went to lift Mr. Evans out of the tub . . . he was probably quite heavy, correct?"

"Yes," Bertie replied.

"And slippery?"

"That too."

"So you might have had a hard time getting a good hold?"

"I did."

"Where on his body did you grab hold of him?"

"Wherever I could," Bertie said. She looked unhappy.

"What does that mean?"

"I started with my arms around his lower torso. That's how I found out he wasn't wearing any clothing."

That wasn't news to Detective Wayne. He pressed on. "And then?"

"I grasped his legs."

"What part of his legs?"

She thought back. "Probably behind his knees."

"It was," I confirmed. "Because that's how you were holding him when you passed him out to me."

Detective Wayne nodded, as if we'd confirmed something he'd expected.

"Does it matter?" I asked.

"There was a significant amount of bruising around

Mr. Evans's ankles. We believe that it occurred while he was still alive, and that that was how he was killed."

"Somebody beat up his ankles?" Bertie asked incredulously.

I was glad she'd asked that. It saved me the trouble of looking silly by doing the same.

"Not quite." Wayne permitted himself a small smile. "We believe that Mr. Evans was seated in the hot tub when someone grasped his ankles and yanked them upward suddenly. That would have caused his head to go underwater."

"Someone who was in the hot tub with him?" asked Aunt Peg.

"Perhaps, but not necessarily. A maneuver like that renders a victim almost powerless. Once a person has been tipped backward under the water, it's almost impossible for them to regain the surface. Using this method, a person can be made to drown in a household bathtub. He can also be overcome by someone much smaller in stature than himself."

We all thought about that.

"So you're not ruling out the possibility that a woman might have been responsible for Charles's death," I said.

"Definitely not," the detective agreed. "We're not ruling out anybody."

I wondered if we were meant to take that as a warning.

"That's all for now," said Detective Wayne. "But please keep yourselves available."

He stood up, then paused and looked at each of us in turn.

"Is there anything else you'd like to tell me? Something you might have remembered since last night?

Anything we haven't touched on? Something you think I need to know?"

"You'll want to talk to Alana Bennett," I said.

"And she is?"

"A participant in the symposium. Someone who knew Charles."

"She said she saw him outside last night in the hot tub," Bertie added. "It must have been right before he was killed."

"She should have come forward," Wayne said sternly.

"Before, you were calling this an accident," Aunt Peg pointed out.

The detective spun on his heel and headed for the door.

"Not anymore," he said.

11

By the time Detective Wayne was finished with us, I'd already missed half the Ibizan Hound lecture. Rather than joining it in the middle, I decided to sit out until the next track of seminars started.

While Aunt Peg went off to meet up with friends and Bertie wandered away in the direction of the health club, I went upstairs to our room. Hopefully I could catch a few peaceful minutes to check in with Sam and Davey and see how they were managing without me.

Once again, I called the home number. This time Sam picked up first.

"So much for sending you on a quiet vacation," he said.

I plumped up the pillows on the bed, then sat down and stretched out. "How did you hear already?"

"Are you kidding? The dog show grapevine travels faster than jungle drums. Besides, Bertie called and told Frank, and Frank called me."

I should have figured on that.

"It was Charles Evans," I said. "Did you know him?"

"Mostly by reputation. Everyone who's been involved in dogs for any length of time knew who he was. Charles was the kind of man who had his finger in a lot of different pies. Judging, lecturing, fundraising—if there was an event or a gala anywhere, you could pretty much figure the Evanses were going to be on hand."

"I guess that's what brought them here. Charles was the keynote speaker."

"Margo Deline must have had a fit when she heard what he had to say. I heard he called for an end to dog shows."

"And a reconciliation with animal rights groups."

"Not a very popular stand to take, considering the audience he was addressing."

"And now he's dead," I said.

"Don't tell me," said Sam. "You think you ought to find out why."

"No, Alana Bennett thinks I ought to find out why."

There was a pause while Sam turned away from the phone and spoke to Davey. I heard him promise my son that he could talk next. Then Sam held out the receiver so Faith and her daughter, Eve, could bark hello.

There are families where this might be considered unusual behavior, but it's pretty normal for us.

"What does Alana have to do with anything?" Sam asked when he came back on.

"She says she was a great admirer of Charles and all that he had accomplished."

"Alana likes to spread her admiration around," said Sam. "In fact, now that I think about it, she and Charles are two of a kind. How is Caroline holding up?"

"I haven't seen her since, but Margo says she's doing okay."

"Caroline would. That lady's strong as hickory. Charles

had the big name and the big reputation but there are plenty of people who would tell you that she was the power behind the throne. You want to go outside?"

I assumed that sudden change of topic was directed at the Poodles, not me. That the guess had been a good one was confirmed when I heard a chorus of happy barking in the background. A moment passed, I heard a door open and shut, then Sam's attention returned to the conversation.

"What about the judging scandal you mentioned last time we spoke?" he asked. "Anything interesting happening on that front?"

"Now that you mention it, not a thing. With everything else that's been going on, I'd forgotten all about it. It seems like everyone else has too. I haven't heard a word."

"Hey!" I heard Davey cry in the background. "Isn't it my turn yet?"

"One more minute," said Sam. "Listen, whatever you decide to do there, I want you to take good care of yourself."

"Is that for Davey or me?" I asked.

"Both of you," Sam said with a chuckle. "But especially you. Don't forget that's my number two son you're carrying around."

"Son? Don't tell me that Davey managed to convince you that I'm having a boy?"

"No, but he hasn't warmed up to the girl idea yet, so we're easing into it. Monday, Wednesday, and Friday we pretend you're having a boy. Tuesday, Thursday, and Saturday we talk about the baby as if she's a girl."

I smiled to myself. Trust Sam to come up with a compromise that worked.

"What about Sundays?" I asked.

"Twins," said Sam. "Think of it. One of each."

"Bite your tongue. It's been a while since I did this, but I still remember three a.m. feedings, schlepping a diaper bag everywhere, and spit-up on the shoulder of every dress I owned. I don't even want to think about doing all that times two."

"Yes, but now you'll have me to handle half the chores—"

"And me!" Davey cried in the background.

Sam laughed. "I think your son wants to speak to you."

"Of course he does," I said. "I'm a wonderful mother."

"And a paragon among wives. Stay out of trouble, okay?"

"I'll try."

Unspoken was the rest of that sentiment. I always tried. I just didn't always succeed.

"Here's Davey."

"Orlando," said my son. "Great name, huh?"

"Orlando Driver?" I couldn't picture it.

"What about Shrek?"

"No."

"You could at least consider it before saying no."

"I did consider it. We're not naming your brother"—it was Wednesday after all—"after a green movie monster."

"Shrek was cool."

"So was King Kong and we're not going there either."

"All right." Davey sighed. "I'll keep thinking."

"How's everything else? Are you taking good care of Sam while I'm away?"

"Everything's under control here."

Coming from a nine-year-old, that line sounded rehearsed.

"Is there anything going on that I need to know about?" I asked.

"Nope. But I hope you like blue because we're painting—"

"Painting what?" I asked.

Suddenly Davey was gone and Sam was back.

"Nothing," he said into the phone. "Just a little redecorating."

"Where?"

"Nothing for you to worry about."

"I wouldn't worry if you told me what you were doing."

"Funny thing about that," said Sam. "I often feel the same way about you."

He had me there.

"I'll be careful," I said.

We'd covered this ground before, but it bore repeating.

"If you want me to come," said Sam, "just say the word."

I felt a swift pang of homesickness, a deep-seated longing for my family, my Poodles, my home. He had no idea how tempting the offer was.

This from a woman who'd always thought of herself as fiercely independent. It had to be hormones.

"Mel?"

"Right here," I said. "I will. Love you."

"You too."

Over and out.

I never made it to the second track of seminars either. Instead I fell asleep on the bed and woke up after lunch. At this rate, I was going to be the only symposium participant who went home at the end of the week without learning a single new thing.

"Good, you're up," said Bertie.

I rolled over and saw her sitting in a chair by the window.

"What are you doing here?"

"Waiting for you to wake up, what does it look like?"

I yawned and sat up. The clock next to the bed said it was almost two. "You let me sleep through lunch."

"Who cares?" Bertie said with a shrug. "You don't eat anything anyway."

Good point.

I stood up and pushed my hair back out of my face. "What'd I miss while I was out? Anything important?"

"Detective Wayne spent the entire morning walking around the inn, asking questions. It's really weird. People seem to be hanging around, hoping that they'll be asked to participate. They're already over being horrified. Now they're all enjoying the excitement."

Bertie paused and grinned. "Oh yeah, and Alana's pissed at us."

"How come?"

"Because we sicced the detective on her."

I contemplated brushing my teeth, then settled for running my tongue over them instead. Sad to say, my standards were definitely dropping.

"Of course we sicced the detective on her. She told us she was the last person to see Charles alive. What did she expect us to do?"

"Be impressed, I suppose. Just like everyone else was. Don't worry, Alana enjoys playing the drama queen. She'll get over it."

Bertie got up, picked up her jacket, and headed for

the door. Since she seemed to expect me to, I followed suit.

"Where are we going?" I asked.

"Remember that German Shepherd you saw yesterday? Peg's still determined to hunt him down. She planned to go looking for him right after lunch. Except that she wanted you to help and nobody knew where you were. You should have seen the look on Margo's face when Peg asked if she'd seen you. After what happened to Charles, I think she pictured you lying dead in a ditch somewhere. She nearly had a cow."

"I was sleeping," I pointed out. "Not missing."

"That's what I figured," said Bertie. "But when you didn't answer your cell phone . . ."

I pulled the darn thing out of my pocket and turned it back on. Yup, I had three missed calls.

Cell phones are supposed to be a great convenience, but I've never grown accustomed to the idea of having to be accessible one hundred percent of the time. Especially not when I was trying to sleep.

I gazed down at the screen. "Should I listen to Aunt Peg's messages?"

"Only if you want to hear a lot of yelling. Me, I'd pass."

I hit the delete button without regret.

"Once I found you here, I called Peg and told her to relax. She's spent the last hour at a lecture on the diagnosis and management of common genetic disorders. . . . "

Aunt Peg's idea of relaxation and everyone else's are slightly different, can you tell?

"And she's set to meet us out on the porch in a few minutes."

There was a bowl of fruit on the center table in the lobby. I helped myself to an apple and a banana as we passed by.

Outside, the air was brisk and refreshing. It quickly cleared the last of the sleep-induced fuzziness from my brain. I was peeling the banana and enjoying the view when Aunt Peg appeared.

"You look none the worse for wear," she said.

"I was *sleeping.*"

"You disappeared."

"I was in my room."

"You might have bothered to check in—"

"I would have if I'd known that sleeping was against the law."

Bertie heaved a sigh and stepped between us. "Stop squabbling. This is going to be the longest pregnancy in history if you two don't figure out how to manage it better."

"Excuse me?" I said. "Aunt Peg is not going to be managing anything, much less—"

"Quit," said Bertie.

She looked as though she wanted to shake both of us. Fortunately she contented herself with giving us a lecture instead.

"It's a beautiful day. The sun is shining. The birds are singing. And somewhere around here, a lost dog is looking for a new home. Now, do you want to stand here arguing or do you want to go help him?"

Point taken.

Once Aunt Peg had ascertained that Bertie and I both had cell phones that were turned on and functioning, we split up in order to cover more ground. Aunt Peg took the path through the woods where I'd seen the German Shepherd previously. Bertie headed down the long driveway toward the main road. I was told to search the vicinity of the inn itself, a less-taxing assignment that my two cohorts seem to think was appropriate, considering my status as *the pregnant one.*

Whatever.

Aunt Peg disappeared into the thick band of trees. Bertie walked away whistling. I went out and stood in the parking lot. I turned and faced the cluster of low buildings that comprised the resort and contemplated my next move.

It was the middle of the day. Cars came and went. People hurried by.

In the eyes of a stray dog, the compound would offer little cover and even less in the way of sanctuary. If I were the Shepherd, this was the last place I would want to be right now. Except . . .

It occurred to me that we'd never made it around to the back of the building the night before. And while I had little hope of finding the dog sniffing around the garbage cans now, there was always the possibility that I might run into some of the kitchen staff who could tell me if they'd ever seen the Shepherd in the vicinity.

The most direct route around the inn took me down the path past the courtyard that housed the hot tub. My footsteps slowed as I approached. I'd expected the entry-way through the hedges to be blocked but it wasn't.

Curiosity is an affliction. I know I should probably try harder to fight it, but instead I ducked my head through the opening and had a look around. The platform, and the tub upon it, were ringed in yellow tape but the remainder of the area looked surprisingly unchanged.

I started to withdraw, then abruptly realized that someone was seated on one of the ornamental cedar benches placed at intervals around the alcove. The woman was sitting quietly. She appeared to be totally absorbed in her own thoughts.

She became aware of my presence about the same time I noticed her. When she looked up, I realized it was Charles's wife, Caroline.

"I'm so sorry," I said. "I didn't mean to intrude."

"You're not intruding." She managed a wan smile. "It's public property."

"Yes, but—"

"Come," she said, patting the bench beside her. "Sit for a minute."

When I hesitated, she said, "Unless of course you don't have time."

"I have time. I just thought you might want to be alone."

"Nobody really wants to be alone, do they?" Caroline asked. "Isn't that why people get married?"

"That's one reason."

Caroline scooted over. She was trim and tiny, and barely took up a quarter of the bench. I walked over and sat down beside her.

"You were one of the people who tried to help Charles last night, weren't you?" she said. "I'd like to thank you for that."

"We did what we could. I'm sorry it wasn't enough."

"Charles was a great admirer of your aunt."

"And she of him. Although he managed to surprise her yesterday."

As soon as I'd spoken the words, I wished I could recall them. There was no point in rehashing Charles's unpopular opinions now, not when it was much too late to make any difference. Fortunately Caroline didn't take offense.

"Charles liked to keep people on their toes," she said softly. "He always said that anyone who stops learning new things might as well just stop living."

12

The irony of that comment hit me like a kick in the gut. Or maybe the baby was just doing back flips. Either way, I felt a jolt.

Considering the circumstances, Caroline seemed remarkably composed. How could she sit there and discuss her husband's death so calmly?

"Now I've shocked you, haven't I?" she said.

"No," I lied, perhaps not too convincingly.

Caroline shook her head. "I've always believed in facing life head-on. The good, the bad, the challenges, the tragedies. I don't hide from any of it. Charles would hate the thought of me packing my bags and running away to grieve in solitude. *Throw a party,* he would have said. *Celebrate my life rather than mourning its passing.*"

"He must have been a fascinating man."

"He was," said Caroline. "He was that and more. Charles was my rock, my anchor. And I was his."

"What will you do now?"

She glanced over. "I take it you're asking short-term?"

I nodded.

"Stay here and finish out the symposium, I suppose. Watch the police do their job. Hope they figure out what in hell happened."

"You wouldn't be happier going back home?"

"Home?" Caroline gave a little laugh. "What is that? People who judge at as many dog shows as Charles and I do spend more time on the road than we ever do at home. We learned a long time ago to make our home wherever we are that week."

Oh.

"Besides," she said, "the police seem to think that I might make a good suspect. That detective, what's his name?"

"Wayne?"

"That's the one. He said something about keeping myself available. I was probably supposed to think that was in case they wanted to ask me more questions, but I could guess what he really meant."

"It's nothing personal," I said. "Unless there's a compelling reason to think otherwise, they always look at the spouse first."

"Yes, well, here's a compelling reason for them. I didn't kill Charles."

"I'm sure they'll figure that out soon enough."

"Easy for you to say . . ." Caroline began. Then she stopped. Her eyes narrowed. "Wait a minute, I just remembered something. You're the one who—"

"Shows Poodles," I filled in quickly.

"Solves mysteries," she said instead.

"Just sometimes," I told her. "Not lately."

"Why not?"

"Pardon me?"

"Why not lately? Lack of interest? Opportunities drying up? Well, then this should be just the thing. It must be fate, don't you think?"

"No, I—"

"Karma, kismet, call it what you will. There's a reason you came to this symposium."

Of course there was a reason. And this wasn't it.

"I wanted a little vacation, a chance to learn about different breeds . . ."

"Don't be silly. Learning about dogs is a lifetime endeavor. It won't matter in the slightest if you take a week off to do something else."

Something else? She made it sound like I might be going on a picnic instead.

"I really don't think—"

"Yes, you do. Of course you do."

Now I was puzzled. "Do what?"

"Think," said Caroline. "You must be a good thinker, just like Peg. Intelligence runs in families, you know. It's the same with dogs. Certain traits are specific to certain breeds."

And I'd inherited my nosiness gene from Aunt Peg? Interesting thought. It actually would have been a good guess except for one thing: she and I were only related by marriage.

"I can see how this could come together quite well," said Caroline. "All your suspects are currently gathered together in one place. Isn't that handy?"

"I'm sure the police think so."

"The police," Caroline scoffed. "What do they know about dogs?"

I swallowed a laugh. Caroline thought like Aunt Peg. No matter how many times the course of events zigged and zagged, in the end everything important always came back to dogs.

Except that I was willing to stake my reputation on the fact that no dog had committed this murder.

"I guess this means you're not placing much faith in the detective," I said.

"Hard to, these days, isn't it? The only good police seem to be the ones on television and they have their plots written for them. In real life, nothing ever gets solved so easily, or so quickly. It's already been almost twenty-four hours. What do you think they've done so far?"

"Mostly ask questions, I guess."

"So they're busy detecting, big deal. What about solving? That's what I'd like to see."

Another woman who knew just what she wanted. Caroline had spoken earlier of fate and this was apparently mine. To always be surrounded by strong women.

I'd been sitting long enough that my legs had begun to go to sleep. I stood up and stretched. Then I began to rock, shifting my weight from one foot to the other.

Caroline eyed me curiously.

"Pregnant," I said.

"Still early, I assume?"

I nodded.

"Boy or girl?"

"We don't know."

"That's the good thing with dogs. You get both."

I laughed. "Thanks, but I don't want a litter."

"Dogs and people," said Caroline. "In some ways, they're not that different. Dogs attack when they feel threatened."

"Or when they're hungry," I said, thinking of the stray I was supposed to be looking for.

"Murder for profit? It's a possibility." Caroline stood up and brushed off her skirt. "But I'll tell you what I think. Somebody here felt threatened by Charles. Now all you have to do is figure out why."

"I'll give it some thought," I said.

"You do that. Somebody took my husband away from me. I'd like to know who was responsible."

Caroline looked as though she was ready to leave. I forestalled her departure by asking a question. One I'd been wondering about since the day before.

"When Charles delivered his keynote speech . . . did you know ahead of time what he was planning to say?"

"No," Caroline replied quickly. "I didn't have a clue. My husband gave many such talks. He spoke to kennel clubs, to judges' groups. He tended to compose his speeches at the last moment. It would have driven me crazy to leave things so late, but that was just his way."

"So he didn't run anything past you? Maybe practice ahead of time?"

"There was never a chance to do something like that. The first time I heard the speech was in the lecture hall along with everyone else."

Caroline began to walk away. Once again I stopped her.

"Were you surprised?"

"Of course."

"Maybe annoyed?"

She spun around to face me. "What would have been the point? The damage was already done."

"Did that worry you?"

"Worry me?" She sounded perplexed.

"Were you concerned about the effect his talk might have on your career?"

"Not in the slightest." Now her tone was firm. "Charles would have found a way to fix things. He was good at that. Given the chance, he'd have made everything right again. I'm sure of it."

I'd spent so long with Caroline that after she left I ended up merely doing a quick walk around the back of the inn. There was nothing notable to be seen: no kitchen workers, no stray dog, just a couple of garbage cans with their lids firmly closed.

Completing my circle of the building, I met up with Bertie in the parking lot. She'd walked the driveway from top to bottom, then back again, and hadn't seen anything either.

"Where do you suppose Peg is?" she asked.

We both turned and looked toward the woods. The trail I'd followed the day before had been no more than a mile long and very well marked. If Aunt Peg hadn't returned yet, it was probably because something was holding her up.

Of one accord, we headed toward the hiking path.

I'm not usually a big worrier, but like so many other things, that had also changed recently. When a vision of Charles, floating face down in the hot tub, teased its way into my subconscious, I pulled out my phone and pressed Aunt Peg's number.

She picked up on the first ring and snapped, "Don't bother me, I'm busy." Before I could say a single word, the connection was severed.

So much for my concern. Aunt Peg was not only fine; she was *busy*.

"I guess that means she's okay," Bertie said with a laugh as she watched me tuck the phone away.

"How much do you want to bet she found our missing dog?"

We were already hurrying, but we quickened our footsteps anyway. As soon as the woods enveloped us, it grew both cooler and darker. The ground felt damp beneath my feet and I gathered my jacket more tightly around me. The smell of pine was everywhere.

"I can see why a stray dog would want to hide out in here," said Bertie. She peered into the dense wall of tree trunks that surrounded us. "Step six feet off this path and you'd disappear entirely."

Up ahead through the trees, I saw a flash of blue, down low near the ground. Aunt Peg's coat. I held up a hand. Bertie and I both slowed.

Creeping along quietly, we could hear Aunt Peg talking. Or crooning really, as the utterance was more sounds than words: a comforting murmur meant to put a skittish animal at ease.

We rounded the next turn and Peg came into view. She was sitting quietly in the middle of the path. The German Shepherd was another ten feet farther away.

The dog had been lying down. His ears were cocked, his head tipping slowly from one side to the other as he listened to what Aunt Peg had to say. Seeing us, however, he leapt to his feet. His body was motionless but only for the moment; the Shepherd was poised for flight.

"Stop right there!" she said. "You'll ruin everything."

We had but it was already too late.

Still half crouched, the Shepherd darted a last, wary glance in our direction. Then he spun around and slunk away into the underbrush.

"Damn," Peg muttered.

"Sorry," I said.

"As well you should be. I think I was finally beginning to gain his confidence."

Bertie reached down a hand and helped Aunt Peg to her feet. "And then we came along and spoiled things for you."

"Never mind." Peg stared off into the trees for a moment, before turning back to us. "There'll be another day. He's a good boy, or at least he wants to be. It looks like he was somebody's pet at one time. He knew how to trust humans once. All we have to do is make him remember how that felt."

"Poor guy," said Bertie. "He's a nice looking dog. I wonder what he's doing out here all by himself."

"He's probably wondering that too." Peg reached around and brushed off the seat of her pants. "He's cold, lonely, and hungry. And I'd be willing to bet that none of it is his fault."

"You'd think he'd want us to help him," I said.

Both Aunt Peg and Bertie shook their heads. Their experience with dogs far outweighs mine. The Poodles I'd left back in Connecticut with Sam and Davey were the first pets I'd ever owned.

"His last experience with people can't have been good," said Bertie. "Otherwise he wouldn't be in this situation."

"He's afraid of people now," Peg added. "And probably with good reason. So it's up to us to change his mind."

"At least he seems to stay around the inn," I pointed out. "So he hasn't gone completely wild."

Aunt Peg nodded. "If we take things slowly and give him enough time, I believe eventually he'll be willing to meet us halfway. And of course the half pound of ground meat I just fed him won't hurt our case a bit."

Trust Aunt Peg to have a plan. Boy Scouts had nothing on her.

"Now he'll go back to his den with a full stomach and think about that for a while. And tomorrow when we come looking for him again, I suspect he might not be as hard to find."

As we walked back to the inn, I told them about my conversation with Caroline.

"She wants Charles's killer found," I said at the end.

"Of course she does," Peg agreed. "We all do."

"But the police aren't looking at all of us as potential suspects."

Aunt Peg thought for a moment. "I wouldn't say that I knew either of them particularly well. But at least from the outside, their marriage always seemed as solid as most."

"That doesn't sound like much of an endorsement."

"No, but it's the best I can do. The older I get the more I wonder if human beings are really meant to live together in monogamous bliss for twenty or thirty years. Even the best marriages aren't necessarily smooth sailing all the time. Caroline's a rather forceful presence. She likes to have her own way. And Charles was very much the same. I could see how that might lead them to butt heads once in a while."

"So you think the police are right not to discount her as a suspect?"

"I think they're right not to discount anyone," Aunt Peg said firmly. "Did you think to ask her if Charles had any enemies?"

"No, unfortunately."

"Not to worry," said Peg. "I'm sure you'll have another opportunity."

We reached the end of the hiking trail, exited the

woods, and came out onto the edge of the parking lot. It was nice to feel the sun on our faces again.

"Caroline seems to think I'm going to figure out who's responsible for Charles's death," I admitted as we headed back toward the inn.

Bertie looked surprised. "You told her you'd do that?"

"Not exactly. But she wouldn't take no for an answer."

"First Alana, and now Caroline," Aunt Peg mused. "I wonder who'll be trying to enlist your services next."

"I'd give it a try if I was innocent," said Bertie.

"Or if I was guilty." Peg opened the door and held it as we all filed through. "In fact perhaps more importantly if I was guilty. You know what they say: keep your friends close and your enemies closer."

13

It didn't take long for me to discover the answer to Aunt Peg's question.

Having had only a small breakfast and then missed lunch entirely, I was on my way to the dining room in search of a snack that I could take into the lecture hall when I was waylaid by Margo.

"Perfect," she said, twining her arm through mine. "You're just the person I was looking for."

Why did I suspect our meeting was going to work out to be more perfect for her than it was for me?

"Where are you going?" she asked. "I'll go with you."

"Food."

I would have said more, but my stomach chose that moment to rumble loudly. I figured that was punctuation enough.

"At this hour? Are you sure? You need to be careful when you're pregnant, those pounds will sneak right up on you. Next thing you know, none of your clothes fit and you look like the Goodyear blimp."

"Food," I repeated firmly. If she protested again, I

was going to take my arm back and chart my own course. "I was thinking maybe a milk shake. Chocolate, double thick."

"Oh my." Margo sighed. "How youth is wasted on the young. A milk shake it is then. I suppose I could do with a cup of tea. It is, tea time, isn't it? Maybe the bartender would be so kind as to lace it with whiskey for me. Or perhaps I'll just skip the tea and go straight for the hard stuff."

Next thing I knew, we were seated in the bar. The first and, so far, only customers of the day. Margo was sipping a whiskey and soda. My milk shake was on the way.

"So," she said companionably, "how are you enjoying the symposium so far?"

"I've seen so little of it I can hardly tell," I said, filled with the unhappy suspicion that I was about to miss yet another lecture. "Is that what you steered me in here to ask?"

"Actually no. That was small talk, meant to put us both at ease."

At least she was honest. That always scores extra points in my book.

"I'm not sure it's working," I said.

"Too bad." Margo looked past me and waved to a waiter who was heading our way. "Maybe this will help."

The milk shake helped a lot. The glass it came in was frosted and nearly a foot tall. The shake itself was rich and dark, and so thick that I had to eat it with a spoon. If there's a better way to take your calcium, I have yet to find it.

"Happy now?" Margo asked.

"I was happy before. You were the one who looked like you had something on your mind."

"I did. And I still do. What have you learned so far?"

I paused to lift the spoon to my mouth and skim off a generous portion of ice cream. The cold went straight to my forehead. I winced and blinked, then said, "About what?"

"Don't be dense. About Charles, of course. You've had all day."

"To do what?"

"Melanie. Sweetheart." Margo braced her arms on the table and stared hard. "Let's not be coy, okay? Your reputation precedes you. Things go wrong when you're around and then you find out why. All I'm asking is what you've found out so far."

"Today I took a nap," I said. "Since breakfast, the only person I've spent any time with aside from Peg and Bertie is Caroline."

"Caroline, good. That's a start. You can build from there."

"I wasn't trying to start. Or build. I ran into her by accident."

"Naturally that's what you would want her to think."

"No, I really did."

"Don't worry." She reached across the table and patted my hand reassuringly. "I won't blow your cover."

"I don't have a cover."

"Your mission will be our little secret."

Sure, I thought. Why not? Since I didn't have a mission, it would be easy enough to have a secret about it. The cover thing, however, had me confused. Had I been pretending to be someone else?

"I just want you to do one thing for me," Margo said. "It's simple really."

Nothing about this conversation was turning out to

be simple. Maybe that was my fault. Maybe the milk shake had given me brain freeze.

Margo leaned toward me. Her voice dropped. "Whatever you find out, I want you to bring the information to me first."

Interesting request.

"Why would I do that?" I asked.

"Because I'm in charge. I'm the one who brought everybody here and now all these people are my responsibility. Everything that happens here reflects upon me."

"Even murder?"

"Everything," Margo repeated. She drained her glass and stood. "Do we understand each other?"

No, I thought. I'd never been able to understand how some people were able to treat death as an inconvenience in their otherwise orderly schedule.

But that wasn't what she was asking.

"I'm sure we do," I said.

I was holding my spoon in one hand. The other was beneath the table, fingers crossed. Because hell would freeze over before I felt the need to report back to Margo Deline about Charles's murder or anything else.

After Margo left the bartender was kind enough to transfer what remained of my milk shake into a paper cup. I carried it out into the lobby, where I consulted the afternoon's schedule.

Currently two lectures were in progress. The first was titled *Junior Showmanship: Fun for the Whole Family.* The second, *Plucking the Terrier Coat, Is It a Lost Art?*

I stood. And sighed. Then read the offerings again just

to make sure that I hadn't missed something. I finally had the opportunity to attend another seminar and neither of the topics was even remotely interesting to me.

Poodles are clipped, not hand-plucked. And Junior Showmanship is a class for children, judged on their handling skills and presentation. While Davey could compete if he wanted to, so far he hadn't shown even the slightest inclination.

I was considering my options when Florence Donner emerged from the library with several friends. Spotting me, she excused herself from the group and headed my way.

I couldn't remember the last time I'd been this popular.

"I'm just going outside to give Button a walk," she said. "Perhaps if you're not busy, you'd like to accompany me?"

It was hard to plead that I was otherwise engaged when she'd just found me standing there, doing nothing more important than sipping a milk shake and staring off into space.

"Sure," I said and we walked outside together.

Florence waited until we'd reached a grassy strip on the other side of the parking lot before leaning down to tip her large purse over onto the ground. Button popped out, looked around, and gave himself a good shake.

"Doesn't he mind being confined like that?" I asked, as the Chihuahua began to sniff around the grass.

"Not in the slightest. Button's a very companionable little dog. The thing that pleases him most is being wherever I am. He'd mind being left behind more."

We watched as the Chihuahua found a patch of lawn to his liking. He lifted his leg and peed, then scratched furiously with both hind feet to cover the evidence. His efforts barely disturbed the grass around him but he looked very pleased with what he'd accomplished.

When he was done, Florence bent down and held out her hands. Button trotted right into them and she placed him back in her purse.

The bag bobbled and rolled as the Chihuahua maneuvered himself around within. A moment later his head emerged from the opening. Button's ears were pricked; his large dark eyes looked around curiously. Despite my reservations, I had to admit that he seemed perfectly happy with the arrangement.

"I didn't ask you out here to talk about dogs," said Florence.

I'd figured that.

I was assuming that Florence—like just about everyone else I'd spoken to that day—was going to request that I apply myself to finding Charles's killer. I wondered what her stake in the outcome of the investigation might be.

"It's your aunt we need to discuss. I want to know what her intentions are toward my son."

"Aunt Peg?" I sputtered. Florence had caught me by surprise.

"Yes, of course, Peg. Do you have any other aunts here who are pursuing my Richard?"

"Well . . . no. But I'd hardly say that Aunt Peg is pursuing Richard."

"I don't know what else you'd call it. First she wangled herself an introduction over the Internet. I gather they met in some sort of *chat room*." Florence spit out the phrase as if she found it highly distasteful.

"Actually I believe it was a message board."

She flipped a hand in the air as if the distinction made no difference.

"Either way, she found out who he was and singled him out for special attention."

"They enjoyed talking to one another online," I said. "They have things in common. Is that so unusual?"

"Their relationship isn't the slightest bit suitable. Something he would have immediately seen for himself if they hadn't met in such an unorthodox fashion. For one thing, she's quite a lot older than he is."

"Richard doesn't seem to care about that."

"Richard is a kind and generous man. It's in his nature to overlook other people's faults."

If Florence thought Aunt Peg's age was a fault, I hated to think how she might feel about her own.

"They don't even live in the same state."

"That's the beauty of the Internet," I said cheerfully. "It makes differences like that one moot."

Florence's brow lowered in what I'm sure she thought was an intimidating scowl. I work with teenage kids for a living, however, and I've seen all manner of body language. She was going to have to work harder than that to impress me.

"I have no idea what you find funny about this situation," she snapped. "Rather than supporting your aunt's transgression, I would think you'd be eager to save her from potential embarrassment."

If there was one thing I never worried about, it was Aunt Peg embarrassing herself. She could smoothly extricate herself from more tight spots than most people even knew how to get into.

"Richard's a grown man," I said. "Surely he must be old enough to make his own decisions about who his friends are."

Florence was looking increasingly annoyed. It was as

if she'd scripted this conversation ahead of time and now I was refusing to play along.

"If my son has a single flaw, it's that he's too much of a soft touch. He would never want to hurt anyone's feelings, whether they deserved such treatment or not. Perhaps he's flattered by your aunt's infatuation—"

Infatuation my foot, I thought.

"Or maybe he returns her affection," I said. "I thought they looked like they made a very nice couple."

"Don't be ridiculous. You're simply wrong, that's all. I want you to talk to your aunt."

Right, I thought. Like that would help.

"You may tell her whatever you like," Florence continued imperiously, "as long as the end result is that she stops following Richard around."

She turned and headed back toward the inn. As far as she was concerned, our conversation was over.

Earlier Florence had dodged my question about her relationship with Charles Evans. Now seemed like a good time to try again.

I caught up and fell into step beside her. Button hung out of her purse and rode shotgun between us.

"You told us this morning that you'd known Charles for many years."

Florence nodded curtly.

"His death must have come as quite a shock to you."

"I'm sure the same is true of everyone else here."

Except for one person, I thought.

"Were you very good friends?"

"We traveled in many of the same circles, we were often invited to judge at the same shows. The dog show community can be a somewhat sheltered environment. Eventually that much proximity begins to feel like friendship."

Once again, I noted, she hadn't exactly answered my question.

"How did you feel about his keynote address?"

"I don't have an opinion about it."

If that was true she had to be just about the only person on the premises who felt that way.

"Why is that?" I asked.

Florence turned her head my way and gave me a long, measured look. "I didn't attend."

Another surprise.

"How come?"

"Occasionally I suffer from migraines. I'm afraid that the thought of someone holding an audience captive while he pontificated on the future of dog shows was enough to bring one on."

"Someone?" I asked. "Or Charles in particular?"

Abruptly Florence stopped walking. Her purse rocked forward, then settled back. Button squeaked in protest and scrambled for purchase.

"Let me tell you something. I've participated in the dog show world since before you were born and I've heard predictions of doom and gloom before. I've seen changes come and go and I've rolled with all of them as necessary. At this particular point in my life, I'd say that I feel as qualified to give that speech as to listen to it."

Well, well, well, I thought. So Florence was a bit resentful of the honor that had been accorded to Charles. Perhaps she'd felt that her seniority should have entitled her to take his place on the podium.

I wondered if I could use her disgruntlement to my advantage.

"Having been Charles's friend for so many years, you'd be in a perfect position to know who he might have annoyed or provoked in the past."

"I might," Florence replied, "if I paid any attention to such things. But I don't. If something is none of my business, I have the good sense to leave it alone."

"So you wouldn't have any idea who among the symposium participants might have been angry enough at Charles to want to kill him?"

"I'm sure I wouldn't. Until I heard that Charles had met his early demise—in a hot tub of all undignified places—I hadn't given him the slightest bit of thought. The only time I'd even heard his name mentioned recently was when I dined with two of Richard's friends that first night."

"Derek and Marshall," I said.

"Precisely. Derek mentioned that he had come to the symposium for the express purpose of meeting Charles. Apparently there was some matter that he intended to discuss with him."

"Did he say what it was about?"

"No, and I didn't ask. I was enjoying my crab bisque at the time and, as I said, it was really none of my affair."

"Do you know if he ever managed to meet with Charles?"

Florence frowned. "You're really very inquisitive. Has anyone ever told you that?"

Little did she know, I thought.

"That's not an attractive trait in a young lady. Men prefer women who are demure and retiring, not pushy and aggressive."

"I'll try and remember that," I said. "But if you don't mind, please just try and think back for a moment. Did Derek tell you whether or not he and Charles had had a chance to meet?"

"I'm quite certain they hadn't. Wasn't that the whole point? Otherwise he wouldn't still have been talking about it. Whatever the topic was that he needed to discuss, it was still unfinished business."

I stood and thought about that as Florence walked away. I wondered if Derek had found Charles the next evening in the hot tub and had a chance to finish his business then.

14

"Wow," said Bertie. "That was great."

I was in the room, preparing to go downstairs for dinner. Bertie had just thrown open the door and walked in.

Her hair was tousled, and her skin flushed. There was a sheen of sweat on her brow. If I didn't know better, I'd have thought she'd just had sex. Really good sex.

"What was great?"

"You have got to visit the spa with me tomorrow."

"That's where you've been?"

"Sure." She flopped down on the nearest bed. "What did you think?"

"Let me see, how can I put this delicately? You look like you're in love."

"I am." She sighed and flopped over on her back. "They do this hot rock massage down there that's to die for. Gunther's hands are like magic."

"Gunther?" I laughed. "You're cheating on my brother with a man named Gunther?"

"As if." She rolled over on one side, propped her elbow

on the bed, and rested her chin in her palm. "Gunther's a sweetheart, but totally gay. He looked at me semi-naked and didn't even bat an eye."

Case closed. Gunther was gay all right.

"Although come to think of it, I wonder if there's a way I could get him and Frank together. I love my husband to bits, but trust me, Gunther could teach him a thing or two about—"

"Stop right there," I said. "That's my little brother you're talking about."

"You know Frank has a sex life. Where else do you think Maggie came from?"

"Well, yes . . . but it's not something I like to spend any time thinking about."

"Trust me. Even Sam could learn a trick or two from this guy."

"*Even* Sam?"

I'd been checking my reflection in the mirror as I brushed my hair. Now I slowly turned around.

"Yeah. That's what I said."

Bertie sat up and crossed her legs, bouncing the bed a few times to demonstrate how good she felt.

"Even Sam?" I repeated.

Bertie stopped bouncing.

"What's wrong with that? I'm not trying to insult the guy. I mean, nobody's perfect. Even Sam. There . . . you see? That's what I meant."

My hand lowered. I dropped the brush on the dresser.

"I'm just wondering how you know," I said.

"Know what?"

Bertie's green eyes were wide and innocent, like she was just now beginning to realize what sort of dangerous territory she might be venturing into. But I'd seen her bat her lashes to great effect before and I wasn't buying her guileless act for a minute.

"Oh, you know," I said casually, "how good my husband is in bed."

Don't get me wrong. I wasn't accusing anyone of infidelity. Sam had been in his thirties when we met. I knew he'd had a life before I became part of the picture.

But every so often in the course of our relationship disconcerting bits of information seemed to rise unexpectedly to the surface. Things that it turned out everyone was already aware of. Except, of course, me. It was a situation that left me wondering why I always had to be the last to know.

One time, the omission had been an ex-wife that Sam hadn't deemed important enough to mention. Another, it was a video game he'd invented that had gone on to earn millions in the marketplace. So there was good reason why I might have been a little touchy about information other people possessed about my spouse.

Or maybe it was just the fact that I was pregnant. And feeling insecure about the shape of my body. And swamped with hormones that made me cranky.

But whatever the reason, I wanted an answer.

Bertie must have read the determined look on my face. She paled slightly. Either that or her post-massage glow was finally fading.

"Ummm . . ." she said.

"Not good enough."

"Well . . . you know . . . it was Alana's idea that we go and get these massages in the first place. She scoped out all the facilities in the health club and spa, and decided that Gunther's room was the place to be."

"And?" I prompted when her story petered out.

So far she hadn't even come close to answering my question. Or had she? My eyes narrowed.

"So you and Alana went and had a massage together?" She nodded.

"And maybe a little girl talk?"

"You know how it is."

Sure I did. They'd talked about men. Jeez, what else did I think would come up while Gunther was applying his magic hands to their half-naked bodies? Certainly not dogs.

"And Alana, well . . ." Bertie lifted her shoulders in an elaborate shrug. "What can I say? She's been a busy girl."

"Alana and *Sam*?"

"She was talking about a long time ago. Like years! Long before the two of you even met."

I'd figured as much. I trusted Sam implicitly. He'd never given me any reason not to. But still, when we'd talked about Alana the other night, it might have been nice of him to give me a little warning.

Men.

Why do they always think that what they don't say won't come back to haunt them later?

"So Alana and Sam had a relationship," I said.

"Alana's had relationships with lots of men. It's what she does for entertainment."

"We're not talking about lots of men. We're talking about Sam."

I almost added *my Sam*, but I caught myself in time. Good thing. That would have sounded whiny.

"It wasn't any big deal," said Bertie. "Probably more like a one night stand. Maybe a fling."

Funny thing about that, I felt like flinging something myself. Hormones again, no doubt.

"Apparently it made enough of an impression on her that she's still talking about him years later."

"That's what Alana does. She kisses and tells. It's not Sam's fault."

"I'm not saying it is. I just . . ." I stopped, frowned, then sat down on the bed. "I just . . ."

"What?"

"I don't know."

Bertie was looking at me with such concern that unexpectedly I found myself dissolving in a fit of giggles. I knew the reaction didn't make sense, but it didn't matter. Pregnancy was a mood swing roller coaster and I was just along for the ride.

"It just feels weird that the two of you were discussing my husband's prowess in bed," I said when I got my breath back.

"If it helps, she said he was stellar."

"I don't need Alana Bennett to tell me that."

"She gave his performance an A."

"Not an A-plus?" I started laughing all over again. "He must have learned a few things since she knew him."

"That's the spirit. For a minute there I was afraid you were going to kick my ass."

"You've been pregnant," I said. "You know how it is."

"Yeah, I do. But now that you're normal again, there's just one more thing."

"Go for it."

"Brace yourself."

"It's that bad?"

"We were feeling so companionable that I told Alana to go ahead and book us a table for dinner."

I knew Aunt Peg had a dinner date with Richard. I'd intended to fall in with whatever plan Bertie had made. That had seemed like a fine idea earlier. Now I wasn't so sure.

"The three of us?" I said.

"And probably a couple of others too. You know Alana, she likes a crowd."

That could work. I'd simply sit at the other end of the table.

"We won't be discussing Sam, will we?"

Bertie choked on a laugh. "I highly doubt it. And certainly not in such graphic terms as she managed this afternoon."

I threw a pillow at her.

Bertie dodged and shut up. Which was just what I'd intended.

The dining room was nearly full by the time we arrived. The buzz of animated conversation was so loud that the sound carried all the way out into the hallway.

It seemed as though Margo had been right. The same people who, only that morning, had been desperate to hear every detail of Charles's death were now busy discussing the information they'd gleaned from another day of lectures and seminars. These were hardcore dog people. The murder had already become old news and they'd moved on.

As Bertie and I were shown to our table, we passed Aunt Peg, who was seated at a table for two with Richard. The pair looked very pleased to be in one another's company. They also looked as though they wouldn't welcome any unnecessary interruptions. Florence, thankfully, was nowhere in sight, so I decided not to worry about the fact that I had yet to deliver her message.

"It's about time you got here," Alana said when we reached our table. "Bertie, back me up. I've been telling Rosalyn and Tubby that they simply have to go spend some time over in the spa, but somehow I haven't managed to convince them yet."

"There isn't time for everything," said Rosalyn. "I signed up for a symposium, not to come and get pampered."

Tubby dutifully hauled himself to his feet and helped me with my chair. He'd been snacking on bread and butter and he wiped his fingers on the napkin he'd tucked into his collar.

"Spas are for women," he said as we settled into our seats.

"Tubby, you're old-fashioned." Alana laughed. "That's a very narrow-minded view."

"I may be old-fashioned, but I know what works. And real men don't get facials and manicures."

"What about a mud bath?" Bertie suggested. "Boys like to play in mud, don't they?"

"I'd consider it." Tubby swung his gaze her way. "If you'd like to join me and show me how it's done."

"Ewww," Rosalyn said under her breath.

She was seated on my other side and I hoped the sound hadn't carried. But if Tubby heard, he didn't respond. He was totally focused on Bertie now.

"Naked," he said. "Isn't that the way you're supposed to do those things?"

"Not me." Alana tossed her head and her silky blond hair lifted, then resettled around her slender shoulders. "That gooey mud seeps into all sorts of little cracks and crevices and it's hell to get out again . . ." She lowered her voice suggestively. "If you know what I mean."

Obviously Tubby did. He turned away from Bertie to leer at the blond appreciatively.

Alana smiled and I realized she was competing with Bertie for Tubby's attention. Not that there was much point. Bertie had no interest in Tubby and I doubted that Alana did either. The only thing he had going for him was that he was the only man at the table. Alana's response was probably just a knee-jerk reaction.

"Ewww again," said Rosalyn.

This time everyone at the table heard her.

"Don't knock what you haven't tried," said Alana. "And let's be clear about something. I'm not against nudity on principle. In certain situations, it can be very liberating. People tend to shed their inhibitions along with their clothing."

"I'd certainly like to hear more about that," Tubby invited.

Was there a woman at the table who hadn't seen *that* coming?

"You know," said Alana, "like at a nude beach."

"Or in a hot tub," Rosalyn added.

That brought the conversation to a stop.

"That's what I heard," she said after a weighted pause. Rosalyn looked around the table. "Charles was naked when they found him."

"He was," I said.

"That's right, I forgot. You two were there."

The gossip mill had been churning all day. By now everybody knew all there was to know about the tragic happening in their midst. Or at least they thought they did.

"Which two were where?" asked Tubby.

"Melanie and Bertie. They were the ones who found Charles."

"Were you? It must have been awful."

Tubby didn't sound sympathetic. Titillated was more like it. I braced myself for the inevitable questions.

"Here's what I want to know," said Rosalyn. "Where were Charles's clothes? I heard he was out there under the stars buck naked with nothing more than a skinny little towel. I've known Charles for years and that pompous prick would never have allowed himself to be caught out in such an undignified position. So what on earth could he have been thinking?"

"Probably that he wasn't going to get caught," Tubby said. His shoulders shook with a little giggle. "Wrong again."

I exchanged a puzzled glance with Bertie. Neither of us had known Charles, but under the circumstances, I might have expected a little more restraint from our companions.

"Had Charles been wrong before?" I asked.

"Not to hear him tell it," said Tubby. "He was like the ethics police. Always trying to tell other people how to live their lives. Not to speak ill of the dead but—"

"But nothing," Alana snapped. Her shoulders were rigid, her cheeks flushed with color. "Whatever your opinions of Charles may or may not have been, I'm finding this whole conversation to be entirely inappropriate. Surely we'd do better to honor his life by remembering the good things about him."

"Like his keynote speech?" Tubby said dryly.

"There was nothing wrong with that speech." Alana's voice had grown shrill. "Charles knew his position would be unpopular and yet still he had the strength of conviction to stand up and make his feelings known. I, for one, think that he should be applauded for that."

"Before we go raising him up on too high a pedestal, let's get real for a minute," said Rosalyn. "Charles wasn't the kind of man who ever had to worry about being unpopular. Probably not even once in his entire, charmed, frat-boy life. So delivering a talk like that wasn't a show of bravery. More like a demonstration of arrogance. It was his way of saying, *Here's my opinion, and everyone should agree with me just because I said so.*"

"Did we even listen to the same speech?" asked Alana. She looked at Bertie and me for confirmation. "Because I didn't hear it that way at all."

"Hard for me to tell what his motivation was," Bertie said with a shrug. "I didn't know him."

"Me either," I agreed.

"No loss," Tubby muttered.

He raised a hand and summoned a waiter. "We'd better order some food, don't you think? Otherwise we'll be sitting here all night. And let's change the subject too. I'll enjoy my meal a whole lot more if I don't have to talk about Charles Evans while I'm eating."

As we opened our menus, Tubby pointed at me. "You. Come up with something better to talk about. Proper dinner conversation."

Just about anything would sound proper compared to what we'd discussed thus far: murder and naked babes.

"I'll do my best," I said.

15

"I don't want to talk about it," said Aunt Peg.

Frankly I wasn't entirely sure I wanted to talk about it either. But here I was and there she was, and that being the case, I was determined to get to the bottom of things.

The "it" in question was the fact that moments earlier I'd seen Aunt Peg rise from her seat across from Richard and fling her napkin down on the tabletop with the flair of a courtier throwing down a gauntlet. Then she'd left the table and stormed from the dining room.

At the time, I'd been seated with my own group of quarrelsome dinner companions on the other side of the dining room. I had been poking at a pasta dish that had seemed more appealing when I ordered it than it did when it actually appeared in front of me. I'd also been wondering how long I had to listen to Tubby, Rosalyn, and Alana disagree about everything under the sun before I could slip away without appearing rude.

Oh, and I'd also been passing the time by spying on Aunt Peg.

I mean really. What fun is it to have a relative—especially one who's friend, mentor, and bane-of-your-existence all rolled into one—dating if you can't keep a curious eye on the proceedings?

So when Aunt Peg stood up and stalked from the dining room, I was only a few steps behind her.

Bertie looked at me with concern when I pushed my plate away and rose. Engrossed in the conversation at the table, she hadn't noticed the events transpiring across the room.

"Everything's fine," I said. "I'm just going to check on Peg. Finish your dinner, and I'll see you later."

By the time I reached the dining room exit, Aunt Peg was halfway across the lobby on her way to the stairs. Breaking into an undignified jog, I caught her as she placed her hand on the banister.

And was firmly rebuffed for my efforts.

"I don't want to talk about it," Aunt Peg said.

"Of course you do," I replied.

"No. I don't."

"Okay, fine." I backed up a step or two. "Go up to your room and sulk. That will accomplish a lot."

Aunt Peg's nostrils flared. "I am *not* going to sulk."

"Are you going to throw things?"

"Maybe."

"Can I watch?"

"At the rate you're going, I might make you the target."

"Done," I said. "Let's go."

But of course because I was now moving up the staircase, Aunt Peg stalled at the bottom.

"You can be a very large pain in the posterior," she said.

"I know." Two steps up, I was taller than her for once. "I get that from you."

She sighed. Aunt Peg is a formidable woman. It was a formidable sigh.

"You probably do," she agreed. "So now what?"

I hopped back down to equal footing, which, of course, made her taller than me again. Aunt Peg liked that.

"Let's go for a walk," I said.

She balked again. "Not back into the dining room."

"No." I steered her the other way. "Outside."

"We don't have coats."

"It's not that chilly. We'll deal."

Besides, I was pregnant. I'd been warm for two months.

Outside, the weather was unseasonably balmy. So much so that several people were seated in the Adirondack chairs that lined the porch. Aunt Peg nodded a greeting but we kept moving, down the steps and across the small strip of lawn.

"I love star gazing," I said, looking upward. "It always makes my own problems seem so much smaller."

Aunt Peg harrumphed. "Your problems *are* small."

"Not always. Besides, we're here to talk about you."

Aunt Peg sighed again. She folded her arms across her chest. She didn't appear to be cold; it was more like she was setting up a barrier while she debated how much she wanted to reveal.

"Now that you mention it," she said after a minute, "I guess my problem is pretty small too."

"Richard isn't as appealing in person as he seemed over the Internet?"

"Something like that."

We'd been strolling along the grassy strip between the parking lot and the inn. Now we came to a corner. We had to either turn left around the building, or head off into the woods. Aunt Peg went left.

Good choice.

"Don't get me wrong," she said. "It's not like Richard is a monster or anything. He just isn't perfect."

"Did you expect him to be?"

"Yes," Aunt Peg said stubbornly, even though we both knew how ridiculous that sounded. "I did. After all it isn't as though we're just meeting for the first time. I've known him for months."

"But not in person."

"That shouldn't matter. We exchanged long messages. We talked about everything under the sun. It was amazing how well we got along."

"By e-mail."

"Yes, by e-mail. But still . . ."

I knew what she was thinking. E-mail, with two correspondents both pouring out their deepest thoughts and emotions, could feel like a very intimate form of communication.

But it was also one where the participants could easily censor aspects of themselves or their lives that they didn't wish to reveal.

"Tonight," I said. "What did Richard do wrong?"

"He called me a sentimental old fool."

"*Really?*" I was shocked.

"No, not really. At least not in so many words. But trust me, that was what he meant."

"And what were you being foolish about?"

She leveled the kind of look that used to scare me. Luckily I'm pretty much immune to them by now.

"Well?"

"It was the dog, the German Shepherd. I mentioned that there was a stray in the area and that I was trying to befriend him."

"That sounds reasonable."

"Of course it sounds reasonable. It *is* reasonable."

"But Richard didn't think so?"

"He said he'd been looking for me this afternoon and wondered where I was. Apparently he'd been hoping that we might be able to spend some time together, which then didn't happen because I was busy elsewhere trying to find a homeless dog."

"I take it he wasn't pleased about that?"

"Richard is a dog person. He should have understood. Instead he had the nerve to say that I'd gone off on a fool's errand. You can't save them all, he said."

"That doesn't mean you shouldn't try."

"My thought precisely."

"Maybe it wasn't the dog. Maybe he was just upset because the two of you haven't had a chance to spend much time together."

Aunt Peg stopped and wheeled around so abruptly that I plowed right into her.

"And whose fault is that?" she demanded.

I paused and thought. After a moment the answer she obviously expected came to me.

"Florence," I said.

"And by extension, Richard. *I'm* not the one who brought my mother to the symposium."

Aunt Peg resumed her walk. She has long strides. I was probably putting in two of mine for every one of hers.

I might be able to worm information out of her, but Aunt Peg was going to make me work for it.

We passed the opening in the hedge that led to the

courtyard and hot tub. All sounded quiet within and neither of us even slowed down. Still, it was hard not to remember and give a small shudder.

"Florence doesn't like you," I said.

"Of course she doesn't like me," Peg said briskly. "She sees me as the competition. All these years she's had Richard to herself and now she's faced with having to share him."

"*All these years* . . . ? You mean he's never had a woman friend before?"

"Don't be literal, Melanie. Certainly he's had girl-friends. He was even engaged once, though it didn't last long. I gather Florence drove the poor woman off."

"She'd like to do the same to you."

"She can try," said Peg.

She drew herself up to her full height and squared her shoulders. It was an impressive sight. Interesting how the prospect of losing Richard to his mother had made her forget that she wasn't sure she wanted him anyway.

That's one of the reasons why Aunt Peg has always done so well in the dog show ring. Right or wrong, she's a competitor.

"So you've been talking to Florence," she said. "What else have you been up to?"

"I've had a busy day. You wouldn't believe all the peo-ple I ended up speaking with. It's beginning to look as though we're going to have to figure out who killed Charles."

"*We?*" Aunt Peg's acting skills were improving. She managed to sound surprised. "We who?"

"Surely you don't expect me to do this by myself."

"You always have before."

That was not true. So not true that it was almost funny.

Aunt Peg loves a good mystery and she loves to take charge. She can never resist getting involved and she's a master at pulling strings from the sidelines.

"I'm pregnant," I said.

"Oh, for Pete's sake. Stop trotting out that excuse every other minute."

"It's not an excuse—"

"I don't know what else you'd call it. So you're incubating, regenerating, with child . . . whatever. Dogs do it all the time and it doesn't slow them down. Drink a glass of milk and get on with it."

Aunt Peg never had children. Can you tell?

"So, does this mean you're not going to help?"

"Don't be absurd. Of course I'm going to help. You couldn't keep me from it. There's a murderer right here among us, how could I not be interested in something like that?"

"Then why are we arguing?" I asked.

"Heaven only knows. You're probably having mood swings. Now come over here and sit down and tell me everything you've learned so far."

Cedar benches lined the walkway that we'd been following through the compound. Lights from above cast a flattering glow. It was warm enough that the thought of sitting outside for a while seemed much more appealing than rejoining the crowds in the inn.

So we sat down and I told Aunt Peg about the conversation I'd had with Margo that afternoon.

"That's three people now who've asked for your help," she said, ticking their names off on her fingers. "First Alana, then Caroline, and now Margo. All women. I wonder if that's a coincidence."

"You mentioned earlier that you weren't sure how happy the Evanses' marriage was. Was Charles a ladies' man? Had he had affairs over the years?"

"I haven't any idea. Which is perhaps indicative considering how quickly gossip finds its way though the dog show community. Let's just say that if he did, he was discreet enough that it never became common knowledge."

"Speaking of common knowledge," I said, "did you know that Sam and Alana . . ."

My voice trailed away. I wasn't entirely sure how I wanted to finish that sentence. Maybe I'd let Aunt Peg do it for me and see what term she used to describe my ex-husband's relationship with the blond party girl.

"Sam and Alana?" She repeated the words, which was no help at all.

Aunt Peg sounded intrigued by the possibility. A tidbit of old information, but it was new to her too. "No, I never heard a thing. It must have taken place years ago and was probably over quickly, but still . . . Sam and Alana . . . *together?*"

"Yes, together," I said irritably. "Otherwise, why would I care?"

"Why do you care anyway? In the grand scheme of things, Alana is a woman of very little consequence. Frankly I would have thought that Sam had better taste."

"I'll ask him about that the next time we talk."

"Or," said Aunt Peg. "you could try being the bigger person and let it slide."

Let it slide. The phrase sounded so simple. As if a potential problem could be made to merely glide away into the recesses of forgotten memory.

"Bertie would agree with you," I said.

"Naturally she would. Bertie's a very sensible girl. She doesn't go out of her way to find trouble."

Which, I guess, implied that I did.

Sheesh, I thought. Who was I kidding? Of course I did. Otherwise we wouldn't have been sitting there having this conversation.

"Back to Charles," I said. I related what Tubby and Rosalyn had had to say about him.

"You wouldn't expect a man of Charles's stature to be universally liked," she said when I was finished.

"No, but I would hardly expect him to be pilloried by his constituents before the body was even cold either."

Aunt Peg nodded. She agreed with that.

"Tubby's manners have always been lacking," she said. "But I wonder what Charles did to Rosalyn to put such a bee in her bonnet."

"And there's something else. Rosalyn brought it up and now I've been wondering about it myself. Where were Charles's clothes?"

"What do you mean?"

"Last night, when we found him—"

"He was naked," Aunt Peg said distastefully. "I know. I was there."

"So where was his clothing? The only thing I remember seeing in the vicinity of the hot tub was that one towel. Are we meant to believe that Charles decided to use the hot tub, took off all his clothes, then walked out of his room and through the inn, wearing only a bath towel?"

"I see what you mean," said Peg. "It does make one stop and wonder."

"And here's something else to think about. *Why* was Charles naked? Bertie had used the hot tub earlier. It was situated in a public place and she said that participants were expected to be wearing bathing suits. So how come Charles wasn't?"

"Maybe he didn't bring one with him?" Aunt Peg guessed. "Maybe the nightly swim was a spur-of-the-moment decision and he hadn't come prepared."

"And so he decided to fling off his clothes and go naked?" I said incredulously. "I don't see it. I didn't know Charles, but everyone who did has talked about his prominence and his dignity. And behavior like that simply doesn't jibe."

"Then what do you think was going on?"

"We're back to what we talked about earlier. I'm wondering if Charles was alone, or if there was someone in the hot tub with him. Someone he'd gone out there to meet."

"You mean a woman?"

"Most likely."

"You think Charles was expecting an assignation and found himself with a killer instead?"

"Something like that."

"He would have to have been very bold to plan that sort of meeting in such a public place."

"Maybe that was the point. You know, hiding in plain sight? If someone else had happened upon them, they could have pretended that the fact that they were both in the hot tub was entirely innocent."

"So why did she kill him?" asked Aunt Peg.

"If I knew that, we'd have the puzzle mostly solved."

"It sounds to me like you need to get to work on it."

"You and everybody else," I said with a laugh.

I stood up and stretched. As I raised my arms above my head, a movement in the shadows beyond the lighted path caught my eye. I turned to have a closer look.

"What's wrong?" asked Aunt Peg.

"I don't know. I thought I saw something." I headed that way. "Tell you in a minute."

To my surprise, what I'd seen turned out to be Button. The fawn-colored Chihuahua was trotting along the grassy verge, carrying a twig in his mouth.

I leaned down and scooped him up.

"Button?" Aunt Peg left her seat and followed me. "What are you doing out here?"

Peg talks to dogs all the time. She expects her own to answer, but then they're Poodles.

Button wasn't nearly so compliant. He lifted his lips and grimaced at us.

"Something's wrong," I said. "Florence never would have left him out here by himself."

Peg and I stared together in the direction from which the small dog had come. Beyond the circle of lights, all dissolved into darkness.

"I suppose we'd better go have a look," she said.

16

"I have a bad feeling about this," I said.

"You're not the only one," Aunt Peg replied. "Florence may have her faults, but neglecting that Chihuahua isn't one of them. If he's out here, it seems like a safe bet that she must be too."

We continued along the walkway that ran between the inn's main building and the tall hedge. Button, nestled complacently in my arms, was perfectly happy to ride along.

"I don't see a thing," I said.

"Pity it's so dark out here. If something did happen to Florence, I'm afraid we'd have to be almost right on top of her before we'd find her."

The walkway intersected with another path. A left turn would take us around behind the lodge toward the kitchens. Right led to the health club and spa.

Aunt Peg hesitated. When I started to speak, she held up a hand for silence.

"Listen," she said.

I did, and for a moment heard nothing at all.

Then, just when I thought I might have heard the merest wisp of a sound, Button lifted his head, pricked his ears, and began to whine. The Chihuahua's small body began to shake.

"Precisely," said Peg. "That's what I thought. I heard a dog crying."

"You're hearing Button."

"No, before that. Button's ears are much better than ours. He didn't start the conversation, he's whimpering in response. This way."

Aunt Peg turned and strode purposefully in the direction of the health club.

Like the one before it, this walkway was lit from above. But although we had no trouble seeing the path, darkness obscured the wide grass alleyways on either side.

"There." Aunt Peg pointed. "Look."

Two yellow pinpricks of light glowed in the recesses of the verge.

Eyes, I realized abruptly, as a wolf-like face took shape in the gloom. The animal stood and growled.

I blinked and stared hard into the dark. Comprehension slowly dawned. It wasn't a wolf I was seeing, it was the stray German Shepherd.

Then I looked down and a mound lying next to him swam into focus. A small human form was lying crumpled on the ground.

Florence.

"Oh no." I inhaled sharply. "Do you think he attacked her?"

"Let's hope not."

Aunt Peg moved forward toward the pair, taking cautious steps.

The dog's stare was fixed and unblinking. He shifted from one front foot to the other uneasily.

"Go on now," she said, her tone equal parts soothing and authoritative. "You're done here. Shoo!"

For a moment, the Shepherd looked undecided. He leaned down and nosed the unconscious woman at his feet, whining softly under his breath. Then with one more anxious look at Aunt Peg, he bounded away and vanished into the darkness.

"Good boy!" Aunt Peg said automatically. She's a big believer in positive reinforcement.

Even as the dog disappeared, she was already hurrying forward to Florence's side. I was right behind her.

"What happened?" I asked. "Is she all right?"

"Give me a chance. I don't know anything more than you do yet."

Aunt Peg reached out and felt for a pulse. When she felt a steady beat beneath her fingertips, her shoulders sagged in relief.

"I don't see any blood," I said.

That was good news, especially for the Shepherd's sake. If he'd been to blame for what had happened, his teeth would have torn through Florence's fragile skin.

Aunt Peg's thoughts must have mirrored mine. "I don't know what went on here," she said, "but it looks as though maybe he was trying to protect her. Keep her warm until help arrived. What a good dog."

We'd been speaking in hushed tones. Now a low moan silenced us.

I had already pulled out my phone. I was about to call for help, but I hesitated when Florence groaned and rolled over.

Her eyelids fluttered. One hand came up and slowly reached for her head.

"Hellfire and damnation," she said.

All things considered, that seemed like a good sign.

"Just lie still," I said. "I'm going to call for an ambulance."

"Put that thing away." Florence struggled to sit up. "I don't need any medical types running around telling me what to do."

Aunt Peg placed a hand on the older woman's shoulder, a gesture of comfort and support. Florence looked annoyed, but she didn't pull away.

"How are you feeling?" asked Peg.

"My head hurts. That's how I'm feeling." Florence looked around in confusion. "What am I doing on the ground?"

"We don't know," I said. "We just found you here a minute ago. You were unconscious."

Still in my arms, Button started to whine again. I put him down on the ground and he quickly scrambled up into Florence's lap.

"I think we ought to call for a doctor," said Aunt Peg.

Florence shook her head, then immediately looked as though she regretted making the sharp movement.

"Nobody asked you to do any thinking," she snapped. "I may look fragile but I'm made of pretty stern stuff. I don't need any damn doctors. What I need is some answers."

At least we were all on the same page with that.

"You said you just found me," said Florence, her eyes narrowing. "Were you looking for me?"

"We were outside walking," I explained. "And then Button came trotting down the path. We knew if he was out here, you had to be close by—"

"So you *were* looking for me."

Aunt Peg frowned. "Does it matter?"

"It does to me," Florence said sharply. "Because I'm still trying to figure out what the hell happened. My head hurts. Did one of you bop me when I wasn't looking?"

The question was absurd enough to seem funny to me. Aunt Peg, however, didn't look amused.

"Certainly not," she said.

"You won't get rid of me that easily, you know."

I had put my phone away. Now Aunt Peg pulled hers out.

"I'm calling Richard," she said.

"Good idea." Florence cuddled Button in her skinny arms. "When he gets here, we'll get to the bottom of things."

Aunt Peg stood up and stepped away to make the call. I took the opportunity to probe for more information.

"What were you doing outside?" I asked.

"Same as you. Taking a walk. At least I had a reason." She nodded down toward Button. "What were you two up to, skulking around in the dark?"

"We weren't skulking. We were talking."

"Normal people would have done that inside the inn. What were you talking about? Something secret, I'll bet. Something private that you didn't want anyone to overhear."

As it happened, we'd been talking about the deficiencies of Florence's only son. Too bad I couldn't tell her that. Instead I changed the subject.

"Lucky for you we *were* out here. Otherwise who knows how long it might have been before someone came along and found you."

Florence waved a hand, dismissing my concern.

"Button would have run to my rescue. Didn't you just say that he found you and brought you to me?"

Maybe when they made the movie version that was how the story would be told. In real life, things had played out a little differently.

Button had been carrying a twig when we'd first seen him. He'd looked more interested in finding a soft spot to lie down and chew than in performing a dramatic rescue. Even now, the Chihuahua was nosing around in Florence's pockets, looking for something to eat. His appetite seemed to be of greater concern than his owner's condition.

Still, I hated to destroy Florence's illusions.

"I'm sure you're right," I said. "Button probably would have run up to the front door of the inn and stood there barking until somebody came out to see what was wrong. Like Lassie racing to fetch June Lockhart so she could pull Timmy out of the well."

"What on earth are you babbling about?" asked Aunt Peg, coming back to join us.

"Button's a hero," said Florence. "He deserves a medal."

Peg looked justifiably confused. "For doing what?"

"Saving my life." She stroked the small body from stem to stern, a trip of mere inches. "What a *good* dog you are."

Aunt Peg had used the very same tone, and words, only minutes earlier. Though neither woman would have thanked me for pointing it out, they might have had more in common than they suspected.

"I'll tell you later," I said to Peg over Florence's head.

"Indeed you will," she murmured, then added in a louder voice, "Richard is on his way. He should be here in just a minute."

"Well, why didn't you say so?" Florence demanded.

She stuffed Button into the purse that was lying next to her on the ground and raised a hand imperiously. "Help me up."

"Maybe you don't want to stand up just yet," I said. "We still haven't figured out what happened. Or why your head hurts."

"My head hurts because some hoodlum knocked me down." Florence grabbed my fingers. She yanked them around to the back of her head. "Feel right there, I have a lump the size of a goose egg. Somebody snuck up on me and hit me, I tell you. It's a wonder I'm even still alive to talk about it."

Florence wasn't kidding. She did have a large knot on her head. Aunt Peg was right. We should be calling for medical assistance.

"Why?" asked Aunt Peg.

"Why am I alive? Because I have a hard head, that's why. If Richard comes out here and sees me sitting on the ground like this he's going to have a fit. Are you two going to help me up or not?"

Aunt Peg held out a hand. I stepped around Florence and braced her from behind. The older woman hardly weighed a thing. Cautiously, we lifted her to her feet. She rocked unsteadily for a moment, then got her balance.

"That wasn't my question," said Aunt Peg. "What I'm wondering is why would someone want to hit you."

"I'm sure I don't know. All I was doing was walking my dog and minding my own business."

"How long were you out here before you were attacked?" I asked. "Did you see anyone else while you were walking around?"

"My head hurts. It's hard to remember."

"It might be important," Peg said.

Florence closed her eyes and grimaced. Despite her protests when we'd tried to call for help, she was clearly in pain.

"Mother?"

We heard Richard before we saw him. The sound of footsteps, racing up the path, announced his imminent arrival. As did his frantic calls.

"Mother, where are you?"

"Over here, darling."

Florence's voice, weak and whiny only a moment earlier, now hummed with vitality. And as I watched, the woman underwent a startling transformation. Florence's head came up and her spine stiffened. She found the will to smile. Only a tightness in the muscles on either side of her mouth revealed what the effort was costing her.

Abruptly Richard seemed to burst upon us out of the darkness. Sparing neither Peg nor me a glance, he went straight to his mother and gathered her into his arms. He drew her close for a moment, then stepped back again, holding her away and examining her from head to toe.

"Thank God you're all right. What happened?"

"Just a little accident. Nothing you need to be concerned about."

Florence was clearly reveling in her son's attentive behavior. Over Richard's shoulder, she gave Peg a triumphant look.

Psychology isn't my strong suit but even I knew that Freud would have had a field day with this.

"It was more than a little accident," I said. "Your mother has quite a bump on her head. It looks as though someone might have hit her. We tried to convince her to let us call an ambulance—"

"And I told them it wasn't necessary," said Florence.

"The last thing I want is for anyone to make a big fuss. I'm sure I'll be fine in the morning."

"You'll be fine in the morning," Richard said firmly, "because I'm taking you straight to the emergency room tonight. I know how much you value your independence, but you're not as young as you used to be. You've got to let me take care of you."

"I suppose you might be right."

The woman's show of bravado was waning. Her voice weakened. When she linked an arm through her son's, her body leaned heavily against his side.

Aunt Peg bent down and picked up Florence's purse, with Button still nestled within. Richard reached out and took it from her. Their fingers touched for a moment. They exchanged a look.

"Do you have any idea what happened here?" he asked in a low tone.

Aunt Peg and I both shook our heads.

"Florence was unconscious when we found her," Aunt Peg said. "There's a good chance she has a concussion. At the moment, that's all we know."

"But why . . . ?" Richard sounded as confused as we were. "My mother's never harmed anyone in her life. Who could possibly want to hurt her?"

"It doesn't make sense to us either," I said.

"Do me a favor," said Richard. "Please? Ask around and see if anyone knows anything. This is a travesty and something needs to be done about it."

Even as I started to shake my head, Aunt Peg was already nodding.

Go figure. I'd been about to refuse for her sake.

"Call me later," said Aunt Peg. "And let me know how your mother is doing."

"I will," Richard promised.

17

By unspoken agreement, Aunt Peg and I took the most direct route back inside the inn. We kept to the well-lit areas of the path and didn't even so much as glance into the shadows. We'd both had enough excitement already.

"Now what?" she asked when we entered the lobby.

I walked over and stood near the fire. Despite the evening's warmth, I was feeling a distinct chill.

"For one thing, I vote that we stop walking around outside the inn after dark."

"Done," Peg agreed. "That's two bodies in as many nights. I don't think I could take finding a third."

"Two bodies?" a voice repeated behind us.

Richard's friends, Marshall and Derek, had been walking past on their way from the dining room. Unfortunately they'd overheard what Aunt Peg had said. The pair stopped in their tracks.

"Did I hear correctly?" Marshall asked. He sidled over to stand beside Peg. "Has there been another murder?"

"Certainly not," Aunt Peg said briskly. "This was merely an unfortunate accident."

The chances of Florence having accidentally hit her head seemed slim to me, but I could understand Aunt Peg's desire to downplay the evening's events. Like me, she could probably already hear the gossip express revving its engines and preparing to leave the station.

"Tell us what happened," said Derek. "Was it anyone we know?"

"Florence Donner," I said. There was no point in denying it, I was sure that everyone would know the rest of the story soon enough. "She was walking Button outside and it looks as though someone hit her over the head."

Marshall gasped. "How awful. Is she all right?"

"No, she's not all right," Aunt Peg said shortly. "The woman probably has a concussion. Richard is on his way to the emergency room with her right now."

"That sounds serious," said Derek. "Why was she attacked? Was she robbed?"

"We don't know. It didn't occur to any of us to check. Florence was unconscious when we found her, but her purse was lying on the ground right next to her."

"Richard must be beside himself," said Derek. "The two of them have an unusually close relationship. His mother means the world to him."

"So we've noticed," Aunt Peg said dryly.

She looked past him to the doorway where Margo was now leaving the dining room with several friends. "If you'll excuse me, I see someone I need to speak to."

As Aunt Peg walked away, Marshall plucked off his wire-rimmed glasses and cleaned them on his shirt. His movements were jerky with agitation.

"This is an outrage," he said. "If you ask me, somebody ought to do something."

"Like what?" I asked.

"I don't know. Maybe hire a security team or make the police post a guard at the perimeter. If it were up to me, I'd lock down the inn until we find out exactly what's going on here."

"*Lock down the inn . . . ?*"

I hoped he was kidding. Marshall was clearly upset, but even so, his suggestions were more than a little extreme. Not only that, but having a guard posted at the perimeter of the property most likely wouldn't have kept Florence safe.

"That's what I said," he said forcefully. "But what's the use in telling you? I should take my concerns somewhere where they'll do some good. This inn must have a general manager. I'm going to find him and demand to know what kind of a slipshod establishment he thinks he's running."

Filled with the power of his convictions, Marshall spun around and stalked away.

Derek watched him go with a small smile on his face. "Don't mind Marshall. When things upset him, he tends to have a very short fuse."

"Whereas you're more willing to take the wait-and-see approach."

"Something like that. At any rate, I have no intention of getting all bent out of shape until I've talked to Richard and found out what happened."

More power to him in that attempt, I thought.

There was an empty couch behind us. I sat down and patted the cushion beside me. After a brief hesitation, Derek settled down beside me.

"You and Florence are friends," I said.

It seemed like a good assumption considering that he and Marshall had had dinner with Richard's mother on the first night of the symposium. But Derek was quick to correct me.

"*Richard* and I are friends," he said. "We've known each other for years. We met in Louisville at the spring cluster, and of course we tend to frequent many of the same shows."

It wasn't unusual for exhibitors to have good friends that lived several states away. Traveling in search of good judges was a fact of dog show life, and close relationships were often forged in the cramped camaraderie of the grooming tent.

"Florence is an admirable woman," Derek continued. "Because of my friendship with Richard, our paths tend to cross quite a bit."

"I just met Richard," I said. "So I don't know anything about his relationship with Florence except what I've observed here. It does seem a little unusual for a grown man to spend so much time with his mother."

"Not to them. I know I couldn't imagine living that way myself, but for Richard and Florence, it seems to work. They share the same interests and their mutual passion for dogs takes them to many of the same places. So I guess it only seems natural that they travel together."

Natural wasn't the word I would have used to characterize Richard's relationship with his mother. But that was Aunt Peg's problem, not mine. I had something else I wanted to ask Derek about.

"I was speaking with Florence earlier," I said. "Before dinner."

"I'll bet she tried to warn you off, didn't she?"

"Warn me off?"

"Florence isn't happy about her son's relationship with your aunt."

"Yes, so I gathered."

"But she's also not the kind of person to confront a situation like that head-on. Florence likes to manipulate people but she would prefer it if they don't realize what she's up to. Did she ask you to tell Peg to leave Richard alone?"

I nodded. Derek had read the situation pretty well.

"And will you?"

"No. And trust me, it wouldn't matter if I did. Nobody tells Aunt Peg what to do."

"Good," said Derek. "That should keep things interesting."

As if that aspect of our lives needed any help.

"It's not like there's been a shortage of interesting things going on at this symposium," I pointed out.

"You're right, of course. Whoever would have thought that a simple little gathering in the Poconos could turn up this many problems?"

While others had been titillated by their proximity to the dire events, Derek sounded genuinely worried. Perhaps because he had been acquainted with both of the victims.

"Charles was a friend of yours, too, wasn't he?"

Derek looked up quickly. "What? No. Where did you hear that?"

"From Florence. She told me that you'd mentioned something about coming to the symposium to talk to Charles Evans."

"Yes, well . . . that was true. But as you might imagine, it didn't happen."

"Was that a problem?"

"Of course not." Derek fidgeted in his seat. He didn't

look nearly as happy as he had earlier when I'd been answering his questions. "Why would it be?"

"Florence seemed to think that you'd come to the symposium for that very reason."

"Florence exaggerates."

"Really?" I tipped my head to one side innocently. "I didn't get that impression."

"You don't know her as well as I do."

I wondered if what Derek had wanted to see Charles about had anything to do with the keynote address. A speech that had, in a span of mere minutes, turned the respected judge into an object of derision from his peers.

Charles had to have known that his stand would be unpopular. But the man was also no fool. It seemed likely to me that before he would choose to deliver that address to this particular crowd, he might have expected to find support from some quarter.

Could Derek be another member of the dog show community who believed in the goals that the animal rights groups espoused?

"How did you feel about Charles's speech?" I asked.

Derek shrugged. "The topic was certainly a surprise."

"You didn't expect him to come out in support of the animal rights' agenda?"

"No. Why would I?"

"I was just wondering if maybe that was what you wanted to discuss with him."

"An end to selective breeding? The demise of dog shows as we know them? Hardly. I don't know what Charles hoped to accomplish by delivering that speech, but he ended up costing himself a great deal of credibility and respect. When he stepped up to the podium,

Charles was a shining star on the dog show horizon. When he left, he looked like a bit of a crackpot."

Derek leaned toward me. He lowered his voice confidentially. "Besides, even if I did happen to agree with what Charles said—and I'm certainly not saying that I did—there's no way I'd cop to that now."

"Why not?"

"Come on. You're kidding, right? That stand not only made Charles unpopular, in hindsight it looks like it might even have gotten him killed. There's a certain irony in that, wouldn't you say?"

His closeness was making me uncomfortable. I leaned back and my shoulders braced up hard against the cushions. There was nowhere left to retreat.

In some cultures, this much contact would have been grounds enough to insist on marriage. Unfortunately, I was too interested in hearing what he had to say to push him away.

"What do you mean?" I asked.

"Those of us who breed and show dogs tend to think of the animal rights activists as a bunch of loonies. Fanatics who would go to any lengths to further their agenda. And yet, in our own way, are we really any different than they are? We're equally fanatic about protecting what we believe in. You only have to look at what happened to Charles to realize that."

"What makes you so sure that it was his speech that got him killed?"

"It seems like the obvious conclusion, doesn't it? The views Charles espoused were clearly unpopular. Someone must have wanted to silence him."

"If that was the case," I said reasonably, "the killer should have gotten to Charles before he delivered the address, not after."

"Not necessarily. Who's to say that whoever murdered Charles even knew what the speech was going to be about? But then after he listened to Charles talk, he became so outraged that he struck out in anger. You know, a crime of passion."

I knew crimes of passion, all right. And at least in theory, that was a notion I could get behind. I just wasn't sure that we'd yet succeeded in narrowing down what the killer had been passionate about.

Derek had been hovering over me for long enough. I slipped out from beneath him and stood up. It felt good to have space around me.

Before I left, however, I wanted to take one last stab at steering him back to the question I'd originally wanted to ask.

"You never did tell me what you wanted to talk to Charles about."

"It's not important."

"You must have thought it was at the time."

"I did." Derek smiled grimly. "But things change, don't they? If you must know, before the conference I'd shared a brief correspondence with Charles about a matter of mutual interest. We had intended to continue our discussion here."

"And did you?"

"No, I never had the chance. But as things turned out, it didn't matter. Someone else was able to solve my problem for me, so I didn't need Charles's intervention after all."

"Problem?" I said with interest.

I hoped Derek would elaborate, but he didn't.

"As I said, it's already been resolved. Which was what I would have told Charles had I gotten the opportunity

to talk to him. So you see, everything worked out all
right in the end."

Easy for him to say, I thought.

I doubted if Charles would have agreed.

18

It wasn't even nine o'clock yet but I was ready for bed. I hadn't seen Bertie since we'd parted in the dining room, and Aunt Peg had gone off with Margo. Presumably both my relatives were capable of fending for themselves for the remainder of the evening. I was going to go upstairs, put my feet up, and watch a television show that had absolutely no redeeming social value.

Inside the room, I pulled out my cell phone and started to hook it up to the charger. Then stopped. I had spoken to Sam and Davey that morning, but it felt like eons had passed since then.

And then there was the matter of that issue which I still wanted to discuss with Sam. *Let it slide*, Aunt Peg had said.

Fat chance.

Davey, who would have been in bed if I'd been home, answered the phone. Thanks to the wonders of caller ID he knew who he'd be speaking to.

"Scarlett," he said. "What do you think?"

"Hello to you too."

"Hi, Mom. What about Scarlett?" When there's something he wants, my son has a one-track mind. "You know, like red?"

"I assume we're talking about baby names?"

"Of course we're talking about baby names. Sam-Dad suggested Angelina. I think it's too long."

At least they were beginning to come up with girls' names. And on a Wednesday, no less. That was progress.

"Too long for what?"

"You know. The baby's not going to be very big when it's born. So you don't want to give it a really big name."

The crystal clear logic of a nine-year-old. You had to love it.

I sat down on the bed and crossed my legs. It felt wonderful to be connected to home.

"What do you think of Katherine?" I asked. "We could call her Kate."

"No way. There's a girl named Kate in my class at school. She's the biggest pain—"

"Davey!"

"Well, she is. You wouldn't like her either. She thinks she knows everything."

Okay, so Kate was out. At least for the time being.

"How come you're not in bed yet?" I asked.

"It's fall break," Davey informed me as if I hadn't known. "Besides, we're having guys' night out."

"Out where?"

"Well, Sam and I aren't actually out. It's more like we're in. You know, like home. But Dad and Frank are here. We're playing poker and drinking beer."

I assumed that was the royal we. Still, Davey would be disappointed if I didn't muster a little outrage.

"How much beer have you drunk so far?" I asked.

My son giggled into the phone. Right answer.

"Winning any money?"

"No, but Sam-Dad's doing okay."

No surprise there. I'd seen my husband bluff. I sus-pected he was cleaning up. The other two guys would probably be happy to take a break.

"Would you ask Sam if they can deal him out for a hand?"

"Sure," said Davey. "I'll go check. Scarlett. Think about it."

He must have set the phone down because now I could hear the keening wail of a jazz trombone, pour-ing from a nearby speaker. It helped to set the mood.

I pictured the four of them hunched around a green baize tabletop, concentrating on their cards, fingering their chips, a veil of dusky smoke hovering in the air above them . . .

"Hey, babe," said Sam.

The image dissolved, replaced by a reality that was much better. It was great to hear Sam's voice.

"What's going on?" he asked. "I didn't think I'd hear from you again today."

"I know. Me either. But it's been that kind of a day."

"What kind?"

"Long. Eventful."

"That doesn't sound good. You're supposed to be taking it easy."

"Believe me, I'm trying. Things just haven't worked out that way."

"But you're feeling good?" Sam sounded anxious.

"I'm fine," I said quickly. "And much better now that I'm talking to you. I hear you've taught Davey to play poker and drink beer."

Sam snorted a laugh. "Every kid deserves a well-rounded education, don't you think?"

"I'm pretty sure that's why I became a teacher. How's the game going?"

"I haven't had to dig into the retirement fund yet."

I smiled into the phone. "That's good to know. Listen, I wanted to ask you about something that came up earlier. Let's try some free association. I'll say a name and you say the first thing that pops into your mind."

"Okay," Sam agreed. "Shoot."

An ironic choice of words, considering that this was suddenly beginning to feel a bit like an ambush.

"Alana Bennett."

"Oh, crap."

"Nice mouth, Driver."

"Who have you been talking to?"

"Bertie, among others."

"Bertie?" Sam sounded perplexed. "What does she know?"

"She and Alana have become best buddies. And apparently Alana's the type who likes to kiss and tell."

"So I guess I'm busted?"

"It looks that way."

"Did she also tell you that it was all over a long time ago?"

"She didn't have to. I could figure that part out for myself."

"Then we're okay—"

"Not entirely," I said. "You know, a heads-up on the subject would have been nice. Since Alana's here and I'm here, and we talked about her the other day, so you knew that we'd met. It would be easier for me if when stuff like this came up, I didn't always feel like I was the last to know."

"Stuff like what?" Sam asked.

He sounded puzzled. Selective memory at its finest.

"Remember Sheila?"

It was a rhetorical question. Of course he remembered Sheila. She was his ex-wife, the love of his younger life. The woman he'd somehow neglected to mention until we were engaged and she'd reentered his life on a mission to win him back.

"Oh, right," said Sam. "Sheila."

"Sheila?" I heard Frank echo in the background. "She was a fox. What are you talking about her for?"

"Give me a minute." Sam turned his mouth away from the phone. "Why don't you guys go take the dogs outside for a walk?"

The yard was fenced. The Poodles didn't need to be walked, merely let out an open door. But either Frank and Bob had drunk enough beer that that didn't occur to them, or else the look on Sam's face told them they'd be better off leaving the vicinity.

I heard the sound of feet scrambling and a couple of random barks. Davey whooped, probably just for the heck of it. A door opened and shut; then all was quiet and Sam was back.

"*Sheila*?" he repeated.

"She was just an example," I said. "Move on."

"I did, didn't I?" Now he was confused. "I thought we were arguing about Alana."

"We weren't arguing, we were discussing."

This whole conversation was starting to wear me out. I was beginning to suspect that Aunt Peg had been right.

"All I'm asking for is a little advance notice before another of your exes pulls me aside to discuss your performance in bed."

"Alana didn't do that."

"What makes you so sure?"

"Well, now that you mention it," Sam said glumly, "I

guess I'm not. She isn't the classiest lady. Want me to call her and tell her to cut it out?"

"No way," I said with a laugh. "Feel free to stay as far away from her as possible."

"That I can do. Listen, not that I'm in any hurry to change the subject or anything but I did a little asking around. Rumor has it—and we're talking unsubstantiated here—that there's a multibreed judge from the Midwest named Tubby Something, whose judging was recently found to be a bit irregular."

"Tubby Mathis," I said. "That could be the scandal Margo was worried about because he's here. And probably greatly relieved that all this other stuff has overshadowed his problems and given everybody something else to talk about."

"Timing is everything," said Sam. "The rest is going okay?"

"Well . . ." I smiled into the phone. "What's this I hear about Scarlett?"

"Hey, you can't blame that one on me. He's your son. It stands to reason he'd be an independent thinker."

Guilty as charged.

"Get some sleep," said Sam. "And try not to do so much tomorrow."

"I'll work on it," I said.

Neither one of us believed me for a minute.

I went to bed and awoke, enormously refreshed, ten hours later. One good thing about being pregnant, you can indulge yourself as much as you want and nobody says a thing.

Bertie was singing in the shower when I opened my eyes. Considering the decibel level she'd managed to attain, the two events were probably related. She emerged from the bathroom five minutes later, wrapped in a towel and smoothing moisturizer on her face.

"I heard I missed out on some excitement last night," she said. "Florence got herself knocked out?"

I sat up in bed. The covers pooled around my waist.

"That's true, unfortunately."

Bertie paused in front of the mirror to study her reflection. She poked at a nonexistent blemish and frowned. If I looked like Bertie, I'd probably spend entire days just staring at myself in the mirror.

"Peg didn't do it, did she?"

"No," I said with a grin. "And I can vouch for that. I was with her when it happened."

"Good thing. But you two were the ones who found her, right?"

"Right. First Button, and then Florence. She didn't have any idea what had happened."

Bertie looked skeptical. "Really."

"She said she was just walking Button and minding her own business."

"It sounds like you haven't heard the rest of the story."

"Tell me."

"You went to bed early last night but I was still downstairs when Richard came back. He said that his mother was probably fine but that the doctors wanted to keep her overnight for observation."

"That's good," I said.

"Wait, there's more. And this part's not so good."

"Now what?"

"After you left the dining room last night, the four of us got the check and went our separate ways. But later, Alana and I were socializing in the bar."

Carousing was probably more like it, I thought. Everywhere Alana went seemed to turn into a party.

"And Rosalyn came back in. Apparently Florence had just called her from the hospital."

"Rosalyn and Florence? When did they get to be such good friends?"

"I have no idea," Bertie said impatiently. "And besides it's not important. What matters is that Florence told Rosalyn that Peg is the one who'd attacked her and that was why she had to be taken to the hospital."

Oh, good Lord.

I pushed away the covers and scrambled out of bed. "Does Aunt Peg know about that?"

"*Everybody* knows about it. Once Rosalyn told a couple of people in the bar, the news spread through the inn like bird flu. Probably the only reason you haven't heard is because you were asleep."

"I assume Aunt Peg put a quick end to that nonsense?"

"Well . . . no," said Bertie. "She wasn't there. She and Margo were holed up somewhere, dealing with official business or something."

I'd been digging through my suitcase, looking for clean underwear. Now I straightened and sighed.

"Then please tell me that *you* told Rosalyn she was wrong."

"I would have been delighted to. But how could I when I didn't have the slightest idea what had happened? So I went looking for you. . . ."

"I was up here sleeping."

"So I discovered. And then Peg reappeared but by then it was too late. Everyone had already heard Florence's version and they all looked at Peg like she was some kind of criminal."

"Don't be ridiculous," I said.

Bertie was exaggerating. She had to be. Really, who was going to take Florence's word over Aunt Peg's?

"Most of the people at the symposium have known Aunt Peg for years," I said. "They know what kind of woman she is. They must realize that she'd never be capable of doing something like that."

"You're right, they should know that. But don't forget, Florence is a fixture in the dog show world too. Or at least she's been around forever. And she looks like a helpless little old lady, plus of course she's the one who's in the hospital. So right away she got the sympathy vote."

From what I'd seen of Florence, she was about as helpless as a boa constrictor. And probably just about as tenacious when it came to getting what she wanted.

In fact, considering how things had worked out, maybe we shouldn't discount the possibility that Florence had hit herself over the head, just to see how much trouble she could cause.

"Wonderful," I said. "Did I miss anything else?"

"Isn't that enough?"

Bertie dropped the towel she was wearing and kicked it under the bed. Supremely unselfconscious about the fact that she was naked, she opened a dresser drawer and rifled through a stack of wispy, lacy underthings until she found the ones she wanted.

As she gracefully stepped into a thong the size of a rubber band, I looked at the panties I'd pulled out for myself. They were big and made of cotton and had a thick elastic waist. A stretchy band in the front allowed for future expansion.

Just another example of the many ways in which life isn't fair.

"I suppose I'd better talk to Aunt Peg," I said. "Do you think she's up yet?"

"Oh, she's up all right." Bertie looked at me meaningfully.

I stared back. Obviously I was missing something. "What?"

"Don't ask me," said Bertie.

Sheesh. I'd only been awake a matter of minutes and already this day was shaping up to be just as confusing as the previous one.

"I don't get it," I said. "What are we talking about?"

"Listen for yourself." Bertie gestured toward the common wall that our room shared with Aunt Peg's. "I have no idea what's going on in there, but I've been hearing strange noises ever since I got up."

"What kind of noises?"

"Thumping, banging . . . you don't want to know the rest, believe me."

I started toward the door that connected our room with hers. "I hope she's all right."

"Mel, wait!"

My steps slowed. "Now what?"

"Think about it. You don't want to just go barging in there. What if she's not alone?"

Oh.

I spun back around. Sank down on the bed.

Oh.

I felt like an idiot.

"You think Richard is in there with her?"

Now I was whispering. I had no idea why. It wasn't as if either one of them could hear us through the wall.

"Somebody has to be. Peg couldn't make that much noise on her own."

"But she was mad at Richard last night. They'd had a fight."

Bertie shrugged. "Maybe they're making up."

I sat on the rumpled bed and stared at the door. For the moment, all was quiet.

"Look on the bright side," said Bertie.

"Please tell me there *is* a bright side."

"If Peg's in her room with Richard, that must mean that he didn't believe that nonsense about her attacking his mother."

I supposed that was something. Not much, but better than nothing. I was beginning to feel like a shipwreck survivor clinging to a splinter of wood.

I'd been staring so hard at the connecting door that when someone suddenly rapped hard against the other side, it was almost as if I'd conjured the sound. I jumped to my feet and looked at Bertie.

She raised her brows and shrugged. "Open it."

What if it was Richard? I was wearing my pajamas. And Bertie was still in her underwear.

"Melanie?" Aunt Peg called from the other side. "Bertie? Are you awake in there?"

I smiled in relief. "Coming."

"Hurry up," Peg ordered. "I have something in here to show you."

19

"It better not be Richard," Bertie muttered.

"Shhh!" I grasped the knob and turned it. "She'll hear you."

"What will I hear?" asked Aunt Peg.

I pulled the door open and there she was, filling the doorway. She was standing with legs braced apart and arms crossed over her chest. She was also looking very pleased with herself.

"Nothing," I said quickly. "What do you have to show us?"

Aunt Peg looked past me and frowned. "Bertie, dear, don't you want to put on some clothing?"

"Right away."

Bertie opened another drawer and yanked out a pair of low-slung jeans and a T-shirt. It took her less than a minute to make herself presentable.

On the subject of clothing, I noted with relief that Aunt Peg herself was fully dressed in an outfit that included both a wool sweater and sturdy walking shoes.

Whatever she'd been up to, it didn't look as though Peg had been cavorting with a lover.

"You're staring," she said. "What's the matter?"

"Nothing," I said again. It was getting to be a habit.

"She's just surprised you're dressed," said Bertie. Tucking in her T-shirt, she walked over to stand beside me.

"Why wouldn't I be dressed?" Aunt Peg asked. "It's nearly eight o'clock. The early bird catches the worm, you know. I've already been outside for a walk."

"Catch any worms?" Bertie said cheekily.

"Better than that, and if you two would stop jabbering for a moment, I'd show you what I've got."

Aunt Peg stepped away from the doorway, allowing us to see into the room. Lying on her bed, a pillow bunched up between his front paws, was the homeless German Shepherd. He lifted his head and cast a wary glance in our direction, then went back to gnawing on his prize.

"Wow," I said. "How'd you manage that?"

"With great difficulty."

Aunt Peg eased back into the room. Bertie and I followed and she slid the door shut behind us.

"Don't make any sudden moves. He's still a bit skittish."

"He's going to shred that pillow," said Bertie. "Any minute now, there will be feathers everywhere."

"I'll survive the loss. Chewing on that pillow is the first thing that's calmed him down since I got him in here. It seems to be acting like some sort of giant pacifier. Earlier he was bouncing off the walls."

"So that's what Bertie heard." I began to laugh.

"It's not that funny," Bertie grumbled, but she was biting back a smile.

"Dare I even ask? I'm beginning to think that letting the two of you share a room was a mistake. It's as though you've developed your own private language that excludes everyone else."

"Bertie heard some noises coming from your room earlier," I said. "She thought you were in here with Richard."

Briefly Aunt Peg looked nonplussed. Then she began to laugh too.

"Oh my, that's rich. You thought that I . . . that Richard and I . . . oh my . . ."

"It was just a guess," Bertie said in her own defense.

"Not a very good one. Though I suppose I should probably be flattered." Aunt Peg stopped and caught her breath. "As it happens, however, you were entirely wrong. What you heard was Walter and me—"

"Walter?"

"He needed a name. He wasn't going to begin to feel at home without one."

"Yes, but . . . *Walter*?"

"I'll have you know that's a perfectly good German name. It's entirely suitable under the circumstances."

If she said so.

"Besides, he seems to like it. Look." Aunt Peg lifted a hand and waved. "Walter, over here!"

The Shepherd raised his head again. His dark eyes darted back and forth.

It was probably the movement, as much as the name, that had drawn his attention. Aunt Peg could have called him Ronald McDonald and gotten the same response.

But she was right, he did need a name. If only so we would stop referring to him as the stray.

"What are you going to do with him?" asked Bertie.

The Shepherd had nosed the pillow into a ball. He

opened up a small hole in one end and went to work on enlarging it.

If Walter had been one of her Poodles, Aunt Peg would have immediately put a stop to such antics. But she watched the Shepherd destroy the pillow with a benign eye.

"For the moment, I'm just going to try and be his friend. Give him some security and see if I can restore some of his faith in the human race. And of course get some food into him. If his coat wasn't so thick, you could see his ribs. You can certainly feel them. He looks as though he hasn't had a proper meal in weeks."

So Aunt Peg had been close enough to Walter to know what his body felt like. That was a good sign. Even with Bertie and me in the room, the Shepherd finally seemed to be relaxing a bit.

I'd seen my aunt use her voice and her calm, supportive manner to soothe anxious dogs before. There was something about the way she handled herself that dogs instinctively responded to. And trusted. It was probably only a matter of time before she and Walter became great friends.

"Speaking of food," she said, "I called Room Service and asked for a triple order of scrambled eggs, bacon, and toast. Later this morning, I'll pick up some kibble, but in the meantime Walter is going to have to make do. That's why I knocked on your door. I told Room Service to deliver the food to your room. There's no sense in alerting anyone to the fact that I've smuggled in an unauthorized pet."

She'd managed to relay that news just in time. As she finished speaking, a knock sounded on the door to the adjoining room.

"Room Service!" a voice called out cheerfully.

Bertie slipped through the common door and went to sign for Walter's breakfast.

While we waited for her to return, I said, "Now that you've got the dog sorted out, what are you planning to do about Florence?"

"Not a blessed thing." Aunt Peg permitted herself a small smile. "At least for the moment, she's out of my hair. It's probably the first time since our arrival that I've been able to say that."

"Don't be too sure," I said. "Florence called Rosalyn last night from the hospital and told her that you were the one who was responsible for what happened to her."

Aunt Peg snorted. "Have you ever heard anything more absurd?"

"No, but that doesn't mean that some people won't believe her."

"Anyone that silly deserves to be misled."

I couldn't believe she wasn't taking the problem more seriously.

"Have you spoken with Richard?"

"Now that you mention it, no." Aunt Peg looked thoughtful. "I expected him to call and give me an update but he never did."

"Probably because Florence had told him the same thing she told Rosalyn. You've got to talk to her and make her stop telling lies about you."

"No," Aunt Peg said firmly. "What I have to do is tend to this poor animal. At the moment, he's my first responsibility."

She opened the door between the two rooms and helped Bertie maneuver a rolling cart through. "Trust me, the rest of that nonsense will sort itself out in time."

She had truth and the power of her convictions on

her side. Even so, I wasn't nearly as complacent as my aunt. I'd seen good things turn bad before. Hopefully it wasn't about to happen again.

Bertie and I left Peg and Walter to their breakfast and retreated to our own room.

"You know you're still in your pajamas," Bertie pointed out.

As if I'd had time to do something about that, but chosen not to.

"What's your point?"

She strode across the room and yanked the curtains open wide. Sunlight came flooding in.

"My point is, if you would get dressed we could go somewhere."

"Do you have any particular place in mind?"

"The spa."

"Not that again." I rolled my eyes. "Do you have another appointment with Gunther?"

"No, but—"

"By the way, I spoke with Sam last night."

"Don't change the subject," Bertie said, then stopped. "Oh, wait. I get it. You're not."

"He and I talked about Alana."

"Big surprise." Bertie marched over and sat down on the edge of the bed. "Did he remember her as fondly as she does him?"

"Not exactly. But that got me thinking. There's something that's been nagging at me. Remember yesterday when we talked to Alana at breakfast?"

"Sure." Bertie chuckled. "She asked you if you'd ever heard of multitasking."

I ignored that. "She also said that she was outside the

other night and saw Charles in the hot tub. Probably not long before he was murdered."

"Right. So?"

"Do you remember what Alana said she did after that?"

Bertie squinched up her face and thought back. After a minute, she shook her head.

"No, does it matter?"

"I don't know. Maybe. Alana said she went back to her room and watched TV. You know her better than I do, does that sound likely to you?"

"Now that you mention it, no." Bertie yanked open a dresser drawer and started tossing clothes at me. "Get dressed, already. Then we'll go find out what Alana has to say."

As it turned out, the path to Alana led us to the health club anyway.

We found her in the meditation garden, an indoor alcove fashioned to look like a peaceful forest glade. Alana was sitting cross-legged on the floor. Her hands rested on her knees, palms turned upward. Her eyes were closed. She was breathing rhythmically in and out.

She looked like she was channeling her inner swami.

At the edge of the room, Bertie and I kicked off our shoes. We padded across the floor in our stocking feet.

"Go away," Alana said as we drew near.

She hadn't shifted position, nor opened her eyes.

"How did you know we were here?" asked Bertie.

"I can feel your negative energy. It's wafting over me like a wave."

"And disrupting your inner harmony, no doubt."

I dropped to the floor beside her and crossed my own legs. I was absurdly pleased to see that I could still accomplish the feat.

"Now's not a good time," said Alana. "I'm meditating."

As if we couldn't have guessed.

"This will only take a minute," Bertie told her.

Bertie was still standing, apparently undecided whether to stay or go. Her social graces must have been better than mine. I was already hunkered down for the duration.

I reached down, grabbed my foot, and flipped it up on top of my knee. To my delight, it went. And I didn't even tip over backward.

"About Tuesday night," I said.

Alana sighed loudly. She still hadn't opened her eyes. I wondered how she could do that. I hate talking to people when I can't see them.

"Why should I tell you anything?" she asked. "Last time I talked to you, you sent the police after me."

"That wasn't our fault. You should have gone to Detective Wayne yourself."

I patted the floor beside me. Bertie finally sat.

Effortlessly, she pretzeled her legs into position. Meanwhile I was still wrestling with my second foot.

Bertie flipped over her hands and closed her eyes too. It was amazing how serene she looked.

How come I was the only one with a shortage of inner peace?

"I don't know anything," said Alana. "I already told you that."

"You also told us that after you saw Charles in the hot tub you went back to your room and watched TV."

Alana gave up trying to block me out. She opened her eyes. Her shoulders slumped.

"So?"

"What was on that night?"

"As if I would remember something like that."

"It was only thirty-six hours ago. What'd you see?"

"Some reality show, with lots of people running around acting stupid. There." She glared. "Are you satisfied?"

Not by a long shot, I thought.

"Speaking of acting stupid," said Alana, "I heard your aunt beat up Richard's mother. That must have been something to see."

"It might have been," I allowed, "if it had happened."

"Florence is in the hospital. If Peg didn't get her, who did?"

"That's something else we'd like to know," Bertie said.

Alana turned and gazed at her friend. "Seriously?"

Bertie opened her eyes. Her fingers curled upward; her hands clenched into fists. Her inner harmony was receding too.

"Seriously. That's two people in two days. And whoever was responsible for those attacks is probably still here among us."

"Wow." Alana exhaled. "I wonder who will be next."

"Nobody, if we're lucky," I said. "That's why we were hoping you might be willing to answer a couple of questions."

"I already told Detective Wayne everything."

"*Everything*?" Bertie repeated skeptically. "Or everything that cast you in a flattering light?"

"Like you should talk." Alana sniffed. "Let's just say that I told him everything I wanted him to know. That's almost the same thing."

A rather warped view of things in my opinion. But then, considering my track record with the authorities, who was I to throw stones?

"Tell us the parts you didn't tell Detective Wayne," I invited.

Alana pushed her lower lip out in a pout. No doubt she thought she looked charming, but the effect was lost on me.

"Why should I?"

"Because you love to gossip," said Bertie. "Face it, it's what you do."

Alana giggled. "Not about myself!"

"That's not what I heard," I said. "Bertie came back from a hot rock massage yesterday with some pretty interesting tidbits about your sexual escapades—"

I'd been referring to the business between Alana and Sam. I guess on some level I'd been hoping that a mention of her previous girl talk might loosen Alana up. But to my surprise, she went positively pale.

"Who told you about that?" she demanded.

About *what?* I wondered. I wasn't about to concede that Alana had lost me, but I had no idea what she was talking about. What was I missing? What did she think I knew?

"Damn," said Bertie.

She was quicker on the uptake than I was. Maybe I was missing out on something by not meditating.

"I can't believe I didn't put it together yesterday. You and Charles?"

Holy moly, I thought. That was serious.

"Why not?" said Alana. "He was hot."

And now he was dead.

20

"For starters," I said, "he was married."

Alana tossed her head. "Like that matters."

It did to some of us.

Alana and Sam. I ground my teeth at the thought of the two of them together.

"*Charles*?" Bertie said again. "Surely you couldn't have been that desperate."

"Desperation had nothing to do with it. Charles and I had a lot in common. We were soul mates."

"Next you'll be telling us you loved each other," I said dryly.

"You're not really that naïve, are you? Love had nothing to do with our relationship. It didn't need to. We had mutual respect, mutual desire. Believe me, that was enough. And for a man his age, Charles had plenty of energy . . . if you know what I mean."

Yup, I thought. We did.

This new information rearranged things. It no longer looked like mere chance that Alana had been the last person to see Charles alive. And perhaps it explained where his missing clothes had gone.

"Tell us about Tuesday night," I said.

"I already did."

"Tell us the truth this time."

Alana looked at Bertie. "Is she always this rude?"

"When she needs to be," Bertie said complacently.

"This glade is supposed to be a place of peace and spiritual harmony."

Like that was going to stop me.

"Just tell us what we want to know," I said. "And we'll leave you alone to realign your chakras."

"My chakras may never recover. First Charles's murder, and now this. You're treating me like I was some sort of suspect."

"You were the last person to see Charles alive," I said. "And you were having an illicit affair with him. The police would have a field day with information like that."

"So now you're threatening me?"

"I'm sure Melanie didn't mean it that way." Bertie was ever the peacemaker.

"Yes, I did."

"Besides," said Alana, "you're overlooking one important point. *I* wasn't the last person with Charles that night. The murderer was."

"Why don't you tell us about it?"

"If I do, will you promise to go away?"

"Scout's honor."

Alana looked dubious.

I doubted she was ever a Girl Scout. But then, just for the record, neither was I.

She heaved a sigh of resignation. Just in case we weren't already aware that this was a *huge* imposition. Then finally she began to talk.

"I went to the hot tub that night to meet Charles. He was already there, waiting for me. With all the other symposium activities, the hot tub didn't seem to be a particularly popular attraction. The alcove is nice and private and we figured there would be nobody there."

"Then what happened?"

"Take a guess." Alana smirked. "The air was cool, the water was warm. The two of us were out there alone together under the stars. Let's just say, the situation was pretty conducive and we both got a little playful. After what Charles had gone through, he deserved a treat."

"You're referring to the keynote speech?"

"That's right. It took courage for Charles to take such a stand. Especially since he knew how unpopular his viewpoint was going to be."

"Either courage or lunacy," Bertie muttered.

"You only say that because you haven't taken the time to stop and examine the issues. Many of the things that Charles talked about in his speech are going to come to pass eventually. Trust me, it's inevitable, and it's only a matter of time before the dog show world realizes that."

Spoken like a true proponent of the animal rights platform.

Abruptly I remembered Aunt Peg saying that Alana liked to take up causes and adopt them as her own. And all at once I suspected I knew what had caused Charles's sudden change of heart.

"You were the one who converted him, weren't you?" I said.

"Converted?" Alana laughed. "What a thing to say. You make it sound like we're talking about a change of religion."

Believe me, as far as dog show people were concerned,

it was almost that serious. And certainly no laughing matter.

"Convinced him, then. Do you like the sound of that better?"

"Let's just say I pointed out the error of his ways."

"You must have done a pretty good job of it." I had to work to keep the admiration out of my voice. "Prior to this symposium, Charles had devoted both his life and his career to the betterment of purebred dogs—"

"But that's what I'm trying to tell you," said Alana. "He was *still* doing that. Don't you see? The only difference was that he'd changed his belief of what constituted working for their good."

"Or you changed it for him," said Bertie.

"You two must have a very high opinion of my capabilities. I didn't make Charles do a single thing that he didn't want to. The keynote speech was entirely his idea—"

"But the understanding that he could come to the hot tub later to collect his reward, I assume that was your doing?"

"Of course." Alana sounded smug. A woman who never underestimated her own appeal—or its effect on men.

"So you and Charles were . . . entertaining yourselves . . . in the hot tub. What happened next?"

"We heard someone coming."

"Who?"

Alana stared. "How would I know that?"

I stared right back. "You were there, weren't you?"

"Not when the other person appeared. As soon as we realized we were about to be interrupted, I knew I had to disappear. The last thing Charles needed was any hint of impropriety. It would have undone all the good he'd just accomplished."

Maybe they should have thought of that before they'd climbed into the hot tub together. Or perhaps I was just too practical to orchestrate an illicit affair.

"Go on," Bertie prodded when I missed my cue.

"Well, I wasn't about to duck under the water and hold my breath. So I jumped out of the tub, gathered up the clothes on the bench, and made a run for it."

"Your clothes and Charles's both."

"As it turned out, yes. Though I didn't realize that at the time. I just snatched up everything I could and ran."

"Naked." Bertie grinned. "That must have been a sight."

"I'm sure it was," Alana said with a chuckle. "Thank God there was no one around to see."

"What about the murderer?" I asked. "Are you sure he didn't see you?"

Abruptly Alana stopped laughing.

"Yes," she said after a moment's hesitation. "I am."

I didn't know if we were hearing the truth. I did know that we were hearing what she wanted to believe.

"And you didn't see him . . . or her?"

"No. Didn't I just tell you that? I had no idea who was coming, and at the time it didn't seem like it even mattered. All I knew was that I had to get out of there."

"So you went back to your room," said Bertie.

"*Naked!*" Alana repeated in case we'd missed that fact earlier. "Where the hell else was I going to go?"

Good point.

"You must have been sorry you'd been interrupted," I said. "Did you think about waiting a few minutes and then going back outside?"

"For what? The mood was pretty well shot, you know what I mean? I figured if Charles wanted to come looking for me, he knew where to find me."

"When he didn't, did that bother you?"

Alana's shrug was deliberately casual. "I didn't think about it one way or the other. And I certainly wasn't about to go chasing after him."

"So how did you hear about what had happened?" Bertie asked.

"Just like everyone else. I waited a little while in my room, but when Charles didn't show up, I went down to the bar to get a drink. By then, the word was out. It was all anybody could talk about."

"You must have been shocked," I said.

"I burst into tears on the spot. In the annals of Alana Bennett, it wasn't my finest moment. Then I bought a bottle of Johnny Walker Black from the bartender, took it back up to my room with me, and drank myself into a stupor."

Alana's shoulders slumped. She exhaled softly.

"He really was a very fine man," she said.

Bertie started to get up. I had one more question.

"Did Caroline know about you and Charles?"

Alana tipped her chin upward, defiant once again. "What could that possibly matter now?"

"Somebody was angry enough at Charles to want to kill him. Under the circumstances, I would think that his wife might have fit that description."

"Caroline?" Alana sounded as if she was considering the possibility for the first time.

"Do you have any better ideas?"

"I don't have any ideas at all. That's supposed to be your department. As for Caroline . . ."

"Yes?" I said when her voice trailed away. "What?"

"She knew. That bitch knows everything."

"No wonder you do this detecting thing," Bertie said.

We had left Alana in the meditation garden and exited the health spa. Now we were on our way back to the inn.

"It's a bit of a rush, isn't it?"

I stopped walking. "What do you mean?"

"You know, convincing people to confess their deepest, darkest secrets."

"When it works," I admitted, "I guess it feels pretty good."

"And when it doesn't?"

"Then I just look like an idiot."

I resumed course and speed.

"Speaking of convincing people to do things," I said, "Alana must have some pretty incredible powers of persuasion to have turned Charles around like that."

Bertie grinned. "To hear her tell it, she does."

"Did you buy everything she told us?"

"For the most part, I guess it sounded close enough. Although Alana's not above shading the truth when it suits her purposes."

"Like when she talked to Detective Wayne?"

"For starters."

"Do you think she did the same thing to us?"

"I wouldn't rule it out."

"Then I guess I know what we need to do next."

"What?" asked Bertie.

We'd stepped up onto the porch. She reached out and grasped the long, curved tusk that served as a handle and pulled the door open. I preceded her into the lobby.

The space was filled with symposium participants. They were milling about in small groups, checking their schedules, perusing the announcement board, and deciding which upcoming seminars to attend.

If only my life were that simple.

"Talk to Caroline," I said. "And hear the other side of the story."

It didn't take long to track Caroline down. According to the roster of events, she was scheduled to lead a panel discussion on genetic anomalies in half an hour in conference room A. I could attend the session and then talk to her afterward, a win/win proposition.

Bertie ran up to the room to fetch paper and pen to take notes. I looked in the direction of the dining room and pondered the possibility of a morning milk shake. Alas, it was not to be.

Margo was standing at the foot of the wide staircase. She was answering questions, giving directions, and basically micromanaging every aspect of the morning's events. Her motions were jerky and manic; she looked like a traffic cop on speed.

As I stood there debating, she caught my eye and waved. It was too late to duck out. Margo motioned me to her side and I obeyed.

"Are you looking for me?" she asked.

"No, Caroline."

"You're sure? Because I thought you might be ready to give me a report."

"No," I said firmly. "I'm not."

A gaggle of chattering dog show judges came walking down the stairs. I side-stepped to let them by and, in the momentary confusion, almost made my escape. But Margo was determined. She left her post and followed me.

"What do you need to see Caroline about?" she asked.

"Just stuff," I said brightly.

"Stuff relating to Charles's murder?"

I shrugged and would have kept walking, except that another group came spilling out of the dining room and blocked my way.

"Because, you know," she said, "you already talked to Caroline yesterday. Wouldn't it be a better use of your time to investigate somebody else? If you broadened the scope of search, maybe you would have something to tell me by now."

"Good thought," I said. "I'll take it under advisement."

Margo's hand snaked out. Her fingers closed around my arm and squeezed shut. Her grip was like iron.

"Don't toy with me, Melanie. This is serious business. I need to know what's going on."

"Why don't you talk to Detective Wayne?" I said. "He's the man in charge."

"You don't think I've already tried that? Whatever the police know, they're not giving out any information to civilians. I need another way to keep tabs on the process and you're it. Now tell me what you've found out."

I'm not good at taking orders. Never have been, probably never will be. So I side-stepped the issue.

"Remember that judging scandal you were worried about? Tubby Mathis is the guy who's in trouble."

"Oh, please," Margo snapped. "Who even cares? So Tubby got caught doing a few illegal favors. Is anybody here talking about it?"

"No, but—"

"You see? It isn't important. Keep your eye on the ball, Melanie. Because I can assure you that I am."

Margo leaned close. Her voice dropped to a whisper. "You know, I heard some unfortunate gossip this morning. A tidbit concerning someone near and dear to us both."

Rats, I thought. Aunt Peg had only just gotten Walter stashed away in her room. How had word gotten out so quickly?

"There are people here who are under the impression that Peg and Florence had a bit of a contretemps in the garden last night."

Oh, *that* problem.

"You, of course," I said, "would know better."

The first person Aunt Peg had spoken to when we'd reentered the inn the previous evening had been Margo. If anyone knew the truth, it was the program director.

"I thought I did, but now maybe I'm not so sure."

Margo's gaze dropped. Her eyes shifted from side to side.

"The court of public opinion can be a very volatile forum. Sometimes even innocent people find themselves tried and found wanting. It would be a real shame if such a thing were to happen to Peg, don't you think?"

"Aunt Peg had nothing to do with what happened to Florence. We were the ones who found her. She was unconscious when we arrived on the scene."

"That's not what I hear."

"Then people are spreading unfounded rumors. I would think you'd want to put a stop to that."

Margo gave my arm a small jerk. Her nails bit into my skin.

"Just as I would think that you'd want to find out what really happened. And to let me know when you do."

Tit for tat. I got it now. I'd give Margo what she wanted, and she'd go to bat for Aunt Peg.

The rules of engagement had been set.

21

"Caroline's in the library," said Margo. "She's not entirely comfortable with public speaking. She likes to gather her thoughts ahead of time and do some positive visualization. I told her I'd make sure she wasn't disturbed."

"Then I should wait—"

She dropped my arm and gave me a firm nudge. "Go. The sooner you finish talking to her, the sooner you can move on to something more productive."

I could either stay and continue to be lectured, or else go and bother Caroline. So I went.

The door to the library was closed, but not locked. I knocked, then pushed it open.

Caroline was sitting curled up on the couch, her shoes kicked off, her feet tucked up beneath her on the plump cushion. Sunlight slanted through the tall windows and fell across her face. She'd applied her makeup with care, but the strong morning light revealed the fine web of lines she'd worked to conceal.

A cup of coffee, full and fragrant, sat on the table beside her. I inhaled the aroma like a junkie in need of a fix. I was trying to keep my caffeine intake down, and of all the things I'd given up for pregnancy, morning coffee was the one I missed the most.

A sheaf of papers rested in her lap, but Caroline was staring out the window. As I closed the door behind me, she slowly turned to see who had invaded her privacy.

"Oh, it's you," she said. "I should have known. Once other people have offered their condolences, they mostly make a point of avoiding me. I think my presence makes them uncomfortable. I remind them of the random nature of life. And death."

I picked up a chair and carried it closer to the couch before sitting.

"You don't scare me," I said.

Caroline offered a wan smile. "Perhaps I should."

"I'll keep that in mind. How are you feeling?"

"Empty."

A single word, so forlorn. I swallowed and didn't reply.

"Funny thing," said Caroline. "Before this week, I would have told you that I led a very full life. I was always going from dawn till dusk, running all day with a million different things to keep me occupied. There were so many obligations that I had to keep lists so I wouldn't lose track. Take one away and I'd have thought that was a blessing. And now look at me. Sitting here, staring out a window, and feeling as though I have absolutely no idea what to do next."

I wondered if I should interpret that to mean that Charles had been just another of her many obligations.

"I guess you go and talk about genetic anomalies," I said lightly.

"There is that." Caroline fingered the papers in her

lap. "Have you come to tell me that you've discovered something important? A clue that will point the way to the solution and allow me to get on with the rest of my life?"

"No," I said regretfully. "I've come to ask more questions."

"I'm afraid I don't see how that will help."

"Sometimes I don't either," I replied.

Caroline's blunt honesty seemed to demand the same of me. I shifted in my seat, leaning forward, bracing my elbows on my thighs, and diminishing the space between us.

"Sometimes solving mysteries is like unraveling a quilt from a dozen different directions. I follow the course of one thread for a while and then switch and pull another. Some of them lead to dead ends, others take me to places I never expected to go. I don't know in advance which ones are going to work and which ones aren't. So I just keep asking questions and see what turns up."

"So now you've come to see what else I might tell you that I haven't already."

"Something like that."

Caroline nodded thoughtfully. I took that as an invitation to continue.

"Where were you on Tuesday night when Charles went out to spend time in the hot tub? Did you know what his plans were?"

"Of course I knew. We were in our room together shortly before he went outside. I knew his schedule and he knew mine."

That statement sounded rather cut-and-dried when applied to the activities of a couple who, to all appearances, had been happily married. Despite what Alana had said, I still wasn't sure I believed that Caroline had known everything her husband had been up to.

"Did you consider accompanying Charles outside to the hot tub?"

"No, it wasn't an option. Charles was free, but I had work to do. Preparation, in fact, for this morning's seminar. I was meeting with the other panelists to discuss the details of our presentation."

Handy that Caroline had an alibi. I wondered how solid it was.

"So that's where you were Tuesday night when Charles was killed? Meeting with . . ."

I looked down at the papers she'd placed on the table between us. A symposium schedule was lying on top. It listed the names of the participants in each event.

"That's where I expected to be," Caroline corrected, following the direction of my gaze. "But when I got to the room where we were supposed to be meeting, I found that only two of us had shown up. Rosalyn Arnold was off gallivanting somewhere and Wanda Swanson simply never appeared. It hardly seemed worthwhile for only half the group to compare notes, so I left."

"And went where?"

"Back to my room. You might remember that I hadn't had the best day thus far. By that time I had a splitting headache."

"I assume your bad day had something to do with the speech Charles had given earlier?"

"Among other things," Caroline said, sounding weary. "All I wanted at that point was to be alone."

So much for the alibi.

"So you didn't think of going outside to join your husband?"

Caroline stared at me across the table. "That's the

second time you've asked that particular question. I imagine you must be fishing around for something that I haven't yet answered."

"Well . . . yes."

"And that would be what precisely?"

There had to be a way to phrase this delicately. If Alana was wrong and Caroline didn't already know about her husband's infidelity, I hated to have to be the one to bring it to her attention. Especially now, after the fact, when she had nothing to gain by the knowledge.

I cleared my throat and said, "Did you expect that Charles was going to be using the hot tub alone?"

Caroline went very still. I watched her nostrils pinch together as she drew in a breath.

"Alana," she said softly.

I didn't confirm. I didn't deny. I just waited.

"I didn't know," Caroline said, then stopped. "Well . . . that is . . . I didn't know she was with him that evening. Other times . . ."

She paused again and shrugged. "I suppose I knew that Charles and Alana had some sort of relationship. Is that what you're trying to ask?"

"I'm afraid so."

"And you're telling me that Alana was with Charles when he was killed?"

"Not when he was killed, obviously. But just before."

"You'll have to pardon me," Caroline said sharply, "if I don't see what's so obvious about that. Of all people capable of playing the innocent, I should think that Alana Bennett might find herself at the bottom of just about anyone's list."

Good, I thought. Now the gloves were off and we were getting somewhere.

"You must have resented their relationship."

Caroline drew herself up. "Don't you dare presume to tell me how I felt."

"Then you tell me."

"Alana Bennett fancies herself as something special, but she isn't. Charles and I were married for a very long time. We knew each other's strengths and each other's weaknesses. We also knew how to give one another what we needed. Sometimes what Charles needed was a loose rein and a forgiving partner."

I was amazed by how coolly she was able to discuss the topic. In her position, I'd have been ready to throttle Sam. Was Caroline really that dispassionate? Or was she instead an accomplished actress, intent on leading me away from the facts?

"So Alana wasn't the first woman he'd had an affair with?"

"No, and she wouldn't have been the last."

"That must have made you angry. Maybe angry enough to do something about his fooling around."

"You've got it all wrong," said Caroline.

"Explain it to me, then."

I settled back in my chair as if I had all the time in the world to listen. Which, as it happened, I did. I wasn't the one whose seminar was fast approaching. But if Caroline wasn't worried about her upcoming obligation, neither was I.

"Something needed to be done," she said, "but killing Charles certainly wasn't the answer. After he gave his speech, I sat him down and gave him a good talking to. He needed to be made to see the error of his ways. Alana was making a fool out of him."

I shook my head. "There are those who would have said that Charles was getting what he wanted and that Alana was making a fool out of you."

"You still don't get it, do you? This has nothing to do with sex. Alana was using him, plain and simple. Make no mistake about it; Charles was very good in bed and I'm sure she saw that as one of the fringe benefits of her quest. But what that twit really wanted was to win him over to her cause."

"The animal rights platform."

"Precisely. On her own, Alana Bennett is powerless. She's nothing more than an empty-headed party girl and everybody knows it.

"But hooking up with those odious animal rights people gave her a network of support and a sense of purpose. Alana had an agenda to promote and she needed someone to help her do it. Someone who had the respect of his peers, someone people would listen to and pay attention."

"And that person was Charles."

"Quite right. She pursued him shamelessly."

"You watched that?" I said incredulously. "And never stepped in to put a stop to it?"

"As I said a moment ago, Charles and I have been married a very long time. You might say that we had an arrangement about such things. I never questioned his taste in extracurricular companions, and in exchange he agreed to manage his affairs very discreetly. Neither one of us had any desire to court scandal. As long as he and Alana had kept their business to themselves, I wouldn't have said a thing."

Amazing, I thought again. The palm of my hand was resting against my stomach. I felt a slight flutter within. A promise for the future, growing within me. And a hope that Sam and I never became this complacent about our relationship.

"All that changed Tuesday afternoon when Charles delivered that deplorable speech. Such is the vanity of a middle-aged man that he was able to delude himself into believing that a woman young enough to be his daughter wanted him solely for himself. He fell for her act hook, line, and sinker. And so he stepped up to that podium and embarrassed both of us."

"After which you spoke with him about their affair."

"What choice did I have? It was clear that he'd allowed his libido to overcome his common sense. I told Charles that he was to break things off with Alana immediately and spend the rest of the symposium undoing the damage he'd done."

"And he agreed?"

"Of course he agreed," said Caroline. "After all, I didn't give him any choice. Alana was a fling and nothing more. I was his wife. Like it or not, Charles was going to knuckle down and do as I said."

A man accustomed to a loose leash being suddenly brought to heel? I doubted that Charles had proven to be that obedient. Indeed, the fact that he'd gone to meet Alana in the hot tub that evening lent credence to the notion that Caroline hadn't succeeded nearly as well as she thought she had.

"So you see," she continued, "if anyone had cause to be angry with Charles that night, it was Alana, not I. She was the one who was about to taste defeat, while I would emerge victorious."

"And yet," I said, "as soon as you left, he went to meet with her."

"He went to break up with her," Caroline corrected me. "After that, he would have come back to me."

She was either lying or else missing a few pertinent

facts. Because if Alana and Charles had indeed been severing their relationship, they'd been doing so outside, under the stars, in a hot tub. Naked.

Not the most likely setting for the scene Caroline had imagined was taking place.

"Are we through here?" she said abruptly. "It's almost time for my seminar. I need to head over to the conference room."

"Of course," I said. "Thank you for your time."

Caroline gathered her notes into a tidy pile, then stood.

As she leaned down to brush the creases from her skirt, I said, "Florence Donner told me that Derek Ryan was rather desperate to meet with your husband. You wouldn't have any idea what that was about, would you?"

"Derek Ryan?" Caroline straightened. Her brow lowered in a frown. "I don't even know who he is. I do know that Charles had several important matters he meant to attend to while he was here. Perhaps that was one of them."

"Do you know if the meeting took place?" I asked.

She walked to the door, turned the knob, and drew it open. "If it did, I never heard about it. That was the thing, of course. Charles thought he'd have more time."

Charles wasn't the only one who'd thought that. We all had.

22

Wonder of wonders, the next thing I did was take in a lecture. My first in two days, in case you're keeping count.

No, I didn't follow Caroline into her seminar on genetic anomalies. Not that it wouldn't have been interesting, but it seemed to me that we'd seen enough of one another for a while.

Upstairs in Conference Room C, three judges and breeders I didn't know were giving a talk on Rhodesian Ridgebacks. A discussion of the sleek, lion-hunting hounds from Africa seemed like just the thing to take my mind off everything else that was going on; and the diversion worked like a charm.

I emerged from the seminar feeling thoroughly rejuvenated. And also starving. About that time it occurred to me that I'd skipped breakfast.

Or, more precisely, watched as "my" breakfast was fed to a hungry German Shepherd.

It was early for lunch, but the dining room had already opened its doors and people were beginning to wander in. I pulled out my phone and called Aunt Peg.

"Where are you?" I asked when she picked up.

"Shopping for kibble and rawhide bones in downtown Mountain View."

We'd passed through the small town on our way to the inn. The shopping possibilities hadn't looked promising.

"I didn't know Mountain View had a downtown," I said.

"It's a figure of speech, and in this case not a very accurate one. It seems to consist of two strip malls and a mini-mart. So far, all I've managed to locate are two boxes of stale biscuits and a pink plastic leash. What are you up to?"

"Looking for someone to eat lunch with. Hear that rumble in the background? It isn't approaching thunder, it's my stomach."

"You'd best feed it, then." Aunt Peg was ever practical. "I wouldn't want my niece or nephew to be going hungry. Try Bertie. I bet she'll be happy to join you."

Bertie might have been, but she wasn't picking up her phone. I hadn't seen her since we'd parted company earlier, and I was willing to bet that in the intervening time she'd found her way back to the health club. She was probably stretched out on a slab somewhere, enjoying Gunther's expertise.

Which left me on my own. I walked into the dining room and stood by the hostess station. "Table for one" sounded pathetic but a quick scan of the room didn't reveal anyone I knew well enough to foist myself upon.

Then Rosalyn came striding through the double doors like a woman on a mission. "Melanie! Perfect. You're just the person I've been looking for. Do you have a minute?"

"As many minutes as you like, as long as they involve food."

Rosalyn grinned. "I never turn down a bathroom or a meal. Lead the way, we'll talk over lunch."

We were quickly seated, and our drink order taken. After weeks of having to force down any food at all, suddenly everything on the menu made my mouth water. If there was any logic to the fluctuations of pregnancy I had yet to figure it out.

Rosalyn ordered a salad. I asked for a bowl of vegetable soup and a turkey sandwich. Then I dug into the bread and butter as soon as they were delivered to the table. Rosalyn watched me with amusement.

"You're pregnant," she said.

I slathered some butter on a roll and stuffed it in my mouth. "Eating for two," I mumbled around the mouthful.

"You're lucky. When I was pregnant, I couldn't keep anything down but dry biscuits for the entire nine months."

"Actually this is the first time I've been hungry in days."

Rosalyn reached for the bread basket and delicately transferred a roll onto her plate. "Adversity does that to a person."

My gaze lifted. I forgot about food for a minute.

"What?"

"You know, hardship?"

"I know what adversity means. I just didn't realize I was suffering from any."

"I'm thinking of your aunt. She must be quite a trial to you."

In oh-so-many ways, I thought. Probably none of which were what Rosalyn had in mind.

Perhaps I'd been entirely too hasty to seize upon her as a lunch companion.

"I'm sorry," I said. "What are we talking about?"

"Florence was released from the hospital this morning. Richard and Derek went to pick her up."

"I'm glad to hear she recovered so quickly."

"Naturally you would be. With Peg being to blame and all."

"Okay," I said, "you can stop right there. You have no idea what you're talking about."

"I most certainly do. Florence called me last night from the hospital. I spoke with her directly. And she told me that Peg Turnbull was the person responsible for her injuries."

"Which you, without verifying whether that was true or not, immediately felt obliged to tell everyone within earshot."

"People deserve to know what happened."

"I agree with you. And that isn't what happened."

"Are you telling me that Florence was lying?"

"Yes."

The word, and the accusation, blunt as I could make them, hung in the air between us.

"I don't believe you," said Rosalyn. "You're protecting your aunt."

"My aunt doesn't need protecting, at least not from a conniving old lady like Florence Donner. She ought to be thanking us rather than trying to stir up trouble. Peg was the one who found Florence, and the one who called for help."

"That's her story."

"No," I said firmly. "That's *my* story. I was there."

"You were?"

Rosalyn sounded surprised. This part was something she hadn't heard.

"Yes, I was. Aunt Peg and I were outside walking. We found Florence lying in a heap near the courtyard. She was unconscious at the time. When she revived, she was pretty confused. She told us that someone had hit her but she didn't know who."

"Hmm." Rosalyn was still reserving judgment. "That's not the version I heard."

The two of us leaned back and made room as the waiter appeared with our food. Too bad all this arguing had made my appetite disappear again. I picked up my spoon and gave my soup a desultory stir.

"Eat." Rosalyn doused her salad liberally with dressing. "It's good for you."

"It seems I'm not as hungry as I thought I was."

"I've upset you."

"No." I sighed. "You're just the messenger. Florence is the one who's upset me. She resents my aunt's relationship with her son and obviously she'd do just about anything to drive them apart."

"Don't tell me you think she hit herself over the head and knocked herself out? Sorry, but I'm not buying it."

"No, I wouldn't go that far. But the story she's spreading is also untrue. I'd love to know what really happened."

Rosalyn paused, a lettuce leaf suspended on her fork between plate and mouth. "You really mean that, don't you?"

"Absolutely. The fact that Aunt Peg has been made to look bad is only part of it. We're four days into this conference. One of the participants is dead and another has been attacked. It amazes me that most people are simply going about their business as if nothing is wrong. I don't know why any of them feel safe here. I know I don't."

Maybe it was all the trouble I'd seen and gotten into in the past. Or maybe it was the pregnancy that was making me feel vulnerable; the responsibility I now had not only for my own welfare, but also for that of my unborn child. But whatever the reason, the threat that surrounded us felt more personal than usual. And more dire.

"Interesting." Rosalyn pushed aside a sliver of cucumber and speared a tomato with her fork. "If Peg isn't the person who attacked Florence—"

"She isn't," I said firmly.

"Then we're left with another mystery."

"Or two facets of the same mystery."

I tasted a spoonful of soup. The broth was rich with flavor and the vegetables were crisp instead of soggy. I felt my appetite begin to revive.

Rosalyn stopped eating to consider what I'd said.

"So you think the same person that killed Charles also hurt Florence?"

"That's the only way things makes sense to me. One crazy person running around a conference seems like plenty. Two would be stretching credibility."

"Unless someone didn't actually want to kill Florence, but rather put her out of commission for a while."

I frowned. Then added a glare for good measure. We both knew which *someone* Rosalyn was referring to.

"Okay," she said, after a moment. "Scratch that. But the one-assailant theory brings up other questions. Like why Charles and Florence in particular? Aside from their long tenure in the dog show world, the two of them don't have anything in common. They judge different breeds, they come from different areas of the country. Granted, Florence may have her moments but basically she's a rather harmless old lady—"

"Tell that to Aunt Peg," I muttered.

"And as for Charles . . . well . . . good riddance to bad rubbish is all I can say."

"I had the impression that you two weren't the best of friends."

"What clued you in? My obvious contempt for the great man himself or my lack of dismay when I heard about his death?"

"Both," I said. "And that puts you in a minority. Scoff if you like, but there are plenty of people here who thought that Charles was, if not a great man, at least one who was worthy of their respect."

Rosalyn laughed derisively. "Trust me, that last speech of his changed a few opinions on that score."

"Maybe so, but Caroline thinks that if he'd had the time, Charles would have been able to change them back."

"Caroline is the little woman. She thought whatever Charles wanted her to think."

The comment surprised me. Rosalyn struck me as a woman who was strong enough, and independent enough, to recognize the same traits in another woman.

"That's not true," I said.

"Isn't it?"

Our waiter had begun to hover solicitously in the background. She lifted a hand and sent him away.

"Charles has been stepping out on her for years. Caroline can't be so stupid that she doesn't know that."

"She knows," I said quietly.

"So why didn't she stop him?"

"She said she didn't mind."

"And you believed her? You must not be very bright either."

"Bright enough," I said, "to recognize a diversion when I see one. A minute ago we were talking about your feelings toward Charles."

"That's old news. I resented the hell out of him, okay? Mostly I just tried to stay out of his way. I found it entertaining when he made an ass of himself delivering his keynote speech and I wasn't sorry when he turned up dead. Is that plain enough for you?"

"Without a doubt. Do you mind telling me why you felt that way?"

"Is it any of your business?"

"Humor me," I said. "I'm pregnant."

Rosalyn had been working herself into a lather of righteous indignation but now, to my surprise, she stopped and laughed.

"I didn't expect that," she said.

"Does it buy me an answer?"

"Hell, why not? Been there, done that, and you're right. Under the circumstances, you probably do deserve a few special privileges. What do you know about the Bedminster Kennel Club?"

Mostly that it was the stuff of legend, I thought. Founded by a very wealthy dog fancier at the turn of the twentieth century, the Bedminster Kennel Club was one of the oldest and most prestigious in the country. Their yearly dog show, held in high summer, was an invitation-only affair.

The event took place on acres of manicured lawn in the high-priced horse country of northern New Jersey. It featured only the best judges and attracted top dogs and exhibitors from all around the country. Over the decades the show had become esteemed as much as a social event as a sporting competition.

Most people in the dog world considered a win at Westminster to be the pinnacle of achievement, but there were others whose reverence for Bedminster placed that event on the same pedestal.

"I've never shown there," I said. "Someday, I'd like to."

"But you know what it's about?"

I nodded.

"Then you probably know that for many years the membership of Bedminster was closed. The entire kennel club consisted of twelve men, all with impeccable credentials, all of whom thought their opinions were sacrosanct. They held quarterly meetings, did a little fund raising and the occasional educational program, and put on the annual show. When one of their members died or resigned, another just like him was elected to take his place."

That was the way things had been run previous to my tenure in the dog show world. I remembered hearing about the "old-fashioned" Bedminster from Aunt Peg. But I was also pretty sure that their mores and procedures had begun to change in the last decade.

"Let me guess," I said. "Charles was a member."

"You're half right. Charles and Caroline were both members. Charles was accorded the honor in the mid-eighties, when it was still a men's club."

"And Caroline?"

"Four or five years ago. About that time, it became clear to the Bedminster board that they needed to step into the twenty-first century. Maybe someone threatened them with a discrimination lawsuit. Or maybe it occurred to them that if they added a few women to their roster, they'd have someone to do all the boring jobs they were too lazy to do themselves.

"Anyway, for the first time in nearly a century, the membership was opened to outsiders. Several dozen people applied for consideration. Caroline was one of the first women accepted."

While Rosalyn was speaking, I'd finished my soup. Since that seemed to be staying down okay, I picked up my sandwich and began to nibble around the edges.

"Is this another diversion," I asked, "or is there a point to this story?"

"I was one of the applicants. Bedminster has members from all over the country, but I grew up in New Jersey. Bedminster felt like my local kennel club. The first show I ever attended as a child was their event. Imagine." She stopped and smiled. "I thought all dog shows were like that."

I smiled with her, thinking of some of the truly terrible venues I'd been to over the years. "That must have been a rude awakening."

"It wasn't nearly as rude as the reply I received when my application was rejected by the Bedminster board. My credentials were good, so was my reputation. I never would have applied if I hadn't thought I stood a good chance of being accepted."

"Did they tell you why they turned you down?"

"Not officially, no. They didn't feel they had to. All I got was a curt, one-paragraph letter on Bedminster parchment stationery, informing me that my request for membership had been denied."

"And unofficially?"

Rosalyn sighed. Even now, it seemed, the memory still rankled.

"I found out later that Charles was the one who had

blackballed me. He didn't give the membership committee a reason beyond saying that in his opinion I wasn't up to Bedminster standards. I barely knew Caroline, but I understand that she backed him up."

Rosalyn put down her fork and pushed her plate away. It looked like her appetite was as capricious as mine.

"You barely knew Caroline," I said slowly, "but you must have known Charles. Do you know why he did that to you?"

"Hell yes, I know exactly why he did it. He blackballed me because a couple of years earlier, when we were both away from home judging at a series of cluster shows, he made a pass at me and I turned him down so fast it made his head spin. I guess his ego couldn't handle the rejection. And isn't it just like a man to take his revenge?"

23

And so the plot thickens, I thought.

"You must have been furious," I said aloud.

"Hell yes. And in my place, anyone would have felt the same. It's one thing to be turned down on my own merits. But to have some pompous jackass step in and turn my life upside down just for kicks . . ." Rosalyn snorted in disgust. "I could have killed him for that."

And now somebody had. Funny how that came together.

"Be careful," I said. "You'll sound like you're giving yourself a motive."

"Too late for that. I've never made any secret about how I felt about Charles. Probably half the people in this room know that I couldn't stand him."

"Do they know why?" I asked curiously.

"No."

She reached for her salad plate and pulled it back in front of her. Apparently confession was good for not only the soul, but also the appetite. Rosalyn dug into her meal with renewed gusto.

"That story isn't anybody's business. Why would I want to advertise that I'd applied for membership in Bedminster and been rejected? Besides, when it comes to motives, I'm certainly not the only person who's got one. Charles and Caroline may have touted themselves as the dog show world's golden couple, but there are just as many people around here who resented them as revered them."

"Really?" I said. "Who else?"

Rosalyn's gaze suddenly sharpened. "The answer depends. What are you going to do with the information? If you're going to go running to the police, then I'm keeping my mouth shut. Why should I get anybody else in trouble?"

"Don't you think the police ought to be told?"

"The police have a job to do and they're the ones who ought to be doing it. That detective is supposed to be tracking down a killer. He doesn't need me to tell him where to look."

"So then I guess you'd be just as happy if Charles's killer wasn't brought to justice?"

Rosalyn scowled. "I didn't say that, did I?"

"You came close enough. And now someone, probably the same person, has attacked Florence. Would that be a better reason for you to get involved?"

Rosalyn was shaking her head again. My arguments weren't making any impression upon her. If anything, they were hardening her resolve.

"That 'getting involved' part? That's not my thing. Sticking your nose where it doesn't belong just makes more problems, and believe me, I've got plenty of my own already."

Our waiter came gliding back. He wanted desperately to find out how we were doing, refill our glasses, and offer us all sorts of things we didn't want. This time, I was the one who waved him impatiently away.

My hold on Rosalyn's attention was tenuous already. The last thing we needed was a distraction.

"Last night when we had dinner together . . ." I said.

"The meal you didn't eat."

That could have applied to any number of meals I'd sat down in front of lately, but it was true enough, so I nodded. "You weren't the only one at the table who wasn't upset about what happened to Charles."

"Yeah, Tubby was there too. He's not my favorite guy by any stretch of the imagination, but I have to say one thing for him. He calls things as he sees them."

"Do you know what his gripe was with Charles?"

"Like what? Like you think everyone who didn't like the guy got together and compared notes?"

Put that way, the question did sound rather absurd.

"I have no idea why Tubby didn't like Charles," Rosalyn said. "Here's my wild-assed guess and you can take it for what it's worth. Knowing what kind of guys they both are, I bet the two of them got tangled up over a woman somewhere, and Charles won. Am I right about that? Who knows? But it makes as good a story as any."

I took a deep breath and looked at her across the table, considering what she'd said. Our plates were empty and the waiter was heading our way yet again. We were just about done.

"Is that what we've been doing here?" I asked. "Spinning tales?"

"You tell me," Rosalyn replied. "Truth isn't absolute, you know. It changes, depending on your perception. Whoever said there are two sides to every story was a fool. There are as many sides as there are storytellers. And that, my friend, is the truth."

* * *

She stuck me with the check. While I was taking care of it, Aunt Peg came sweeping into the dining room.

Her height, her demeanor, and her confident stride would have drawn attention anywhere. But while Rosalyn and I had been eating, the room had filled; and in this crowd Aunt Peg was a woman of some renown.

Half the diners knew her personally, the other half knew her by reputation. And I bet that nearly all of them were privy to the story that had been circulating since the previous evening: the one that placed the blame for Florence's condition squarely on Aunt Peg's strong shoulders.

Voices lowered as she passed between the tables, gazes slipped away. Anyone who hadn't heard the gossip previously was certainly being treated to its more juicy aspects now.

Aunt Peg might have heard the whispers that followed her across the room if she'd been listening. Instead she appeared oblivious, moving fast, and intent on her own concerns as she zeroed in on my table.

"I see I've missed lunch," she said, slipping into the chair Rosalyn had recently vacated. "I hope you ate something."

"Soup and a sandwich."

Aunt Peg's stern gaze scanned every inch of the table as if she was looking for evidence. "Did you actually eat the food or just push it around your plate before sending it back?"

"I finished most of it."

The talk in the room hadn't stopped when Aunt Peg sat down. If anything, the buzz was building. Now people were turning to stare covertly in our direction.

Florence had been due to return from the hospital that morning. I wondered if she was indeed back at the inn—and what she was saying now about the previous evening's events.

Even if she recanted her story, the version she'd fabricated was already out there. Judging by the reaction I was seeing, the news had taken on a life of its own. Why was it always so much easier for people to believe the bad rather than the good?

"You've got to do something," I said.

"About what?"

"How can you even ask that? Surely you can't be that oblivious. Everyone in the dining room is talking about you."

"Surely not *everyone*."

Aunt Peg turned and had a look. Catching several friends in the act of staring, she gave them a cheerful wave.

"You see?" she said, turning back to me. "Not everybody at all. At least half of them are eating, as well they should be."

"They're eating *and* talking about you."

I tried to sound stern, but it was difficult in the face of her relentless disregard for the situation. While I was upset, Aunt Peg was looking remarkably upbeat. And if she refused to be worried about the damage that was being done to her reputation, who was I to insist that she should be?

"Let them talk," she said. "Sticks and stones and all that rubbish. Listen, I was hoping you might have a left-over or two. Canine supplies in Mountain View left a lot to be desired. I finally succeeded in finding some kibble, but I doubt that it's very palatable. A little turkey or hamburger mixed in might go a long way toward making it a more decent meal."

"You're talking about a dog who's been living out of garbage cans. I'm sure whatever you've found will look like prime rib to him."

"Oh, I know he'll eat it. He'll probably even be grateful. But after all he's been through, I feel as though he deserves a bit of a treat. For all his issues, he really is a rather lovely dog."

"Issues?" I sat up straight. "What issues?"

But Aunt Peg wasn't paying the slightest bit of attention to me. Instead she'd turned away to survey the tables around us. I realized with some dismay that she wasn't looking at the occupants, but rather at their plates.

"You wouldn't dare," I said.

She had her eye on a juicy piece of uneaten steak sandwich.

"Why not? We're all dog lovers here. Anyone would understand."

No, they wouldn't, I thought. They'd think she'd lost her marbles. And crazy behavior now, coming on top of Florence's accusation, would only lend credence to the earlier report.

"Nobody's supposed to know you have a dog in your room," I hissed under my breath. "They can't understand what they don't know about. You'll look like you're begging for food off people's plates—"

"With good reason," said Aunt Peg. "As that's exactly what I intend to do. Excuse me . . ." She leaned across to a neighboring table and gestured toward the bit of steak. "Are you going to eat that?"

The startled diner broke off her conversation and shook her head.

"Would you mind if I took it and wrapped it up in my napkin?"

With a little more notice, I might have made my escape before she started this lunacy. As it was, I was stuck there at the table, pasting a sickly smile on my face, and trying to look as though Aunt Peg's behavior was perfectly normal.

She reached over with a fork and snagged the tidbit, plopped it into her napkin, and slipped it into her purse. Maybe she'd been fast enough that no one else had noticed, I thought hopefully.

Fat chance.

Once again, heads were turning. This time, people didn't bother to hide the fact that they were staring.

"Did you have to do that?" I asked.

"Well, I didn't *have* to. But it certainly made sense to."

Aunt Peg reached over and patted my hand comfortingly. Like that was going to help.

"Walter will thank us later, you'll see."

Somehow I doubted that a dog's gratitude, no matter how sincere, would make me feel better about this incident, which had to rank as a new lifetime low for public displays of eccentric behavior.

"Besides," said Aunt Peg, "you can't blame this entirely on me. If you'd had the decency to leave a little something on your own plate, I wouldn't have been forced to resort to such drastic measures, now, would I?"

Of course. This humiliating episode was all my fault. I should have known.

* * *

After that, I couldn't get out of the dining room fast enough. Booty in hand, Miss Lack-of-Manners and I went out to the parking lot to retrieve the bag of kibble and other assorted supplies from the van. We then snuck up the back stairs to the second floor.

As we turned onto our hallway, I was relieved not to hear any barking coming from the direction of our rooms. Aunt Peg, I saw, had taken the liberty of posting DO NOT DISTURB signs on both her door and ours. I supposed that meant Bertie and I would be making our own beds.

"Where did you leave him?" I asked as she juggled the twenty-pound sack of kibble into her other hand and slipped her card through the lock.

"It was damn inconvenient not to have a crate on hand. Who knew what he might get it into his head to chew on? I had to lock him in the bathroom, poor dog."

The door opened and we walked inside. Both of us immediately looked toward the bathroom door. All was quiet.

"Walter?" Aunt Peg called. "I'm home."

A happy whine answered her greeting. It was quickly followed by a series of small yips. Whether the Shepherd was responding to his name or simply the sound of Aunt Peg's voice, it was clear that he was happy to hear from her.

I shoved the outer door shut as Peg pushed the bathroom door open. Walter came flying out and bowled right into us.

I caught only a glancing blow but Aunt Peg was knocked over backward. The bag of kibble went flying. She landed in a heap on the floor, with the German Shepherd straddling her body.

Walter's tail whipped back and forth. He was wuffling softly under his breath. As Peg sat up, he sniffed her face, then her hair, then her hands, as if anxious to reassure himself that she was truly there.

"I see you've made some progress since this morning," I said.

Aunt Peg smiled at her star pupil. Gently she braced her hands on his chest and eased him away so she could get up.

"He's coming along wonderfully. And of course the fact that I was holding a piece of bacon in my hand when we began our lessons didn't hurt one bit."

Speaking of food, as soon as the Shepherd had stepped away from Aunt Peg, his nose had led him unerringly to her purse, which had fallen on the bed. Good thing the clasp had remained fastened; otherwise the steak she meant to add to his dinner would already be gone.

I reached around the big dog and rescued the handbag. Walter gave me a remorseful look, but didn't object to my intervention.

"Good boy!" Aunt Peg said. "You are such a smart dog."

Walter wagged his tail happily in agreement. He *was* a smart dog, and wasn't it nice to have people around him again who cared about things like that?

I let my hand drift downward until it rested just behind his ears. I half expected the Shepherd to scoot away, but he didn't. Instead, he remained motionless. Still a bit wary, but hoping for the best.

When I scratched the base of Walter's ears with my fingers, he closed his eyes and leaned into me. I could hardly believe he was the same half-wild dog who'd been crouched on the bed earlier. Aunt Peg's magical touch had worked wonders.

"Now that you've got him," I said, "what are you going to do with him?"

"What? I can't hear you."

Aunt Peg had gone into the bathroom. She was gathering up the towels Walter had pulled off the racks and used to make a nest on the floor while he awaited her return.

Even so, she wasn't that far away. I was sure she'd heard what I'd said. And if Aunt Peg was dodging a perfectly sensible question like that, I knew there had to be a reason. Probably one that I wasn't going to like.

"Tell me you're not planning to take him home with you."

She appeared in the doorway, arms gathered around a mound of towels.

"Not if I can help it."

"What does that mean?"

"It means there are plenty of other avenues I can explore first. Best case, he can go back home to whoever lost him."

"Unless he was abandoned," I said. "And not lost."

"Either way, the situation Walter finds himself in isn't his fault. I'm going to make up some fliers and post them at the local vets and markets. Check with the nearest pound and maybe the dog warden if I can find one. Don't worry, I have plenty of ideas."

Aunt Peg smiled down at Walter, who reciprocated by flapping the tip of his tail against the rug. The two of them were bonding right before my eyes.

"If that doesn't work, I'll contact the local German Shepherd affiliate club and see what their rescue people are up to. Maybe they can find a home for him. Perhaps they have one waiting even now. It seems like the least I can do. After all, it's not as though I lack for resources in this area."

This area being dogs and anything that pertained to them. No, no one had ever accused Aunt Peg of lacking resources. Or good ideas.

"Isn't it interesting how things work out?" said Peg. She sounded quite pleased with herself. "It looks like you're not the only one with a mystery on her hands."

24

"Here's a thought," I said.

I sat down gingerly on the edge of the bed, weight still balanced mostly on my feet. Just in case I needed to make a quick getaway.

"About Walter?"

"No, about Florence."

"I don't believe I need a thought about Florence."

No one, least of all me, ever said that my aunt wasn't hardheaded.

"I was thinking you could call Richard and get him to talk some sense into her."

"That's not a good idea," Aunt Peg said shortly.

"It's a very good idea. Just because you're in denial doesn't mean you don't have a problem. Florence needs to step up and tell the truth. Otherwise these rumors flying around here are only going to get worse."

"Since when have you paid attention to gossip?" Aunt Peg demanded. "I thought I raised you better than that."

Aunt Peg hadn't raised me at all, which was probably

beside the point. And I *always* listened to rumors, because they often contained a kernel of truth.

Now, however, didn't seem like the time to mention that.

"Here's another thought," I said instead. "Maybe Richard has succeeded in getting more information out of his mother. Wouldn't you like to know what really happened—"

"No."

"*No?*" I echoed.

The answer defied credibility. Aunt Peg was the nosiest person I knew. She always wanted to know what happened. This whole conversation was beginning to take on a slightly surreal cast.

"I'm not calling Richard, and that's final."

"Why not?"

"Because the man is an ass."

My aunt rarely swears, so that got my attention. But to tell the truth, where their relationship was concerned, I was beginning to feel like I had whiplash. The last time I'd seen Aunt Peg and Richard together, they'd at least been speaking to one another, hadn't they?

I sat back on the bed and settled in to hear the rest of the story. Peg, meanwhile, had begun to pace. Her steps carried her from one end of the small room to the other.

Walter chose an out-of-the-way spot and hunkered down to watch. His dark eyes followed her every move.

"What's happened now?" I asked.

"For starters, Richard owes me an apology, which I've never received. . . ."

Presumably that was for the argument that had preceded Aunt Peg's storming from the dining room the previous evening. I nodded.

"Not to mention a thank-you for helping his mother . . ."

I nodded again. I readily concurred, but even if I hadn't it hardly seemed like a prudent time to disagree.

"And then, as if that wasn't enough, I never heard from him last night. Richard was supposed to call me from the hospital, which he never bothered to do. Instead his mother was the one burning up the telephone lines, telling the rest of the inn's guests some crazy, trumped-up story that never should have been allowed to surface in the first place."

"You're right," I said. "The man is an ass."

"That's not all." Aunt Peg was getting warmed up now.

"What else?"

As if she needed an invitation. I probably couldn't have stopped her if I'd tried.

"So, being the big person that I am, I decided to give him the benefit of the doubt. This morning, I called him. And he *whispered* into the phone that he couldn't talk."

"He must have been with Florence."

Aunt Peg scowled mightily. "Of course he was with Florence. He's *always* with Florence. He said he'd come to my room to see me. Well, as you can imagine, I couldn't have that."

As one, we turned to look at Walter. Tongue lolling out of the side of his mouth, teeth shiny and white, the German Shepherd grinned back at us. No, this was not the time for Aunt Peg to be entertaining Richard in her room.

"Why didn't you meet him downstairs?"

"Because that would have been too easy," Aunt Peg snapped.

She turned and stared out of the window. When she

continued speaking, I couldn't see her expression, just the stiffness in her shoulders and the rigid set of her spine.

"After what happened last night apparently Richard doesn't want to be seen with me in public."

"*He told you that?*"

"Not exactly. He hasn't got the guts to be that truthful. But from the way he danced around the topic, it was easy enough to figure out. So you can just forget any notion you might have about him worming the truth out of his mother and setting the record straight. It isn't going to happen."

"What a louse." I was furious on her behalf. "Florence must have told him the same story she told everyone else. But he should have known better. He was there. He saw that we were trying to help her. Why would he believe such a thing?"

"She's his mother."

"Even so."

She turned and nailed me with a glare. "Let this be a lesson to you."

"To me? What did I do?"

"You're pregnant, remember?"

Trust me, pregnancy is one of those things that's hard to forget.

"When that baby arrives, don't smother him. And don't tell him lies. And while you're at it, don't let him pick up any women on the Internet."

All those things seemed very far in the future. But Aunt Peg didn't want to hear any protests. She was looking for agreement.

"Yes, ma'am," I said.

Luckily, before Aunt Peg could offer any more parenting advice, a knock sounded at the door.

"Hey in there," Bertie called. "Who am I supposed to be not-disturbing? Can I come in?"

I jumped up from the bed, opened the door, and slipped out.

"You could," I said. "But you don't want to. Let's take a walk."

I grabbed her arm and pulled her down the hallway.

"Where are we going?"

"Anywhere but here."

"Why?" She skidded to a stop and gave me a suspicious look. "Who else is in there?"

"Aunt Peg. She's holding a postmortem on her relationship with Richard."

"That's dead? When did that happen?"

"It's a new development."

Bertie brightened. "I wouldn't mind hearing about that."

"Aunt Peg is also offering advice on how to be a good mother."

"Oh."

Bertie resumed walking. A mother herself, she had been treated to Aunt Peg's parenting advice before. On more occasions than she cared to count. Like me, she knew the value in making herself scarce when Aunt Peg was on a tear.

"Okay, new plan," she said. "Let's go downstairs and see what's new."

We descended the wide staircase into the lobby. The afternoon seminars hadn't started yet, which meant that most of the symposium participants were either gathered in small groups talking or else milling around trying to look busy.

"I don't see Tubby," I said.

"No great loss."

"I want to talk to him."

"Yuck." Bertie paused at the foot of the steps. "Why would anyone want to do that on purpose?"

"Because he and Charles didn't like each other. And since Charles is dead, I'd like to know why. I was thinking you might want to come along for moral support."

"You mean so he can grab my ass instead of yours?"

"Whatever works."

"Easy for you to say." Bertie was not amused. "If you want to sacrifice yourself on the altar of private detection, feel free. Me, I'll find something else to do."

"Come on," I said. "Be a sport."

"I will. I'll tell you where to find Tubby. After that you're on your own. Keep an eye on his hands at all times and don't let him lure you into any dark corners."

"Do I look that stupid?"

"No, but neither does Alana, and you should hear the Tubby stories she tells."

"Alana has a story for every occasion," I pointed out. "And every man."

"Of course she does. It's part of her mystique." Bertie saw someone she knew on the other side of the room and lifted a hand to wave. "Gotta go. Look for Tubby in the bar. He's nearly always there."

"This early in the day?"

"Some detective you are," Bertie sniffed. "Tubby starts drinking as soon as they start serving."

"Thanks for the tip."

"It's your funeral. Ta!"

Bertie's guess was spot on. Only two tables in the bar were currently in use and Tubby was seated at one of them. His hands were curled around a glass of whiskey, and his eyes were fastened on a flat screen TV on the wall.

ESPN was showing soccer and, lucky for me, Tubby was alone.

"Mind if I join you?" I asked.

Tubby tore his eyes away from a beer commercial. He didn't look entirely pleased to see me. "I guess not. To what do I owe the honor?"

"I was hoping I could ask you a couple of questions."

"I heard you've been running around bugging everybody. I suppose this means it's my turn."

"I'm interested in seeing Charles's killer brought to justice," I said. "Aren't you?"

"Not particularly. But then you probably already know that. Otherwise, why would you be here?"

Score one for Tubby. He wasn't as dumb as he allowed himself to look.

"Did the police question you about what happened?"

"No, why would they? There are over a hundred and fifty judges and dog fanciers here. It's not like they can talk to every single one."

"Even so, I'd think they would have wanted to talk to you. You haven't made any secret of your contempt for Charles."

Tubby smiled complacently. "That doesn't mean that I killed him."

"Ma'am?" The bartender appeared at my elbow. "Can I get you something?"

I started to shake my head but Tubby answered for me. "Bring the lady a white wine."

"No," I said quickly, "I'm not drinking."

"Oh yeah, I forgot. You're the water lady. Just one won't hurt."

"I'm fine, really."

"Jeez, have *something*, would you?"

So I ordered more water.

"You must not be much of an interrogator," Tubby said. "Don't you know that the first rule is to put your subject at ease?"

"There are rules to this? I didn't know that."

"You're a treat, aren't you? Okay, since you missed out on the first opportunity to gain my cooperation, let's go for number two. What are the chances you could set me up with that girlfriend of yours . . . you know, the redhead?"

"Bertie?"

"Yeah, that's the one. She's a fine looking lady."

"She's a fine looking married lady. Bertie's married to my brother."

"And he lets her go running off all over the country on her own? He must be some kind of idiot."

"He's not an idiot. He trusts her."

"Right." Tubby smirked. "So what *are* you going to offer me?"

"Nothing," I said. "Talk is cheap, haven't you heard?"

"Funny girl. All right, let's quit wasting each other's time. Ask me what you want to know. Maybe I'll answer, maybe I won't."

"Why did you dislike Charles so much?"

"The man was a prick. Next question."

He wasn't going to get off the hook that easily.

"Define prick."

Tubby frowned. "It's got different meanings for different people. In Charles's case, I'd say we're talking pompous, sanctimonious, self-serving. You know, the basic prick-like qualities."

"Last night at dinner you said Charles liked to tell other people what to do. I think you called him the ethics police."

"What of it?"

"I heard you might have had a little problem in that department yourself."

Tubby took a long swallow of whiskey, then said, "I don't have the slightest idea what you're talking about."

He was going to make me work for it. No problemo, I could do that.

"The first night we were here, Margo was talking to my aunt. She mentioned that she was worried about a judging scandal that was about to explode."

"Really? What kind of scandal?"

Once again I suspected that Tubby was cagier than he was letting on. He wasn't so much pumping me for information as trying to find out how much I already knew.

"Someone was rumored to have been taking kickbacks for putting up undeserving dogs."

The beauty, and the basic flaw, of the judging system was that it was totally subjective. Every breed standard was open to interpretation by each judge. Given a class of dogs to preside over, ten different judges might place it ten different ways. And as long as a judge could defend his choices, there was no way to prove him wrong.

Most times, judges did their best and the system worked as it was intended to. But the possibility for taking advantage definitely existed. And in a sport where people took themselves, and their dogs, very seriously, there were always those exhibitors who wanted to gain an edge any way they could.

"And you think that was me?"

"That's what I heard."

"Do you have any proof?"

I shook my head.

"Talk like that is slander, you know. It could get you in a lot of trouble. If I were you, I'd watch what I was saying."

"I always do," I replied mildly.

Tubby raised his glass and drained the rest of the whiskey. He set the tumbler back down on the table with a thump.

"Time's up," he said, pushing back his chair.

"What's your hurry?"

"Let's just say the company isn't as entertaining as I thought it was going to be. You've got a lot of nerve thinking I might be implicated in something shady like that. I'll point out the obvious here—nobody's tried to kill *me*."

Tubby marched over to the bar, slapped down a couple of bills, and left.

My water hadn't even come yet.

Just as well, I wasn't thirsty anyway.

25

It was early afternoon and I had nothing on my schedule. I could have gone looking for an interesting panel or seminar, but there was something else that I wanted to attend to first.

Someone needed to confront Florence Donner and tell her to put a sock in it. Since Aunt Peg apparently had no intention of doing so, I figured that made it my job. And while I was there, I could speak to Richard too.

Between the two of them, mother and son were making Aunt Peg miserable. I'd been patient long enough; now it was time for them to cut it out.

Once again, Margo was directing traffic in the lobby. She was also holding a clipboard that looked like it was likely to contain all sorts of useful information. I squeezed through the throng until I reached her side, then held out my hand.

"Can I see that for a minute?"

She pulled the clipboard away and hugged it to her chest. "Why?"

"I want to find out the room numbers for a couple of guests."

"I'm not sure I should be giving out that kind of information. Who are we talking about?"

"Come on," I said. "Tit for tat, remember? You share with me and I'll share with you."

"Good," said Margo. "Finally. You first."

Okay, that was a problem. So far all I had was bits and pieces of information. Unfortunately I had yet to discover a pattern that would knit them all together. Which meant that there were no earth shattering developments to report.

"You want me to tell you *here?*" I raised my voice slightly. Just enough to make a few heads turn. "Because I'm really not sure that's a wise idea."

"You might be right," Margo said with a frown. "And this place is a madhouse. I can't get away right now."

What a shame.

She held out the clipboard. "I'll tell you what. Let's meet after the next set of programs. You can tell me everything then."

By my calculation, that gave me about two hours to come up with some really good stuff. Good luck with that.

I skimmed quickly down the roster of participants. Florence Donner was in room 302. Richard Donner, listed just below his mother was . . . also in room 302.

I read that again just to be sure. The result was the same.

How incredibly Oedipal.

And to think, Aunt Peg had imagined she had a chance with this guy. It was beginning to look like she'd had a lucky escape.

I handed the clipboard back to Margo and debated my next move.

There was a house phone on the registration desk. Calling ahead would let me know if anyone was at home in room 302. But what if I called and was told not to come?

In my experience, people taken by surprise are much more likely to entertain nosy visitors than those who've been given fair warning. Bearing that in mind, I headed over to the stairs. Exercise is good for pregnant women, at least that's what my doctor told me.

I reached the third floor and turned toward the northern wing of the building. This was, I noted with interest, the side of the building that overlooked the courtyard between inn and health club. At ground level, that enclosure was screened by walls of high hedges that lent privacy to those making use of the hot tub; but I wondered what could be seen from the rooms up here.

Room 302 was at the end of the hall. No privacy sign was on the door. I didn't hear any sounds from within.

So I knocked and waited.

After a minute the door opened. Richard stood in the doorway. He looked both surprised and irritated to see me standing there. It wasn't an auspicious beginning.

"What do you want?" he asked.

"To talk to you and your mother."

"Mother isn't here. There was a program this afternoon that she particularly wanted to see and luckily she felt well enough to go down and participate. So I'm afraid you'll have to come back another time."

He didn't wait for my answer, he just started to push the door shut.

"Wait!"

My hand came up. I braced my palm against the panel and pushed back. The door stopped midway.

"I want to talk to you too."

"About what?"

"About what happened to your mother."

Richard's stony expression didn't change.

"And to Charles."

Still no reprieve.

I tried again. "And to Aunt Peg."

Finally I got a response. Richard looked uncertain.

"Did something happen to Peg?"

I nodded. After a brief hesitation, Richard stepped back, allowing me through the doorway.

The room turned out to be a suite, which made me feel a little better about the living arrangements, though I still suspected that Freud would have had plenty to say about the Donner family.

The outer room contained a double bed and a sitting area. Richard remained standing but he waved me toward a small couch beside a picture window. Taking a seat, I glanced out at the view.

All I could see was building and parking lot, with just a sliver of the courtyard on one side. The hot tub wasn't visible at all. Rats.

"Is Peg all right?" Richard asked. "I haven't spoken to her since first thing this morning. What happened to her?"

"For one thing, she thought you were her friend and you treated her like she was some sort of pariah."

"I beg your pardon?"

"That won't help," I said. "Aunt Peg is the one you should be apologizing to."

"Now, see here. You don't have any idea what you're talking about."

"I most certainly do. I was there last night, remember? Peg and I found your mother lying unconscious on the ground and tried to help her. We would have called for an ambulance except that when she revived she wouldn't let us."

"That's not . . ." Richard stopped and shook his head. "Mother said the two of you insisted she wasn't badly hurt and didn't require additional care. Even though she was feeling woozy, you made her stand up and told her she was going to have to walk back to the inn."

"Utterly ridiculous," I scoffed. "The only reason Florence got up was because she didn't want you to see her sitting on the ground. She was afraid you'd worry about her."

"Of course I was worried. And with good reason. The doctors at the hospital told me that she had a concussion. Considering the blow she'd sustained, it's lucky her injury wasn't worse."

"At least we agree on that," I said.

"Then why did Peg tell Mother that the injury was nothing? That she must have tripped and fallen?"

"Aunt Peg didn't say that. Nobody did. We had no idea what had happened. That's what I've been trying to figure out."

I stared at him in exasperation. "You do remember asking me to do that, don't you?"

"Yes, of course. But that was before I knew the truth."

"Your 'truth' is nothing more than a story concocted by someone with an ulterior motive. Florence has been trying to drive a wedge between you and Peg ever since we arrived. And now she's succeeded. See how that works?"

Richard folded his arms over his chest. His expression grew more obstinate.

"No, frankly I don't. Because the blow that my mother suffered was very real. Somebody tried to harm her last night."

"Somebody, yes. But not Peg. I suspect that your mother's injury was related to what happened to Charles Evans—"

"Now, really," he said, his face suddenly red. "That's going too far. My mother is a kind and gracious woman. She couldn't possibly have had anything to do with a murder. And if you're thinking about repeating that nonsense to anyone else, you'll find yourself speaking to my lawyer next."

I was trying to be reasonable. Really I was. But the man was truly an idiot. What on earth had Aunt Peg ever seen in him?

I stood up and walked toward the door. I'd had enough, but I couldn't resist firing a parting shot.

"My aunt thought you were her friend," I said. "She believed that the two of you had gotten to know one another through your correspondence. If that's true, if you know anything at all about Peg, then you know that what Florence is saying about her is a lie."

I grasped the knob and turned it, but before I could open the door Richard was there.

"Wait," he said.

For a moment, neither one of us said a thing.

"Look," he said finally, "this whole episode has been incredibly stressful. For me and Mother both. Maybe we haven't handled it in exactly the best way."

You think?

"The fact of the matter is, I don't know what happened last night. And I'm not sure Mother does either.

The doctors said that was normal. That her recollection of the events leading up to the concussion would be somewhat hazy. Maybe her memory will return, maybe it won't. At the moment, all she knows is that she was outside walking Button . . ."

Richard shrugged helplessly. "The next thing she remembers with any clarity is feeling a sharp pain in her head and waking up to find Peg bending over her. She put two and two together . . ."

And came up with a very convenient total of five.

"Do you really think Aunt Peg is capable of doing what Florence has accused her of?"

"To be honest, no. But I do know that the two of them weren't getting along. Peg seems to think that Mother is a bit over-protective."

"Peg might have had a point," I said.

Thankfully, Richard didn't take offense.

"Maybe she does," he admitted. "My father died when I was an infant. As a result, Mother raised me entirely on her own. She and I have always been very close. She likes to think she's looking out for me."

"And you like to let her."

"She's my mother. What can I do?"

"For starters, you might try telling her that she needs to rescind her story."

"She won't do that. Mother never does anything that would make her look foolish."

"Then maybe you should do it for her," I said firmly. "At the very least, you should apologize to my aunt."

"Peg's a little upset right now. I don't think she wants to talk to me."

Jeez, I thought. This guy really was a weenie.

"Maybe she doesn't want to hear from you, but she needs to. Trust me on that."

I let myself out and headed back toward the public areas of the inn. Turning the first corner in the hallway, craning my head to check the view from each passing window, I ran into Marshall Beckham. Literally.

"Hey," he said, grabbing my shoulders to steady me. "Sorry about that."

"No, my fault. I wasn't looking where I was going."

"I haven't seen you up here before. Your rooms are down on the other side, aren't they?"

"Right, but I needed to see Richard about something."

Marshall nodded. The movement fast and jerky. "Great guy, Richard. One of my best friends."

Sometimes you have to make your own opportunities. And sometimes they just seem to arrive gift wrapped.

Marshall had a habit of speaking very quickly. I suspected he didn't always think before he blurted out what was on his mind.

"Derek is a good friend of yours too, isn't he?" I said.

"Sure. He's another great guy."

My smile was disarming. "Derek mentioned the other day that he had come to the symposium to talk to Charles Evans, but he never got around to telling me why. Do you know what that was about?"

As I'd hoped, Marshall didn't stop to consider his reply. He was as eager to please as a Labrador puppy.

"Some judging snafu, is all I heard. Derek was showing somewhere and thought he'd gotten a raw deal. I think the plan was that Charles was going to help him make it right."

"How?"

Marshall shrugged his shoulders once, then a second time. He was a man in constant motion.

"I don't know, we never got into it. I got the impression

Derek believed that he needed someone with standing and power to be on his side when he filed a complaint. Maybe that's what Charles was for? But then it didn't matter anyway, because Derek changed his mind about the whole thing."

"Changed his mind? What do you mean?"

"Before we got here, he was all 'Charles is going to fix things' and then later he said someone else had solved the problem for him."

"Someone else?" I said, surprised. "Do you know who?"

"One of the other judges. The big guy. You know, the one who does hounds?"

Tubby Mathis.

26

Well, hot damn.

Maybe I'd been wrong earlier. It was looking like I might have something interesting to tell Margo after all. But what exactly? What had Derek been up to? And how did that fit in with everything else I'd learned?

What I needed was a sounding board. Someone to run through the possibilities with.

Aunt Peg was no good. She currently had problems of her own. I got out my phone and called Bertie.

"Yo!" she said.

"Where are you?"

"Guess."

"The health club."

"Right-o. Who would have guessed that an educational symposium could be so much fun?"

Certainly not me.

"I'm on my way," I said.

Bertie was just finishing a hot rock massage, courtesy of Gunther, who was tall, teutonic, and had shoulders like rolled hams.

"All is good," he said in heavily accented English as Bertie sat up and switched her towel for a robe. "Come back and see me tomorrow. We make more steam together."

"It's a deal."

Bertie had a dreamy smile on her face. She looked limber, and languid, and very happy. It was a good thing this guy was gay; otherwise Frank might have been in trouble.

Then Gunther caught sight of me.

"Your turn next," he said. "Take off your clothes. Gunther has magic hands and secret European techniques to make you feel better."

"No, thank you. I'm just here to meet Bertie."

"You should think about it," she said.

"Yes, think about it." Gunther stepped over beside me. Hands the size of baseball gloves began to knead my shoulders. "You are tense here, ja?"

"Probably." My entire body was rolling with the rhythm of his hands.

"Tension not good. Much better if you relax. Gunther show you how. Special European—"

"Techniques. Yes, I know. I'm sure they're excellent, but no, thanks."

I stepped out from under his hands and straightened. What do you know, the kink in my back was gone.

"I need help," I said to Bertie.

"Name it."

"Give me half an hour of your time."

"That sounds easy enough."

Gunther insinuated himself between us. "In half an hour, Gunther could make you feel like a queen."

"Buzz off," Bertie said mildly. "Or your tip is going to suffer."

Gunther laughed and the sound bounced off the soothing, cream-colored walls. "I like you."

"I like you too," Bertie replied. "But now we're busy with something else. Girl talk."

"Gunther is very good at girl talk."

No doubt.

I took Bertie's arm and steered her out of the room. Gunther stared after us wistfully.

"Where to?" I asked.

"The locker room. It's this way."

Bertie led the way through a maze of corridors, all with the same creamy walls. Signs pointed the way to the various amenities. The spa offered everything from mud baths, to facials, to rock climbing. Despite all the choices, we didn't see anyone else making use of the facilities.

"Is this place always so empty?" I asked.

"Apparently only when the inn is filled with dog people. The rest of the year I gather it's very popular."

She pushed open the door to the locker room and I followed her inside.

Rows of lockers lined the walls. Several benches sat between them. One wall was mirrored. A countertop beneath it held a large stack of thick, cream-colored towels.

This room, too, was empty. The majority of the lockers sat open and unused. There wasn't so much as a discarded sneaker out of place.

"I've got a great idea," said Bertie. "I know you didn't want a massage, but Gunther was right, you do look tense. That can't be good for you or the baby. Does it matter where we talk?"

"I guess not. Though I'd rather we weren't overheard. What do you have in mind?"

"How about taking a nice, relaxing break in the steam

room? We can sit around naked, open up our pores, and talk until we're blue."

"Or pink as the case may be," I said.

The steam room opened directly off the locker room. I walked over to have a look. Not surprisingly, the small window in the door was fogged over.

"Is this thing coed or women only?"

"Just for women. The men have their own on the other side, connected to their locker room. Come on, it'll be fun."

I had to admit, the prospect did sound appealing.

"I wonder how good this is for women who are pregnant."

"*Nothing's* good for women who are pregnant," Bertie said with a snort. "Cats, water beds, aspirin, fish . . . I know all about this stuff, I was just there. Do you know you're even supposed to stop eating hot dogs?"

"Thankfully that particular restriction hasn't put much of a crimp in my diet."

I opened the door and peered inside the small room. A cloud of warm, damp steam billowed out. I could feel my hair begin to curl.

"Anyway, I asked my doctor about saunas and he said I could go ahead as long as I didn't overdo. They've done a bunch of studies on women in Scandinavia and they do this all the time. Look, here's the thermostat. If you're worried, we can turn it down a few degrees. There's nobody even around but us. No one's going to care."

"Sold," I said. "Go ahead and dial it down. I'll grab a locker and a towel."

It took me only a minute to get naked, and considerably less than that to wrap up in a big fluffy towel. I stuffed my clothes in the nearest locker and slammed the door shut, then padded, barefoot, across the cool tile floor. Bertie was waiting for me by the door.

"Say good-bye to your mascara," she said and led the way inside.

The steam swirled around the room in silent jets, enveloping us like a dense cloud of fog. But instead of being clammy, this mist felt warm and inviting. I inhaled sharply and felt my sinuses open.

"Take a seat," said Bertie.

Wide benches, slightly elevated, ran along the tile covered walls. She stepped up and settled down on one. Loosening the knot of her towel, she allowed it to slide down and pool around her hips.

I chose a similar bench several feet away. Already the steam was having a therapeutic effect. I could feel the coils in my body beginning to unwind.

"This was a terrific idea," I said.

"I told you so. Do I know hedonistic, or I do know hedonistic?"

"Both," I agreed, leaning back and closing my eyes. "I could fall asleep right here."

"Don't you dare. We're supposed to be talking, remember? Who's the first subject, Peg?"

"Among others. We'll get to her in a minute."

"Fine by me," Bertie said easily. "Who's first?"

"Well . . . Charles."

"Oh, right, I should have known. We're solving a mystery. Excellent. The first thing we need is suspects."

"No problem. There are plenty of those."

"Caroline," said Bertie.

"Interesting you should mention her first."

"She's the spurned wife. I'd have her on the top of my list. She's a very strong-willed woman, one whose reputation means a lot to her."

"More than her husband's life?"

"Could be that Charles's antics were getting to be an embarrassment to her. Maybe that speech he gave was the last straw and she decided she had to get rid of him."

"Speaking of spurned women," I countered, "what about Alana? According to Caroline, she knew all about their affair. She said that Charles had gone to meet with Alana that night so he could break things off with her."

"That's not true."

"According to whom? Alana? If Charles had just dumped her and she drowned him in a fit of rage, she'd hardly be likely to admit it, would she?"

Bertie opened one eye. "What kind of person invites his lover to a hot tub so he can dump her?"

We both thought about that for a minute. Inconceivable as it sounded, we could both see it happening.

"Men," we said together.

"All right," Bertie conceded. "Leave her on the list. Who else?"

"Rosalyn Arnold."

"What did Charles do to her?"

"Blackballed her so she didn't get accepted into the Bedminster Kennel Club. Apparently it was a life-long dream of hers to be a member."

"Who would want to join that bunch of snooty old farts?"

"Rosalyn apparently. It meant a lot to her and she's never forgiven him."

Bertie lifted a hand and fanned her face.

We'd been in the steam room for a few minutes, but rather than adjusting to the temperature, I could feel myself growing warmer too. I loosened my towel and let some air circulate around my body.

"There are hundreds of kennel clubs," she said. "I can't imagine being tempted to kill someone over a membership in one of them."

"You're thinking too logically. Committing murder never makes sense to a normal person. It takes someone crazy or deluded for that."

Bertie began to laugh. "Crazy and deluded. That must bring us to Tubby. I swear. Where that man got the idea that he's God's gift to women, I haven't a clue."

"Me either," I agreed. "And he hated Charles too. He called him a prick."

"Pot calling the kettle black, don't you think?"

"Absolutely. Now listen and tell me what you think of this. The first night we were here, Margo mentioned hearing a rumor about a judging scandal."

"You mean there's hot gossip going around that I missed out on?"

"Apparently so. Some judge was supposed to be getting into trouble for taking kickbacks."

Bertie sat up and opened both eyes. "Who?"

"That's what I'm trying to tell you. It was Tubby."

"Wow," said Bertie. "That'll shut down his career."

"Right. If it gets reported through the proper channels. Which I don't think it has been, because when I asked him about it, he demanded to know if I had any proof. Then he told me that what I was saying was slander."

"It's not slander if it's true."

"Precisely. Except that whoever it is that knows the truth doesn't seem to be talking. Tubby isn't in trouble if his accuser doesn't come forward."

"Good point."

"I know," I said with a grin. "And I have an idea who

that missing person is. Let me backtrack for a minute. Florence told me—"

"Oh, goody," Bertie broke in. "Does this mean it's finally time to talk about Peg?"

"No, we were on Tubby—"

"Bite your tongue! Nobody wants to be on Tubby. Besides, Peg's problems are much more interesting."

There was that. Besides, the heat in the room was having a positively enervating effect. Reasoning things out was beginning to seem like a chore. Exchanging gossip was much more fun.

"I talked to Richard earlier," I said. "He admitted that Florence doesn't really know what happened last night. With the concussion and all, her recollection of events is pretty hazy."

"So she'll tell everyone that she was mistaken about Peg attacking her?" Bertie asked hopefully.

"Not so fast. What Richard will admit and what Florence will admit are apparently two very different things. And by the way, while we're on the subject, Florence resented Charles too."

"My, how that man got around. What was her beef with him?"

"She thought that she should have been the one delivering the keynote speech."

"And killing him after the fact would help how?"

"I'm only mentioning . . ."

"Knock yourself out," said Bertie. "I like the idea of putting Florence on a list of suspects. It seems like the least she deserves."

So we were back to that again.

"What do you know about Marshall Beckham?" I asked.

"Who?"

"Tall, skinny, glasses? He's a friend of Richard's."

Bertie shook her head. The description didn't ring a bell.

"He owner-handles Bichons and he's the kind of guy who always seems to be skulking around somewhere in the background. He has this hero-worship thing going on with some of the judges. I swear he nearly bowed when he met Aunt Peg."

"That must have gone over well."

Sarcasm coated her tone. I let the comment lie.

"Anyway, Marshall felt really let down when Charles gave that speech. It was as if Charles had disappointed him personally."

"Charles aggravated a lot of people with that speech," Bertie pointed out. "Including the one person you haven't mentioned yet."

"Who's that?"

"Margo Deline. She was really angry at Charles for turning her symposium into a platform for his own, unpopular views. Margo put a lot of work into this event and its success means a great deal to her. She was livid after Charles gave his speech. The very subject made a mockery of everything she was trying to accomplish here. If she'd had a gun in her purse when he stepped down from the podium it wouldn't have surprised me to see her use it."

"Except that she didn't," I said. "In fact Margo's been one of the people pushing me to solve this thing. We're supposed to get together in a little while so I can tell her what I've found out."

"That doesn't mean a thing," said Bertie. "If I was the guilty party, I'd want to keep abreast of new developments too. If you're planning to talk to her, be careful, okay? Don't go off alone or anything."

Under the circumstances, that advice made sense with regard to just about everyone at the symposium. I had every intention of watching my step.

Bertie lifted her towel and flapped it loosely around her body. "Is it hot in here, or is it just me? Because all of a sudden I'm sweating like a pig."

Me too, I realized. The room did feel inordinately warm.

"I guess that means we've been in here long enough."

I stood up and stepped down from the bench. Bertie rose as well.

"I'd give my right arm for something cold to drink. Out by the registration desk, there's a snack bar that sells these to-die-for banana peppermint smoothies. I'll race you there."

Bertie might be planning to run through the health club clad in only a towel, but I was definitely going to stop in the locker room and get dressed first.

"Order two," I said with a grin. "I'll be right behind you."

She strode to the door and gave it a shove.

When it didn't move, Bertie walked right into it.

"Ow!"

I stepped up behind her. "What happened?"

She rubbed her shoulder. "I don't know. The door seems to be stuck."

I placed my hand against the solid panel and pushed hard. Nothing happened.

This was *not* good.

Next we both tried together. Still nothing.

I cleaned the steam off the little window and looked out. The locker room was empty.

Standing on my toes and peering downward, I could
see the legs of a chair. It had been tipped back and
wedged beneath the door handle.

"What?" said Bertie.

She pushed me aside and had a look too.

"Damn," she said under her breath.

This was no accident. Somebody had locked us in.

27

"I think we're in trouble," said Bertie.

I tried giving the door a series of hard, abrupt shoves, hoping that might jiggle the chair free. It didn't.

All I succeeded in doing was making myself hotter. Hair hung down in a damp clump over my forehead. I reached up and raked it back.

Over here by the door, the temperature felt a little cooler. But behind us, steam continued to billow from the jets.

"Really? What clued you in?"

"This is no time to be rude," said Bertie. "We need a plan."

"I don't suppose you have a cell phone on you?"

I know. That sounded stupid. All she was wearing was a towel. But even so, I had to ask.

"Outside in my locker."

"Mine too." I sighed.

Bertie peered through the small window.

"If we yell, do you think anyone would hear us?"

"I doubt it. I don't think there's anyone around. Plus, these walls look like they'd be soundproof."

"If we had a piece of paper," said Bertie, "we could slip a message under the door."

Oh yeah. That would help.

"Nobody would see it," I said, starting to giggle. "It would be hidden beneath the chair."

I had no idea why I found that so funny. Maybe this was what budding hysteria felt like.

"They ought to have a phone in here." Bertie turned away and began to look around. "You know, like they do in elevators for when people get stuck?"

"Except I'll bet that nobody ever gets stuck in here."

While Bertie poked around, I stayed by the door. Steam was hissing through the vents with increasing force now. It hadn't been our imaginations; the room was definitely heating up.

"Want to hear the rest of the bad news?" I asked.

"Lay it on me."

"I think whoever jammed the door also turned up the temperature gauge."

Bertie was no more than ten feet away from me, but I could barely see her through the undulating wall of vapor. When she spoke, her voice seemed to come out of nowhere.

"I guess that explains why I'm beginning to wilt like a piece of broccoli. I'll never be able to steam clams again."

I heard her padding toward me across the floor. When she emerged from the billowing cloud, she was only a few feet away.

"Not that I'm ready to panic or anything, but I think we really need to get the heck out of Dodge. Come up with any big ideas yet?"

"I was wondering if we could break that window," I said.

The single pane appeared to be pretty solid, but it was all I'd come up with so far.

Bertie came closer and had a look. "It'd be easier if we had a hammer," she said.

"Good thinking. I don't suppose you found one tucked away under one of the benches?"

"Just for future reference, adversity doesn't bring out your better qualities."

"I deal better when I'm not pregnant."

"Oh, crap, I'm sorry. I forgot all about that."

Bertie gathered me into her arms for a hug. Her skin felt hot and damp against mine and we separated quickly. Still, I appreciated the support.

"Here's the thing," I said. "I'm thinking this much heat is probably not great for the baby. Plus, I hate to say it, but I really have to pee."

"Got it. All right, stand back. One broken window, coming up."

I retreated several feet.

She whipped the towel off her body, wrapped it around her hand, and made a big, padded fist. Then she lifted her arm, took careful aim, and let fly.

Bertie's a bit of an amazon and there was considerable power in her punch. Even so, when hand and window connected, the window won. Not only did the glass not shatter; it didn't even crack.

She swore under her breath.

"How's your hand?"

She jerked the towel tighter. "Could be better. One more try."

The second attempt did more damage to Bertie's

curled fingers than it did to the window. Her eyes welled briefly with tears. She blinked them fiercely away.

"That's enough," I said.

Bertie was staring at the window in frustration. I pulled her away and made her sit down. Her hand was going to hurt like hell in the morning. I hoped we'd be around to care.

"There has to be something in here that we can break, or jimmy, or undo," I said thoughtfully. "Too bad the door hinges are on the outside. What about the drain in the floor?"

"I thought of that too. But I can't figure out a way to make use of it. Where's a guy like McGyver when you need him?"

"Who needs McGyver? I'd settle for Gunther. Even Florence could manage to tip that chair back down."

"Unless she's the one who wedged it up there in the first place."

Irritating thought. Trapping us in here had been so easy to accomplish that even a child could have done it.

Annoyance got me moving again. I marched back to the door and pounded on it with my fist.

"Hello?" I yelled. "We need help in here!"

My words were swallowed by the steam. Even to my own ears, they didn't sound very loud. Nor did they produce a response.

When I started to pound again, Bertie came over and caught my hand in hers. I was still aggravated; Bertie was beginning to look resigned. I wasn't sure I liked that.

Nevertheless, I pulled my hand away and let it drop to my side.

"I know we ought to be conserving our energy," I said. "But I hate just sitting here doing nothing. There must be something else we can try."

"If there is, I can't think of it." Her voice sounded very small. "Sooner or later they'll come around and shut things down for the day, don't you think?"

"I hope so."

Neither one of us wanted to think about how long it might be before that happened. Or what kind of shape we might be in when it did.

Beside me, Bertie slipped down and sat on the floor.

"Heat rises," she said. "Even though there are jets down here, this is still probably the coolest part of the room."

She didn't have to tell me twice. I got down and stretched out on the tiles beside her.

"All this warm air is making me drowsy," I said. "Either that or I've gotten used to napping in the afternoons."

"Don't you dare fall asleep!"

"I'll try not to."

"Keep talking."

Usually not a problem for me. But along with filling the room, the mass of swirling steam seemed to be clouding my brain.

"Did you hear what I said?" Bertie reached over and gave me a poke with her finger. "Keep talking to me."

"I'm sorry."

"Don't be stupid. You have nothing to be sorry for."

"Look around," I said with a small, mirthless laugh. "I'm the one who got you into this mess. Somebody locked us in here on purpose."

"So your snooping around is making someone uncomfortable," said Bertie. "Let's try and figure out who. Who have you talked to today?"

"All sorts of people." I worked my way back through the day's events, ticking off the list of names on my fingers. "Marshall, Richard, Margo, Tubby, Rosalyn, Caroline, and then Alana first thing this morning. You were with me for that."

"Good grief. You have been busy."

Tell me about it.

Bertie lifted a hand and pushed her limp hair up off her face. "Okay, that gives us a list to start with. I'm thinking we ought to concentrate on the women."

"How come?"

"Because this steam room opens off the women's locker room. It would have been harder for a man to slip in unnoticed."

"Not today," I said. "This whole building is just about deserted. We saw that for ourselves when we were walking around. Big Bird probably could have slipped in here without being noticed."

"Okay then, you come up with somebody."

Bertie's breathing had grown shallower, as had my own. It was increasingly hard to draw the hot, heavy air into my lungs. Pretty soon the two of us would be panting like a pair of dogs.

"All right," I said. "Here's something I've been thinking about. When the symposium began, Margo was worried about two things that might interfere with her event. The first was Charles's keynote address and the second was the judging scandal."

"Tubby's transgression."

"Right. But here's the thing: while the first one became a really big deal, the second hasn't even caused a ripple. Mostly it's been a nonissue."

Bertie rolled over languidly on the clammy tiles. "And we care about this, *why?*"

"Because what if Charles's problems and Tubby's

problems were related somehow? I'm pretty sure that Tubby was about to get into serious trouble. The kind of trouble that would make the A.K.C. consider rescinding his judge's license. And then, poof! Somehow the whole thing just disappeared."

"I bet you have a theory about that," said Bertie.

She didn't sound particularly curious to hear it. But then again, at the moment, I was having a hard time working up much energy about anything myself. Conversation seemed preferable to silence, however, so I pressed on.

"According to a couple of people I've spoken to, the whole reason Derek Ryan signed up for this symposium was to met with Charles Evans. Derek had a problem that the two of them had discussed earlier. The plan was that Charles was supposed to help him fix it."

"That's the thing about problems," Bertie said dreamily. "Everybody seems to have them."

Sad, but true. And unfortunately not helpful. I kept talking.

"Derek's friend Marshall said that the problem had to do with a dog being beaten when it should have won."

"Big deal," said Bertie. She flapped a hand in the air. "That kind of thing happens all the time. Every exhibitor always thinks that their dog should have won. Otherwise why would they bother showing in the first place?"

"I know, and under other circumstances I wouldn't have given this another thought. But Derek Ryan shows Beagles and Tubby, who's supposedly about to be implicated in some sort of scandal, judges hounds."

"Lots of people judge hounds," Bertie pointed out.

"You are *so* not helping with this."

"That's not my fault. I'm trying to be the voice of reason."

Maybe I didn't want her to be the voice of reason. Maybe I just wanted someone to agree with me.

"There's more," I said. "Derek meant to get together with Charles, but he never got the chance. But then it turned out that it didn't matter, because Tubby solved the problem for him."

"You see?" Bertie murmured vaguely. "Everything worked out and you don't have to worry about them anymore."

"Yes, I do," I insisted. "Because it occurred to me that I had been thinking about these things in a linear way. You know, like going from point A to point B? But maybe they're not a straight line. What if they're meant to form a circle instead?"

"Oh God, don't start with geometry now. You know I was never any good at math—"

Abruptly she stopped speaking and lifted her head. "Do you hear something?"

I didn't, but I scrambled to my feet anyway.

As soon as I stood up, I felt light-headed. My limbs were limp as spaghetti. Stars swam before my eyes.

As I put a hand on the wall to steady myself, Bertie slipped past me. While I was trying to find my balance, she began to bang on the door with both fists.

"Help!" she yelled. "We're in here!"

All at once the door flew open. Weight angled forward, Bertie went tumbling out.

A draft of cool air came rushing into the room. It felt like heaven on my heated skin.

"Oh my word!" I heard Aunt Peg say.

Margo was standing right behind her. Peg caught Bertie and lowered her gently onto a bench.

"Where's Melanie?" Margo asked anxiously. "She's missing too. Is she with you?"

"I'm here," I said. The words were scarcely louder than a whisper.

I stumbled through the doorway and right into Aunt Peg's arms. The embrace was everything I needed. For the moment all I could do was stand there and let her strength support me.

I burrowed my head beneath her chin like a child. Aunt Peg pulled her arms tighter and held me close.

"I told you so," she said to Margo.

28

"What did you tell her?" I asked.

I stepped away from Aunt Peg and stood on my own. The cool air felt amazingly good. It was as though I could feel my body temperature dropping. Within moments, I began to revive.

Bertie was also looking better. Margo rushed from the room and reappeared a minute later with two big bottles of cold water. Bertie and I each grabbed one and guzzled them down.

Aunt Peg was still watching me, a worried look on her face. Since she hadn't answered, I turned to Margo and repeated my question.

"What did she tell you?"

"That if we had an appointment to meet this afternoon, you wouldn't have stood me up. When you never reappeared after the session let out, I called Peg and told her that you were being willful and irresponsible."

"When I heard that, I began to wonder where you'd gone off to," said Aunt Peg. "So I tried to call you, but you didn't answer."

"Mel and I left our phones in our lockers," Bertie said. "Neither one of us could get to them."

"So I discovered," said Aunt Peg. "Because when I couldn't locate Melanie, I tried you next."

"And when Peg couldn't reach either one of you," said Margo, "that's when we began to worry. Peg said it wasn't like the two of you to just disappear."

"What made you look for us in the health club?" I asked.

"For one thing," said Margo, "between the two of us we'd searched almost everywhere else."

"And then I ran into Alana." Aunt Peg picked up the story. "A most distasteful girl, but helpful on the day. She told me that Bertie planned to spend the afternoon over here and it seemed like a good guess that you might have joined her. Then that large German fellow came along and pointed us toward the locker room, and here we are."

Bertie strode over to her locker, pulled out her clothes, and began to get dressed. I hung back for a minute.

"Thank you," I said to both our rescuers. "I don't know how much longer we would have lasted in there."

"Do you know what happened?" asked Margo. "Who locked you in?"

"Unfortunately Bertie and I didn't see anything. We had no idea something was wrong until we tried to leave and couldn't get the door open."

I joined Bertie by the lockers and began to get dressed as well. Suddenly I couldn't wait to get out of there.

"I think we should call the police," said Peg. "They could dust that chair for fingerprints and find out who did this."

"Fingerprints won't do any good unless the perpetrator already has his on file," I said as I pulled on my pants.

"Nevertheless." Aunt Peg refused to be deterred. "By my estimation, the authorities only have one more day to solve Charles's murder. When the symposium ends tomorrow, everyone will scatter across the country. If the police don't get things figured out soon, it's going to be too late."

"All the more reason to light a fire under them," Margo said firmly. "I'll go make some calls."

Energized by the thought of her next mission, the director spun on her heel and left the room.

"If nobody needs me for anything," said Bertie, "I'm going back to the inn to shower and change. I'll meet up with you later, okay?"

Peg and I both nodded and Bertie left too.

"You're coming with me," my aunt informed me. "There must be an OB/GYN on duty somewhere in Mountain View. Perhaps the emergency room can arrange an examination to let us know that everything is all right."

I opened my mouth to speak, but Aunt Peg was faster. "I don't want to hear a single argument."

I hadn't been about to argue, but I closed my mouth anyway.

Sometimes it's just easier to let Aunt Peg think she's running the show.

True to the ways of doctors and emergency rooms, several hours passed before Aunt Peg and I made it back to the inn. But by then I'd had an ultrasound and been assured that the baby was doing fine; so the trip, and the time it took, was well worth it.

While we were waiting, Aunt Peg and I discussed and

dissected every aspect of our time at the symposium. We began with the opening reception and worked our way through that afternoon's events. By the time I was finished, Aunt Peg knew as much as I did about each of the various suspects.

Not only that, but when I ran my circle theory past her, Aunt Peg's eyes lit up. Unlike Bertie, my aunt is very good at math.

When I was whisked away for tests, Aunt Peg continued to ponder the subject. By the time we were in the car and heading back to the inn, she had reached a conclusion.

"Derek's up to something," she said. "And I'm betting that makes him the key to this whole situation. We ought to go talk to him."

"I've done that," I replied. "And Derek's not talking. If he's mixed up in Charles's murder, there's no way he's going to give anything away if he doesn't have to. We need another angle."

Aunt Peg thought for a minute as she drove.

"Florence," she said finally.

"What about her?"

"She's our angle."

I shook my head. "According to Derek, he and Florence barely even know one another."

"Pish," said Aunt Peg. "For one thing, I'm not at all sure we need to believe everything Derek says. And for another, if Florence isn't part of this mess, why was she attacked?"

"Maybe she was just in the wrong place at the wrong time."

"Or perhaps she knows something. Something the killer would rather have stay hidden."

"If that's the case, her concussion seems to have done

the trick. Richard says her memory of last night is hazy at best."

"That may be." Aunt Peg slowed as we approached the driveway and turned on her signal. "Or it could be that's just a convenient ruse that allowed her to place the blame on me. At any rate, it never hurts to ask. The worst she can do is tell us to go away."

I suspected that Florence was capable of far worse than that, but I've found it's best not to get in Aunt Peg's way when she's settled on a course of action.

"Florence it is," I said. "Let's go find her and see what she has to say."

That objective had to wait, however. When we got back to the inn, our first duty was to retrieve Walter and take him outside for a much-needed walk. Solving a murder was important to Aunt Peg, but responsible dog ownership still took precedence.

She attached Walter's new leash to his equally new collar and led him down the back stairs and out the side door. Immediately the German Shepherd lifted his nose to sniff the air, then took off at a steady walk around the side of the building.

The dog had been cooped up in the hotel room for much of the day. Now that he was finally free, Aunt Peg allowed him to choose his own course. She held the end of the leash and followed along behind.

"Where are we going?" I asked.

"I haven't a clue. Walter thinks he smells something interesting."

"He's taking us back to the kitchens. What he smells is probably the remains of tonight's dinner."

We'd been on this particular walkway on several of the previous evenings. On each of those occasions our night had ended badly. Aunt Peg might have forgotten our resolution not to return to this area after dark, but I most certainly had not. Hopefully Walter and his nose weren't leading us into more trouble.

"Announce yourselves or suffer the consequences!" a voice cried out.

Aunt Peg stopped abruptly. When she tugged on the leash, Walter halted too.

"Florence? Is that you?"

"Who wants to know?"

The older woman was standing around the corner of the tall hedge. She couldn't see us any more than we could see her.

"It's Peg Turnbull. And Melanie is with me."

"So you say. If this is a trick, I should warn you I'm armed with a weapon and I know how to use it."

Aunt Peg and I exchanged a look.

"It's not a trick," I called into the darkness. "We're just out here walking our dog."

"Ha! You can't fool me. You don't have a dog."

Oops. I'd forgotten Walter was a secret.

Florence peered cautiously around the corner of the hedge. Below, much closer to the ground, Button's small head appeared at the same time as his owner's. His must have been the scent that Walter had picked up.

"So it is you." Florence's eyes dropped to the Shepherd. "Where did *he* come from?"

"We found him a couple of days ago," said Aunt Peg. "He's a stray who's been living in the woods near the inn."

"Pretty fancy collar and leash for a stray." Florence sniffed. "Just because you've got a big dog don't think you're going to get the better of me again."

Her arm snaked out from behind the hedge. Light glinted off a long metal bar she brandished above her head. "I've got a tire iron and I'm not afraid to use it!"

"Oh, for pity's sake," said Aunt Peg. "Put that thing down."

Florence glared at us for a moment, then complied. Her arm was probably getting tired anyway.

"What are you doing out here in the dark?" I asked as Button scampered out from behind the hedge.

Walter leaned down and the two dogs touched noses.

"Same as you, can't you tell? I'm walking my dog. Just because people behave like idiots doesn't mean the whole world can come to a stop. Trouble or no, Button still has to do his business."

"You shouldn't be out here alone," said Peg. "It isn't safe."

"Don't you worry about me." Florence hefted the tire iron again. "I've got my own protection."

She didn't look nearly as tough as she thought she did. Even after a night in the hospital, Florence still appeared wan and frail.

"How are you feeling?" I asked.

"I got a concussion twenty-four hours ago. How do you think I feel?"

"I imagine your head hurts," said Aunt Peg.

"Damn straight."

"Maybe you'd like to help us figure out who hit you."

"Why should I help you do anything?"

"Because you're involved in this mess whether you want to be or not. If we pool our knowledge, maybe we can come up with some answers."

When Florence hesitated, I added, "You should know there's a good possibility that several of Richard's friends are to blame."

"Who are you talking about?"

"Derek Ryan and Tubby Mathis."

"Tubby's no friend of Richard's," Florence said firmly. "Nor of mine. And if that man's in trouble, he brought it on himself. I heard he only came to this symposium to do damage control. Tubby's had his hands in other people's pockets for years. He's the kind of judge who gives all of us a bad name. Now he's about to get his comeuppance. It's about time if you ask me."

"I heard someone was about to report Tubby to the A.K.C.," I said. "Was it Derek?"

"Good question. I wondered about that myself. Not that I lost any sleep worrying about it, mind you. But now things have changed, haven't they? Maybe the answer makes a difference."

Florence paused and looked at both of us in the half-light. "Heaven knows you're not the partners I'd have chosen, but you're here, so I guess you'll have to do. Someone needs to put a stop to this idiocy. I don't see anyone else volunteering, so that just leaves us. Fair enough. I've always enjoyed a good tussle myself."

Like that was a surprise.

"Last night," said Florence. "You were the ones who found me."

"That's right."

"I didn't remember much at first. But little by little, things began to come back. That's why I brought Button out here tonight. I thought maybe if I recreated the scene, something might jog my memory."

"Good for you," I said and my admiration was genuine. Florence was braver than I'd have given her credit for.

"Did it work?" asked Aunt Peg.

"Maybe. I wouldn't say that things are exactly clear,

but I'll tell you what I do know. I heard someone talking when I was out here last night. You know, people holding a conversation. They must have been standing on the other side of the hedge and they didn't realize I was here."

"Who was it?" I asked.

At the same time, Peg said, "What were they saying?"

"Both of you just slow down. Back off and let me tell my story."

Aunt Peg was as impatient as I was, but we waited quietly until Florence had gathered her thoughts.

"One of them was Derek. It sounded like he was arguing with someone. That's why I could hear what he was saying, because he was so angry.

"He said something like, 'You idiot. I told you I could turn this around. Once I talked to Charles there would have been nothing more he could do. Everything would have been fine.'"

"Who was he talking to?" Aunt Peg asked.

I didn't need to hear the answer. I already knew.

"At the time, I wasn't sure," Florence replied. "But now, listening to you lump the two of them together, I realized that you were right. The other man had to have been Tubby.

"And he was threatening Derek. He said, 'This is all your fault, not mine. We're both in this together now, and you're in as much hot water as I am.'"

29

"Florence, you're a genius!" I cried.

I leaned down and kissed the tiny woman on the cheek.

"I am?" She sounded pleased. "All I did is tell you what I heard."

"You heard Tubby confessing to Charles's murder."

"That's what it sounds like to me too," said Aunt Peg. "It's one thing to believe that, however, and quite another thing to prove it."

"Maybe we won't have to," I said. "Derek knows what Tubby did, that's what they were arguing about. We can give this information to Detective Wayne and let him pressure Derek into telling what he knows."

Aunt Peg nodded. She pulled out her cell phone and began to punch out a number.

"That may not be possible," said Florence.

"Why not?"

"On my way outside, I saw Derek at the reception desk. He was checking out. He said he had a plane to catch."

"We've got to stop him!"

I'd directed the statement to Aunt Peg, but she wasn't the only one who leapt into action. Florence reached down, scooped up Button, and plopped the little dog into her purse.

"I'm ready," she said. "Let's go."

"But—"

"But nothing. Don't you dare think you're leaving me behind."

We must have looked like a strange procession. Three women and two dogs, all racing around the side of the inn.

By the time we reached the parking lot, Aunt Peg had finished her call. Now Florence was on her phone. It sounded as though she was talking to her son.

Was I the only one who didn't have someone to call for backup?

"Look," said Aunt Peg.

Twenty feet away, standing in the glow of one of the overhead lights, Derek was throwing the last of his bags into the trunk of a dark sedan. Hearing Peg shout, he looked up briefly. Then he slammed the trunk shut and quickly slipped inside the car.

We heard the engine turn over. Backup lights came on.

"He's getting away!" yelled Florence.

She leaned down, picked up a rock, and hurled it at the back of Derek's sedan. Her aim was surprisingly good. The rock bounced off the car's rear window.

"Take that," she cried.

When she lifted her hand again, I saw the glint of metal in the light. I'd forgotten she still had the tire iron.

Arm raised in the air, Florence charged toward the car like a woman possessed.

"Think you can hit me over the head and get away with it, do you? I'll show you a thing or two."

It was a good thing I ran after Florence because the car had already begun to move. Derek must have pushed the gas pedal to the floor. The sedan came flying back out of its parking space.

"Look out!"

I grabbed the older woman's arm and snatched her back. Florence's purse slid down her arm and we both grabbed for it. Button yelped as we jumped to one side, yanking him with us. The car skimmed past the three of us with only inches to spare.

I spun around to give chase, but luck was with us. Either that or good karma.

Derek was in such a hurry to get away that he misjudged the distance to the next row of cars. The sedan was moving too fast and didn't turn in time. Instead it shot straight back, hitting the SUV behind it with a resounding crash.

Derek's head whipped back, then forward again, with the impact. By the time he got himself sorted out, the three of us, plus Button and Walter, were arrayed in a line in front of his grill, headlights illuminating our angry faces.

I could see Derek through the windshield. His eyes were huge, his expression panicky. For a horrified moment, I thought he might try to drive right through us.

Time seemed to stretch forever as he deliberated. Then, finally, thankfully, Derek threw up his hands in surrender.

Right about then, I realized that my knees were shaking. I felt weak with reaction. Not Florence. She hefted the tire iron upward, then brought it down hard on the hood of the car.

"Get out here, you coward!" she yelled.

Derek reached down and turned off the ignition. He opened his door and slowly climbed out.

In the time it took him to do that, he must have decided that he needed a good offense because when he stood up and faced us, he'd arranged his features into an expression of injured innocence.

"Are you people crazy?" he demanded. "Look what you've done. You made me crash my car."

While I sputtered, Florence shouted right back at him.

"It serves you right, you . . . you . . . hooligan. That's what you get for trying to run away."

The tire iron pounded the hood again for emphasis. I winced as the blow landed but Derek didn't look overly concerned. The sedan must have been a rental.

"I wasn't running anywhere," Derek said. "Except to catch my plane back to Kentucky."

"You can't leave yet," I told him. "Not before you talk to the police. Detective Wayne is on his way."

"I don't know what you're talking about. I have nothing to say to him."

"We're talking about Charles Evans's murder," said Aunt Peg. "The attack on Florence last night, and the fact that someone tried to harm Melanie and Bertie at the health club earlier."

Something registered in Derek's eyes, a quick fear that came and went as he deliberately didn't look my way.

"It was you, wasn't it?" I said. "You were the one who locked us in."

When Derek didn't answer, Florence took a step forward.

"You better talk," she said, waving the tire iron like a baton. "Don't make me beat it out of you."

"Florence, let's be reasonable—"

She hauled off and hit him in the leg.

I gasped. Derek yelped in pain. He tried to jump back but the car was right behind him.

"Next one breaks your knee," she said. "Your choice. That's as reasonable as I get. I'd talk if I were you."

Jeez, I thought, I would too. Florence was serious.

"I wasn't trying to hurt anyone." Derek reached down and rubbed his thigh. "I just wanted to slow you down a little."

"So you could escape," Florence accused.

"I didn't do anything wrong. . . ."

"Then why were you in such a hurry to get away?" I asked.

My memory of the afternoon's events was still too fresh. I wasn't about to cut him any slack. Florence looked as though she felt the same way about the bump on her head.

"Look, it wasn't me—"

She went for the other leg this time. Her aim wasn't as good; the metal bar bounced off the car's bumper and didn't entirely connect, but Derek still got the point.

He grunted with the impact, then glared at me. "Can't you do something? I'm going to be covered with bruises tomorrow. Make her stop."

"Why would I want to do that? All you've done so far is make excuses. Maybe if you tell us what really happened, Florence will give you a break."

Poor choice of words on my part. But effective as it turned out.

Derek looked from me, to Florence, to Peg, and found no sympathy anywhere. I could see the moment he decided to capitulate. His shoulders slumped. He expelled a long sigh.

"I had nothing to do with what happened to Charles. You've got to believe me."

"Then tell us who did."

"It was Tubby. I didn't know anything until after, when it was too late."

"Why did he do it?" Aunt Peg asked quickly.

Now that Derek had decided to talk, none of us wanted to give him a chance to catch his breath. Or change his mind.

"It's a long story."

"Tubby's an idiot," said Florence. "We all know that so you can skip that part."

"We also know that he was about to be reported to the A.K.C.," I said. "Was that your doing?"

Derek nodded reluctantly. "What choice did I have? Showing dogs is hard enough. Hell, just breeding good dogs is harder still. You try for years to get that once-in-a-lifetime dog and even then you're still up against it. Between the pros with their enormous strings of dogs and all the bullshit politics . . ."

I couldn't help feeling a modicum of sympathy and I suspected Aunt Peg did too. We'd both been there.

Derek's voice rose in anger as he continued to speak. "When Tubby dumped me in a group that I should have won and then pulled me aside afterward and told me I could win the next time and as many times after that as I wanted as long as I was willing to pay the price, I got so mad I guess something inside me just snapped. I looked at Tubby and thought, *By the time I get through*

*with you at least there will be one less crooked judge for ex-
hibitors like me to contend with."*

Except that wasn't what had happened, I thought.
Tubby was still judging and Charles was dead. Somewhere along the way, things had gone horribly wrong.

"You planned to turn him in," said Aunt Peg. "But
you didn't. What stopped you?"

Derek gave a small, mirthless laugh. "I've been involved in the dog world long enough to know how
things work. Shows aren't the only place where politics
is the name of the game.

"After I calmed down, I thought about how it would
work. Who was going to take my word over that of someone like Tubby? He's approved to judge two groups and
he has big assignments almost every weekend. I realized
I needed to get someone bigger than me . . . someone
important . . . on my side to speak for me."

"Charles Evans," I said. He'd been a man of stature
and, according to most of those who knew him, a man
of principle. Derek had made a good choice.

"That's right. I contacted him by e-mail a couple of
weeks ago. Told him enough of the story to see whether
he'd be interested in getting involved. He e-mailed back
and said that we should get together and talk about it.
That's why I signed up to come to the symposium."

"Tubby found out what you were going to do, didn't
he?" Aunt Peg said. "You were threatening not only his
career but his entire way of life."

Florence nodded in agreement as Aunt Peg spoke.

The two women understood Tubby's predicament in
a way that few other people would have. Both of them
had devoted decades to the sport of dogs. Their social
group, their hobbies, their livelihoods, everything that

was important to them revolved around their involvement in the dog show world.

Derek had given us a motive for what Tubby had done, but there was still a big piece of the puzzle missing.

"There's something you're not telling us," I said.

"What do you mean?"

"So far you've made yourself sound like a pretty upstanding guy. So how did you get from wanting to do the right thing to knocking Florence out and locking me in the steam room?"

"Oh, that."

"Yes, that," Florence repeated sharply. "You're lucky I have such a hard head. Otherwise, you might have killed me."

"You have that part all wrong," said Derek. "You ought to be thanking me for saving your life. Last night when Tubby realized you'd overheard us, I was afraid he was going to do something drastic. It's a good thing for you I was there. If I hadn't knocked his arm away, he would have hit you harder than he did."

"Mother?"

The door to the inn opened and Richard came hurrying out. He saw our group standing in the parking lot and headed our way.

"I just got your message. What's going on?"

He slowed as he drew near and took in the entire scene. "Has there been an accident? Is everyone all right?"

"Everyone is fine, dear," Florence said. "I thought we might need your help, but it turns out we're doing just fine on our own. So stand aside for a moment and let us beat the rest of the confession out of Derek here."

"What confession?" Richard sounded more confused

than ever. "What are you talking about? And why are you holding a tire iron?"

Florence didn't bother to reply. Like a Cocker with a bird to flush, she had her attention focused on Derek.

Richard looked to Aunt Peg. "Can you explain this to me?"

"I'm afraid not," she said crisply. "Listen to your mother, and stand aside. We've got work to do."

"No, you don't," said Derek. "There's no reason for me to remain here any longer. I have a plane to catch."

Unfortunately Richard's arrival had given Derek the breather he needed to think things through. Now he was finished answering questions.

"You'll stay here until the police arrive if I have to knock you down and sit on you," Florence threatened.

"Mother, what's come over you?"

Richard sounded horrified. We all ignored him.

"The police have no reason to detain me," said Derek. "I don't care what you tell them, I'll deny everything."

"Good idea," said Aunt Peg. "Although you're going to have a hard time denying this."

She held up her cell phone and showed us the screen. Derek's face appeared center stage. Aunt Peg had recorded our entire conversation.

Derek swore vehemently. He glared at Florence.

"I'm going to press charges for assault," he said.

Florence smiled back at him. "Me too," she replied.

"Would somebody *please* tell me what's going on?" Richard pleaded.

The sound of sirens silenced all of us. I could see flashing lights heading our way through the trees.

"I told them it was an emergency," said Aunt Peg. "After all, we still have to round up Tubby."

"That's not all," I said.

All eyes looked my way.

"There's one last question we haven't answered. Derek says he came here to ally himself with Charles against Tubby. Yet when Charles died, Derek didn't go to the police. He didn't turn Tubby in—"

"I didn't know what he'd done—"

"Not only that," I continued, "but Florence overheard Derek telling Tubby that he'd been planning to make everything all right."

I nailed Derek with a hard glare. "You changed your mind about which side you were on, didn't you?"

"No, I—"

"Tubby offered you something for your silence, didn't he? Money maybe, it doesn't matter what. You were going to go back to Charles and recant your story."

Derek looked sullen. "Not money, who cares about that? Tubby had the Hound group assignment at the Bedminster show this year. He told me I could have the win, and we'd call it even. Of course I was tempted, anyone would have been."

Sadly, he was right.

"Charles and I were supposed to meet Tuesday night after he gave the keynote address. That's when I was going to tell him I'd been mistaken. But then he stepped up to the podium and gave that crazy speech. Who expected him to do something like that? Then everything seemed to go wrong. First Charles canceled our appointment. He said something had come up."

Alana, I thought. And her offer to give him his reward in the hot tub.

"Then Tubby and Charles ran into each other later that night. Tubby thought I'd already spoken to Charles.

He was feeling pretty good and he started heckling Charles about his speech. He called him a fool.

"Well, Charles wasn't having any of that. He said to Tubby, 'By the time I'm through with you, I won't be the only one who looks foolish.' I guess Tubby just lost it then. He thought his problem had been solved and when he found out it hadn't, he took matters into his own hands."

Derek looked around at all of us beseechingly. "It's like I've been trying to tell you. None of this was my fault."

Maybe the police would buy that line. I certainly wasn't.

Two patrol cars pulled up next to us. Several policemen piled out. Their guns weren't drawn but their hands rested on the tops of their holsters.

Detective Wayne arrived in a third, unmarked car. He pushed his way to the front of the crowd and went directly to Aunt Peg. "Do you want to tell me what's going on here?"

"I'd be happy to," she said.

"I'll help," Florence announced.

They both seemed to have the matter well in hand.

Which was good because all at once I wasn't feeling very well. Usually I deal pretty well with excitement but I was, after all, *pregnant.*

"If nobody needs me," I said, "I'm going to bed."

"Go." Aunt Peg shooed me away with her hands. "I'll fill you in later."

For once in my life, it felt nice to be expendable.

30

So we dumped the whole mess in Detective Wayne's capable hands. As I found out later, he coped admirably.

While Derek had been in a hurry to get away, Tubby remained brazen to the end. When the police found him, he was sitting in the bar among a circle of friends, enjoying his last night at the symposium like a man without a care in the world. Arm draped casually over Alana's shoulder, Tubby was drinking whiskey and pontificating about the joys of judging.

All that came to an abrupt stop when Detective Wayne strode over and asked him to step outside. Tubby sputtered, and protested, and proclaimed his innocence, but in the end both he and Derek were taken down to the police station for questioning.

Thanks to the evidence on Aunt Peg's cell phone, Derek didn't require much convincing to tell the detective everything he knew. Last I heard, he and Tubby were busy implicating one another as fast as they could.

Of course that wasn't the only matter that needed to

be wrapped up before we left Pennsylvania. While I'd been running around chasing a killer, Aunt Peg had been hard at work looking for a home for Walter.

Along with investigating various other options, she'd also gotten in touch with the local German Shepherd affiliate club. Their rescue program had pointed her toward a young couple who'd been waiting for some time to adopt.

Aunt Peg has stringent requirements for anyone who expects to acquire one of her dogs, and having spent the previous two nights on Peg's bed, Walter now qualified as an honorary Cedar Crest canine. Accordingly, the prospective owners were subjected to a home visit.

Aunt Peg checked out every aspect of his new situation thoroughly. In the end, she was delighted to give passing grades to the spacious fenced yard and the sensible, dog-savvy husband and wife whom she found to be well equipped to deal with a large dog who had been living on his own for longer than any of us wanted to think about.

Friday afternoon on our way out of town, Aunt Peg delivered Walter to his new family. Any regrets she might have felt about leaving the German Shepherd behind were quickly dispelled by the eagerness and enthusiasm with which the young couple and the homeless dog greeted one another. Clearly this was a match that was going to endure.

Still, Aunt Peg carefully wrote down her contact information and obtained a promise from the new owners that if they were ever unable to care for Walter, she would be the first person they called. I doubted that she'd hear from them, but it never hurt to cover all the bases.

So Aunt Peg returned to Connecticut without a new dog.

She also returned home without a new boyfriend.

It took Bertie and me half an hour to pry her away from Walter. Richard, she left behind without a second glance.

Aunt Peg succinctly summed up her recent dating experience for us in the car on the way home. "It wasn't a total failure, after all. Richard became annoying after a while; but as things turned out, I found I quite liked his mother."

She and Florence have pledged to keep in touch by e-mail.

I have to confess, I never saw that one coming.

As you might imagine, I'm spending a lot of time thinking about mothers and children myself these days. After five days away, it was utterly wonderful to be home again, surrounded by my family, both human and canine.

In my absence, Davey and Sam had painted the nursery a gorgeous shade of aquamarine. White and yellow sailboats skimmed across the walls. Clouds drifted lazily over the ceiling. If there was meant to be a message in the colors they'd chosen, I declined to make an issue of it. Little girls look good in blue too.

Now that I'm back, I'll be sticking close to home for a while. Five or six months at least. I think I've had enough excitement recently and it's time to take things a little slower. At least until the baby arrives anyway.

I wouldn't be surprised if that stirs things up again.

In fact, I'm pretty much counting on it.

Melanie Travis thought her sleuthing days were behind her. She has a new baby to take care of, not to mention five Standard Poodles—and Aunt Peg is getting Davey ready for his debut as a junior showman. These days, the closest Melanie gets to detective work is scoping out the scene at the local doggie day center for her friend Alice Brickman.

As Melanie learns, it's a dog's life at the Pine Ridge Canine Care Center—and life is good. The dogs are living large with a team of groomers and handlers at their bark and call. Everyone seems blissfully happy. Everyone canine, that is. For Melanie soon discovers there are some simmering resentments among the Pine Ridge staff and when Steve Pine, the center's charming, good-looking co-owner, is found shot to death on the floor of his office, there's no shortage of suspects. His sister, Candy, stands to inherit their lucrative doggie day care operation. His neighbor, Adam Busch, still blames Steve for paving the way for the other businesses that now exist in the once quiet, all-residential town. And then there's Lila Bennington, the disgruntled client who wanted to sue Steve following an embarrassing "incident" involving a Shih Tzu and a Beagle mix. And lastly, the string of female customers Steve bedded and jilted. But which of these suspects was desperate enough to commit murder?

With the police at a loss for leads, it's now up to Melanie to go undercover and sniff out a killer whose secrets lie buried in a dog's paradise that's proving to be anything but . . .

Please turn the page for an exciting sneak peek at DOGGIE DAY CARE MURDER coming next month from Kensington Publishing!

1

A baby changes everything. Don't ever let anyone tell you that it doesn't.

Once upon a time when I was younger and more foolish, I thought that new puppies and new babies had a lot in common. I must have been deluded, or maybe just oversimplifying. Because now it's clear to me that I was insanely wrong.

For one thing, when a puppy doesn't sleep through the night, nobody has to get up and feed him and rock him back to sleep. For another, puppies are happy to entertain themselves for a while if you need your hands free to do something else. But perhaps the biggest difference is that new puppies, wonderful as they are, don't turn your whole world upside down in that mystical, magical way that somehow simultaneously reconnects you to the cosmos and to that vast well of human experience, while at the same time making you feel that if your heart expands any more it might possibly explode.

Trust me, it takes a baby to wreak that kind of havoc.

Having been through this once before, you'd think I

might have remembered how it went. But that was nine years ago when I was in my early twenties. I was young enough then to bounce back from almost anything: stretch marks, ten hours of labor, or the aggravation of a mostly absent husband.

In the intervening years, my life had changed dramatically. Now I had friends and relatives I could depend on, a terrific son in fourth grade, and a second marriage that was eons better than my first. In short, when my second son was born on a wintry March night, my world was complete.

The doctor placed him in my arms while my husband, Sam, dashed out of the delivery room. He returned moments later with our son Davey. The two of them stood on either side of the bed, and Davey stared at the new arrival in awe. Or maybe consternation.

"I didn't think he'd be so red," he said.

"Don't worry," said a nurse, passing by, "that goes away."

Busy cleaning up, she took time to lean in for a closer look. Snuggled tight in his receiving blanket, the infant's face was the only part of him that was visible. His eyes were closed, his expression peaceful. Oblivious to all the activity around him, he was enjoying a brief, post-delivery nap.

"He's a cute one," she said. "What's his name?"

Davey, Sam, and I looked at each other. We'd been working on this for months. Boys' names, girls' names, unisex names, we'd had them all. But right that moment, in the magnitude of him actually *being* there, my mind was utterly blank.

"Kevin," said Sam.

"Kevin," Davey echoed. "He's my little brother."

"And aren't you the lucky one?" asked the nurse. "You be sure to take good care of him now."

Davey reached up and placed his hand on the tiny, sleeping form. He looked like he was taking a vow. "I will," he said firmly.

Now, three months later, Kevin was no longer a newborn. He was a member of the family, his presence so entrenched in our lives and our hearts that it was hard to remember what life had been like without him.

With everything going so well, I knew I shouldn't complain. But there was just one thing I desperately needed. Six hours of blissful uninterrupted sleep. Did that seem like too much to ask?

"I have a problem," said Alice Brickman. She was standing in my kitchen doorway and looked like a woman with a lot on her mind.

"Welcome to the club," I replied. "My hormones are bouncing around like a Ping-Pong ball, Kevin's decided he prefers bottles to breast feeding, and just about every piece of clothing I own has spit-up on it. Have a seat and let's compare notes."

Sam and Davey were off running errands. Kevin had just been fed. A couple of our Standard Poodles had gone along on the car ride, the other three were snoozing contentedly at my feet. Alice's timing was perfect, which is no small feat in a home that has a new baby.

But then, right from the start, Alice and I had been on the same wavelength. We'd met at a play group right after the birth of our first children and been best friends for nearly a decade. I'd married Sam the previous year and moved to a different Stamford, Connecticut, neighborhood. Before that, Alice and I had lived right down the road from one another.

The shared experience of motherhood is a powerful bonding tool. Through car pools, PTA meetings, and soccer games, we'd compared notes, juggled juice boxes, and covered one another's backs.

Davey and Alice's son, Joey, had finished fourth grade together the previous week. Alice also had a seven-year-old daughter named Carly, who was a budding ballerina. Her husband, Joe, was a partner in a prestigious law firm in Greenwich.

Alice was every bit as comfortable in my house as she would have been in her own. And since my dogs were equally comfortable with her, none of them had bothered to get up for her arrival. Three big black Standard Poodles were asleep on the kitchen floor. Alice navigated her way through the recumbent canine bodies and headed directly for the play pen in the corner.

Kevin was lying on his back, kicking his feet in the air and eying a spinning, pinwheel-colored mobile I'd just fastened above him. Alice leaned down over the side bar, inhaled his baby smell, and sighed deeply.

"Aren't babies the best?" she said.

I'd been on my way to the refrigerator. Alice and I always seem to talk better when our mouths are full. Now I stopped and turned.

"You're not," I said.

"Not what?"

"Pregnant."

"Oh that." She laughed. "No way. I'll amend my earlier statement. *Other* people's babies are the best."

I opened the fridge and pulled out a couple of diet sodas.

"Believe me," I grumbled, "there are times when I feel the same way."

"And then you get over it," Alice said practically.

No whining allowed around here.

I nodded in agreement and handed her a drink. We both found seats at the kitchen table. Kevin gurgled, and cooed, and looked cuter than anybody had a right to, as he tried valiantly to insert his toes into his mouth. At moments like that, it was hard to remember why I was feeling grumpy.

Alice popped the top on the soda can, tipped back her head, and took a long swallow. "When did you start drinking diet?"

"Guess."

"How much baby weight do you have left?"

After Carly was born, Alice had struggled with the last ten pounds for years. Finally she'd given up the struggle and simply resigned herself to buying clothes in a larger size. By any standards, except those promoted by celebrities and fashion magazines, she wasn't plump, just pleasantly rounded.

But still, I noticed, she hadn't given up drinking diet soda. For every woman who accepts herself as she is, there's another who's angling to raise the bar ever higher. Sisterhood indeed.

"Five pounds," I said. "But it's not the weight, it's the shape. None of my clothes fit the way they used to."

Alice stared at me over the top of her soda can and lifted a brow, a small gesture every bit as telling as the words it replaced.

"I know, but this didn't happen last time."

"Right. And how old were you when you had Davey, seventeen?"

"Twenty-five," I corrected primly.

"Same thing," Alice sniffed.

She was five years older than me. As if *that* made a huge difference.

"And now you're thirty-five," she said. "Things change."

"So I've noticed. I thought gravity wasn't supposed to start having its way with me until I turned forty."

"Good luck with that."

Alice got up, walked over to the pantry and had a look around.

"Oreos on the left," I said.

She grabbed the bag and brought them back to the table. This wasn't going to help anyone's diet. We each fished one out, twisted them open, and ate the cream filling first.

"Have we talked about your problems long enough?" she asked. "I don't want to seem insensitive here, but I haven't got all day."

Newly fortified by sugar, I was good to go.

"Your turn," I said. "Have at it."

"This part isn't a problem, exactly. It's an announcement."

I sat up straight and paid attention. In my experience, announcements don't always augur well.

"I'm done with being a stay at home mom," said Alice. "I'm going back to work."

This was momentous. And very exciting, as news went. In this one particular aspect of our lives, Alice and I had always been opposites.

I'd been a working mother, and a single mother, for most of Davey's life. Alice, meanwhile, had a husband who went to work and supported the family, which gave her the luxury of staying home to take care of the kids.

Now it looked as though our roles were reversing. At

he end of the previous semester, when my pregnancy had reached the six month mark, I'd taken a leave of absence from my job at a private school in Greenwich. While I'd be staying home for the near future, Alice was gearing up to rejoin the workforce.

"Congratulations," I said, tipping my cookie in salute.

"Not so fast." Alice laughed. "It's been years since anyone offered to pay me for what I can do. Let's see if I can make this thing work first."

"What kind of job are you looking for?"

"That's the good part." Her laughter faded. "At least I hope it is. I already have a job."

"Wow, that was fast. Am I totally out of the loop or did that happen overnight?"

"Kind of the latter," Alice admitted. "I'm going to work for Joe's law firm."

"Plummer, Wilkes, and Hornby?" I said, even though we both knew the name. I was buying time and thinking fast, wondering what she'd be doing there. Finally I gave up and just asked.

"You know, the usual paralegal stuff."

That brought me up short. I even put down my cookie.

"What usual paralegal stuff? When did you become a paralegal?"

"Right out of college. That's what I did before I met Joe."

Utterly amazing, I thought. "How can I have known you for ten years and not known that?"

Alice shrugged. "With the kids around all the time, I guess it never came up. But now Joey and Carly are both in school full time for most of the year. And even their summers are filled with activities. Joey will be at soccer camp for eight weeks."

I nodded. Davey was doing the same thing.

"While Carly's doing a ballet program over at the Sil vermine Guild. So I've been thinking about this for a while. Neither one of them needs me to be home all the time anymore. Which makes me feel kind of superflu ous—like all I do is sit at home and wait for the people who are out doing interesting things to come back. So enough of that. It's time for me to see what else I can be besides just a mother."

Just a mother. The phrase made us both wince, but neither of us bothered to comment on it. I knew what she meant.

"Congratulations," I said again, applauding the deci sion as much as its execution.

"Yeah, well. It'll be interesting to see how this all shakes out. The good thing was that I got a job without having to apply to a million places, go through some huge interview process, and then justify what I'd been doing for the ten years that are missing on my resume. The bad news is, I'll be working for Joe."

I liked Joe. He was a good father and a nice guy. But even so, I could see how all that togetherness might strain things around the house.

"What does Joe think of the idea?" I asked.

"He's the one who came up with it. At first he wasn't crazy about the notion of me going back to work, but eventually I managed to convince him that the kids wouldn't miss me when they weren't even around to know that I was gone. Oh yeah, and that I'd still make sure that the dry cleaner put the right amount of starch in his shirts."

She paused, rolled her eyes, and grabbed another Oreo. "Then he thought of this. I think somehow it made the whole thing seem more palatable to him, like maybe e thought he could keep an eye on me or something. Plus, as he said, think of all the gas money we'll save!"

Alice and I laughed together. I could just hear Joe saying that. He was the kind of guy who liked to keep his eye on the bottom line.

"So give it a try," I said. "If it works, great. If it doesn't, quit and go somewhere else."

"That's what I'm thinking," Alice agreed. "Flexibility's a good thing. There's just one problem with the plan. In fact, that's why I'm here."

Sad to say, that's the story of my life. People always seem to bring their problems to me.

"I need to find something to do with Berkley. If I'm going to be gone all day, I can't just leave him sitting home by himself."

Berkley was the Brickmans' eighteen-month-old Golden Retriever. Though he'd been purchased as a pet for Joey and Carly, predictably the bulk of his care had fallen to Alice. He was a beautiful, smart, rambunctious, teenage dog; and as long as he had company, he mostly managed to stay out of trouble. Bored and left to his own devices, however, I could see how he might be tempted to entertain himself by tearing the place apart.

"That's where you come in," said Alice.

I opened my mouth but she hurried on before I could speak.

"Don't worry, with a new baby and all, I wouldn't dream of asking you to look after him. So I found a place in town that offers doggie day care."

Now she paused. Like it was my turn to say something. For a moment, I couldn't think what that should be.

"*Doggie* day care?" I managed finally.

Despite the subject matter, none of my Poodles even

looked up. Though they understand most things I say, the Poodles possessed far too much dignity to ever think of themselves as doggies.

"Don't make fun," said Alice. "Apparently it's a very successful facility. And hard to get into. There's a waiting list."

"A waiting list," I echoed faintly. It was all I could do to keep a straight face.

"The place is called Pine Ridge Canine Care Center. And you know I'm hopeless when it comes to things like this. I wouldn't have the slightest idea what to look for. But you know all that important dog-type stuff. So I was wondering if you could go and check it out for me. You know, see if it's the kind of place where Berkley would be happy."

She'd played the flattery card and no surprise, it was working. Besides, while I was delighted to have the chance to stay at home and take care of Kevin, Alice wasn't the only one who'd spent some time recently looking around the house and wondering what to do next. A job like this sounded like it would be right up my alley.

"Sure," I said. "I can do that. No problem."

You'd think I'd know better than to make predictions like that.